Sharp Turn

Tara Sharp Book Two

Sharp Turn

Marianne Delacourt

deadlines

For Colleen

by **deadlines**

www.twelfthplanetpress.com

This edition published by Deadlines, November 2016
First published in Australia in 2010 by Allen & Unwin.
Copyright © 2010 by Marianne Delacourt

National Library of Australia Cataloguing-in-Publication entry

Creator: De Pierres, Marianne, author.
Title: Sharp turn / Marianne de Pierres.
ISBN: 9781922101310 (paperback)
Series: De Pierres, Marianne. Tara Sharp; 2.
Subjects: Private investigators--Fiction.
Telepathy--Fiction.
Automobile racing--Fiction.
Murder--Fiction.
A823.4

Chapter 1

My mother is an expert guilt-maker. Joanna Sharp, the Rani of Reproach, the Shazadi of Shame. When she turned her talent on me, it was usually about the fact that I didn't date the right sort of guy. Unfortunately, my mother's idea of a suitable male was someone like Phillip Dewar: privileged, pasty and pissy. But since I'd moved back home, due to loss of employment and a spot of pennilessness, Joanna had broadened her guilt trip to include my latest career venture.

'Why can't you just get a good job in the government, darling? Or let your father help you find work?' she asked me with unrelenting regularity.

My reaction was consistently emphatic: 'I can look after myself, Mum!'

Of course that meant that I had to come good on my statement, which meant earning money, which explained why I was currently on my way to a meeting with a brothel madam.

'And it's all good … it's all go-oo-ood!' I sang the Hill Top Hoods chorus line to Crosby Sweater and sent my 1980s Holden Monaro—aka Mona—into a sharp left-hander with only the faintest squeal of her wheels.

I've always been a great believer in affirmations. I CAN eat less chocolate. I CAN do more exercise. I CAN meet a perfect man. No, scrap that last one. I don't believe in perfect men.

That said, my current date, the gorgeous Edouardo, came close. He was a model, a good egg and he seemed to like me—all of which made me uneasy. He was really too good to be true. My lovelife had been littered with unfaithful Lotharios and even a furniture-stealer (my last boyfriend sent me to a day spa as a treat and proceeded to clean out my flat), which made it almost impossible for me to just enjoy Edouardo's attention and not try to second-guess the whole thing. Ed and I were still pretty casual but Second-Guess is my new middle name. Tara Second-Guess Sharp.

Not just about men, about everything: a legacy from the fact that I have an unusual gift. I can see auras around people, and sometimes around objects. Occasionally, I even smell or feel things or see energy trails.

I'd been to the shrink about my gift and, instead of whacking me on antipsychotic meds, she'd sent me off to Hoshi Hara's Paralanguage School. Betsy, my psych, was an old family friend and turned out to be more alternative than I'd ever expected for a woman who favoured Brendan

O'Keefe glasses.

The end result of getting to know Mr Hara was that my gift didn't go away; it got stronger. Now I was a fully accredited reader of paralanguage and kinesics with my own business, and I was starting to get jobs that used my skills. Like the one I was going to now.

One of my previous clients had recommended me to Madame Vine, a brothel owner. It seemed the madam was a forward-thinking entrepreneur who needed my skills. In return, I hoped she'd bolster my bank account and we'd all be happy. She wasn't exactly the kind of customer I'd expected to attract when I set up my own business, and certainly not the kind of work I'd be telling my mother about, but I wasn't going to knock back a funds infusion because of my mother's delicate western suburbs sensibilities.

'IT'S ALL GOO-OO-OOD! 1-2-3-4...'

I cruised up a tiny side street in Leederville that was crammed with red-brick, Federation-style semi-detacheds, and pulled up outside number nine. It didn't look like a house of ill repute. In fact, with its minimalist garden and locked letterbox, it was much tidier and more dignified than its neighbours. No red light or gaudy lace curtains in the windows. Madame Vine ran a tasteful establishment that didn't accommodate riffraff—at least that's what my Google search had told me.

I parked Mona and reached down to my bag, sighing at the sight of the sequinned palm tree decorating the side.

I'd given my favourite imitation Marc Jacobs handbag to a feral kid out in the Bunkas after she did me a solid, and bartered my beloved backup Mandarina Duck in a second-hand shop. That left me with my old beach bag. Hopefully this job for Madame Vine would bring me enough cash to buy something halfway respectable. I'm not a snob about anything in life except handbags. I guess my mother had to rub off on me in some way.

Scrabbling in the bottom of my Hawaiian beach bag turned up my hairbrush. I dragged it through my shoulder-length hair, and deliberately avoided the rear-view mirror which I knew would reveal my slightly wild-eyed look. Too much adrenaline and too little sleep.

'It's all good...'

I forced my legs out of the car and told myself off for feeling nervous.

It had nothing to do with moral judgments about ladies of the night. As far as I was concerned, you did whatever you needed to get through life; I saved my disdain for bad people.

No, my angst was more about what they would think of me, Tara Sharp, western suburbs ex-private school girl with the posh voice. Maybe the sequinned beach bag was the least of my worries.

The woman who answered the door was dressed in an elegant black suit, sheer stockings and killer black heels. She could have been thirty or fifty, depending on how closely you looked. I had the advantage of being able to see her aura. It was a nice sunny-day blue with the faintly fuzzy edge that older people tended to get, which inclined me to think she was closer to fifty.

'Tara Sharp here to see Madame Vine.'

The woman frowned, sucked in her cheeks and stepped back to let me inside, then she clip-clopped off down the polished wood corridor at an impressive pace considering the height of her heels. I followed more slowly, trying not to gawk at the plush lounge area or through the open doorways into the equally opulent bedrooms.

Ms Clippety-Clop halted in front of an ornate door and knocked.

'Entrée.'

'It's Ms Sharp, Madame Vine,' my guide announced, in a plummy voice. She ushered me in, stepped inside, shut the door behind us and waited. My guide, it seemed, was the PA.

I stared at the woman seated behind a large, decoratively carved cedar desk. Madame Vine was roundish, with her hair cut in a bouncy blonde bob. From what I could see, she was dressed in a silk kaftan and a LOT of bling; fingers, neck, wrists, ears. Old school, though. No piercings. If I didn't know better, I'd have picked her to be in real estate.

'Ms Sharp?' she said.

'Madame Vine,' I squeaked.

The two women exchanged a look, then Madame Vine smiled at me the way an animal handler might at a new, frightened zoo inmate. 'Why don't you sit down? Thank you, Audrey.'

Audrey nodded, and walked through into an adjoining room. As she passed Madame Vine's desk, the two women's auras blended snugly together. There was something more than the usual work relationship going on there.

I plopped into the brown leather armchair and cleared my throat. Time to be a businesswoman. 'Err... Lloyd Honey said you wished to discuss some potential work.'

'Aaah, Lloyd. Dear man.' Madame Vine slipped one outrageously long, diamanté-studded fingernail between her lips and sucked on it, then removed it to stroke an equally ridiculously long eyelash. 'He claims you have a unique ability to read situations. Is that so, Ms Sharp?'

'Tara, please. And yes,' I said, 'my business is reading paralanguage and kinesics. I usually lean towards investigative jobs but I do consider other things. What did you have in mind?'

Madame Vine got up from her chair and moved around to stand directly under the airconditioning vent. She couldn't have been much over five feet tall and her shrewd, plump face was shiny with moisture. A red aura punctuated with blue flashes ringed her ample frame. I mentally reviewed the aura colour code Mr Hara had taught me. People with red auras tended to be materialistic and pragmatic. The brilliant turquoise flashes signified energy and influence. This woman could probably move mountains if she set her mind to it.

'I run a superior business, Tara, and I'm always looking for ways to improve the quality of the service we give.

And to be honest, the economy hasn't been kind to the more … upmarket establishments like us.'

I nodded encouragingly and she went on.

'It's important that we provide a positive environment for our customers. I sense some … problems amongst my girls but haven't been able to get to the bottom of it.'

'What kind of problems?'

She hesitated. 'I believe that someone in my employ is disgruntled.'

'How do you mean?'

'Dead animals on the doorstep, threatening text messages, that sort of thing. I wondered if you might be able to mingle with them for a few days, maybe a week or so, and see what you can learn.'

'Mingle with?'

Madame Vine picked up a long, thin, ivory-handled envelope knife. 'The girls get together regularly in the client lounge. I can introduce you as a trial employee— that way they'll be relaxed about your presence.'

'Let me get this right. You're suggesting that I pretend to be one of your … escorts?'

She gave me a keen smile. 'You wouldn't need to take on any clients. Just interact with the girls. The remuneration for uncovering the perpetrator would be substantial.'

I clutched my sequinned beach bag, trying to ignore the thought of my mother's reaction if she heard about me 'mingling' in a brothel. My sweat snap-froze on my skin. It suddenly felt hard to breathe.

'I-I'm not sure this is really my line of work. And frankly, Madame Vine, I'm sure your girls would see through me in a heartbeat,' I managed to gasp out.

'I can see my proposal has taken you by surprise. Perhaps you should think on it and we can talk again?' she said.

I nodded and sprang up.

Madame Vine pressed her intercom. 'Audrey. Please see Ms Sharp out.'

Audrey appeared. Her eyebrows lifted slightly and her aura surged towards Madame Vine's. I felt a slight snap of a mild electric shock as their energies met, before she led me out into the corridor. These two definitely had something going on.

As I passed the archway that opened into the front lounge area, I couldn't resist a peek inside.

Two men sat at the small bar. One, his sharp-looking Zegna suit not quite hiding a middle-aged paunch, was skimming a newspaper. He glanced at me then kept on with his reading.

The other was drinking from a bottle of Coke while he pored over a small tablet. And, God save me, I knew him.

My mouth fell open. 'Whitey?'

His head jerked up, the bottle halfway to his mouth. 'Sharp?'

It was a bit hard to know where to go from there.

I knew Greg Whitehead—Whitey—at school. After graduation he'd asked me out on a date and, to my dismay, had turned out to be a horny toad. I'd avoided him ever since. But Whitey became a cop, and not so long ago he turned up to a crimescene I'd accidentally stumbled upon. Short story: long outcome. A photo of Whitey and me appeared in the local paper that made his jealous wife, June, furious.

Now it looked like Whitey had found another way to well and truly piss her off. And, as usual, I happened to be in the right place at the wrong time to see it.

'It's only ten in the morning! Can't you keep your fly zipped until after lunch?' The words fell out of my mouth before I could stop them.

Mr Zegna Suit sank further behind his newspaper.

'Why do you care, Sharp? Are you offering your services?' Whitey fired back at me.

'Not if you were the last shag on earth!'

Ignoring Audrey's disapproving look, I flounced out of the front door on enough indignation to float a hot air balloon.

Chapter 2

Whitey's lewd suggestion stayed with me all the way home. I parked Mona outside my parents' home on Lilac Street, Eucalyptus Grove, and stomped down the driveway to the birds' cage, which was back in its usual spot at the front of the house.

Hoo barrelled straight up to the bars to greet me, but Brains was still a bit skittish after a recent bird-napping episode and wouldn't come unless I had food in my hand. Scrabbling in the bottom of my beach bag, I found a bit of stale pie crust and made clicking noises with my tongue to woo her over. She sidled along a branch and swiped at the crust, which crumbled and fell to the floor.

'Serves you right,' I told her and went back to scratching Hoo.

She didn't like that either and bit Hoo on the foot. Much squawking and fluffing of feathers ensued.

People say galahs are as smart and self-centred as three year olds. Frankly, JoBob's—my name for the collective that was my parents—birds were smarter than a lot of adults I'd met and their self-centredness made them extremely honest pets. In galah language, Brains had just said, 'Pay attention to me, not him!' You can't get much more direct than that.

I left the birds and headed down to my flat/apartment/garage where things were in their usual state of immaculate order: my entire wardrobe on the couch, laptop buried underneath somewhere, microwave door open with half a packet of popped corn inside, and a sticky fruit treat (for the birds) attracting a small army of ants on the sink.

Moving back home meant my mum knew way too much about what I was doing, but at least being in a detached flat in the back garden meant I still got to be as messy as I liked.

I plopped onto my bed and buried my face in my pillow. What would Whitey tell the cops at the Euccy Grove station? Tara Sharp's working in a brothel. The very thought of my mother hearing about my visit to Madame Vine made me want to run to the toilet.

Mum and Dad were comfortably off, semi-retired Euccy Grove gentry. While Mum worshipped at the sacred altar of snobbery, Dad was her quiet backstop, preferring Foxtel to the Euccy Grove social scene. I sometimes wondered how they ever got together. Then occasionally I witnessed their perfectly complementary rhythm: Joanna says it and Bob does it. Unless, of course, he gets really ticked off about something. Then watch out!

Unfortunately for them, they gave birth to a slightly offbeat, flaky daughter who showed an aptitude for contact sport quite early and got into frequent fights with the boys at primary school (usually, I might add, to protect my best friend, Martin Longbok). Joanna tried in vain to nurture a more ladylike and refined streak in me, but I just kept turning up with impulsive and boisterous. On top of that, I kept on growing—until I was bigger than either of them and most of the guys I knew. It was about then she gave up the battle and let me be. Well, sort of.

My phone rang. 'Sharp.'

'Tara?'

Every molecule dissolved into one gooey mass at the sound of that voice. Nick Tozzi: hunky, filthy rich and married. I hadn't spoken to him in quite a few weeks. Not since he'd brought me flowers in hospital to thank me for saving him from financial ruin and other things. Why did I keep thinking about him and wondering if he would work things out with his wife, socialite and cokehead Antonia Falk?

'Yo, Tozzi.'

'How are you?' he enquired politely.

Words ran out of my mouth like tap water. 'I just ran into a policeman I know in a massage parlour in Leederville. Now he's going to tell the entire force I'm a "working" girl. It'll get back to my mother and she'll disown me and throw me out of home. I'll end up destitute and alone. Apart from that … everything's shiny.'

'And you were in a brothel for what reason?' I could hear the edge of laughter in his voice.

'Business,' I said stiffly. 'Now what can I do for you?'

'I'm ringing on business as well.' His voice sounded a bit strangled still, like he might let a guffaw slip at any moment.

'Oh?'

'It's an unusual job. So I thought of you straightaway.'

'I'm listening.' It had to be better than Madame Vine's offer, didn't it?

'I'm working from home today—what say I drop past and take you for a coffee? We can talk about it in person.'

I sat up. This sounded good and bad. Seeing Tozzi was good. Not knowing what to wear was bad. 'How do you know I'm even free?'

'I'll be there in ten minutes,' he said and hung up.

Ten minutes! I needed longer than that to work a miracle on my appearance, especially when I didn't have either of my two fashion advisors on hand. My best friends Martin Longbok and Jane Smith-Evans—aka Bok and Smitty— were busy being upright citizens. Smitty was at home being a three-sprog matriarch, and Bok was at his office being a hot-shot magazine editor.

I checked the time. Noon. Smitty might have a window of opportunity. I called her.

'T,' she cried. 'Thank fucking buggery. I thought you

were going to be one of the Kinder mums.'

'Nope. Definitely not. Problem?'

'Yes. But I won't bore you with it.'

'Bore me,' I said in my saintliest BFF manner. Eight minutes left.

'Joe punched one of the other kindy kids and gave him a bloody snout. The mother's been ringing me threatening legal action.'

'Legal action!' I shrieked. 'That is the most ridiculous thing I've ever heard.'

Smitty groaned. 'Thank God you said that. I thought I was losing it. I have to meet with the mother on Thursday.'

'Shall I come with you?'

I was offering out of guilt not saintliness. I was the one who'd taught Joe how to punch.

I babysat Smitty's kids when she went to pilates, and occasionally when she and her doctor husband, Henry, had a dirty overnighter at a posh hotel. Champagne and Cock Night, Smitty called it, without even a flush of her expensively creamed cheeks. Anyway, babysitting was a chance for me to make sure Smitty's kids learned some decent life skills. Some boy had been picking on Joe, so I'd taught him how to defend himself. Xavier, his twin, wanted in on the action after that, and so did Claire, their gorgeous nine-year-old sister.

Claire suffers from Crohn's disease and her frail frame and constant fatigue meant she wasn't up to punching, kicking and blocking. Instead I'd shown her the eye gouge (to be used only in case of assault, of course) and coached her in how to verbally tear shreds off bigots and bullies.

'Would you really come along, T?' Smitty said, her voice lightening. 'I'll love you forever.'

'You already love me forever.' Four minutes. 'Text me the time and place and I'll be there. Now, I need some fashion advice. I have four minutes to make myself look good before Nick Tozzi picks me up to take me for a coffee.'

'Tozzi!' she squealed. 'Why didn't you say something? Okay. Listen. Sleeved white tee, blue jeans and your flat, strappy blue sandals. Don't be a try-hard. What handbag do you have?'

I swallowed. 'My beach bag.'

'The one JoBob gave you for your twentieth?'

'Uh-huh,' I said.

'With the sequinned palm tree on it?'

'Uh-huh.'

'Okay. No bag. Phone and cash in jeans pocket. Lipstick and blush on at the last minute. Go!'

I was already doing the jeans dance as I hung up, squirming and hopping about the place, tugging them on. With no minutes to go, I got up close to the mirror to daub on lippy and scrape some mascara across my lashes.

As I tugged the brush through my hair there was a knock at my door. I didn't have time for a JoBob lecture and an excuse was already tumbling off my lips as I swung back the curtain.

Nick Tozzi grinned at me from the other side of the fingerprint-smeared glass door.

'You were supposed to ring!' I said. 'And I'm supposed to meet you outside on the pavement.'

'Aren't you going to invite me in?'

'Why?' I asked, pulling the curtain around me to hide the pile of dirty clothes spread across the couch.

'Because that would be polite,' he said.

I couldn't tell whether he was teasing me or chiding me, but polite was the farthest thing from my mind when I had knickers hooked over my bedhead and a bra drying on the curtain rail above the sink.

'Wait there!' I said, before turning and grabbing my tragic bag—totally forgetting Smitty's advice. I stuffed my phone and purse into it, then slid open the door and stepped out, forcing Tozzi to retreat. I locked the door before he could utter a word.

'Right,' I said brightly, 'where are we going?'

He was too polite to push it, but showed his annoyance at being outplayed by turning on his heel and striding off down the driveway. Fortunately, I could stride with the best of them and was in step with him by the time we got to the kerb.

His Lamborghini was parked there in all its silver, bat-winged glory. My dream car, owned by my dream man. (Did I say that?) Damn it, Tara, I scolded myself, get the man out of your head! But the thing was Ed and I were only casual still, and that kept allowing room for Tozzi thoughts to creep in.

Tozzi knew I'd give my teeth and ovaries for a drive in his car. He clearly wanted to sell something to me bad.

'You tease,' I said crossly.

'What do you mean?' he said, innocently.

'Bringing the car.'

'It's my car. Why wouldn't I bring it?'

'Because you know what effect it'll have on my brain stem.'

He grinned at that and pressed the key. The doors swooshed open and I peered into the boudoir of his sex-on-four-wheels. Trying to control my excitement, I lowered myself into the passenger seat. The leather glove-snugged around me.

I squirmed in ecstasy as Tozzi accelerated out onto the highway.

'Aaaah,' I said involuntarily.

'Enjoying yourself?' he asked as he slowed down for the traffic lights.

I blushed and looked out the window. The driver in the next car was trying to peer in through the Lambo's tinted windows to see who was driving.

I sighed. 'I suppose you get that all the time?'

'Comes with the deal. And all the revheads try to race me.'

'I get that too,' I sympathised. 'Everyone wants to drag a Monaro.'

He nodded, a smile playing around his lips.

We pulled into a parking spot outside Latte Ole.

'Wait,' he instructed, and a moment later he was around my side of the car, offering his hand to help me out.

I levered out one leg, then the next.

His gaze fell appreciatively to the strip of flesh that momentarily showed between my top and jeans.

I sprang up and into his face. 'I could eat a horse. Hope you're paying.'

He took a quick step back. Seemed I had a natural talent for keeping him off balance.

I strode off ahead of him into the café. It was one thing to be seen with a Tozzi, but another to be seen with a very married Tozzi. Last thing I wanted was his wife, Antonia, fronting up and causing a scene.

Nick followed more slowly with his usual confident gait, smiling and nodding to people. When you're that tall and that rich and you live in a small city, you can't expect to go anywhere without half the room knowing you.

'Why do I get the feeling you don't want to be seen with me?' he said as he folded his huge frame into the opposite side of the darkest booth I could find.

I shrugged and did an average job of looking dismissive. 'Think that if you want.'

I glanced around the café. The closest table was inhabited by a middle-aged couple deep in conversation.

Divorce negotiations, I guessed, from the way their auras were pounding at each other.

The rest of the place was in morning beat. The slight scent of last night's spilled beer clung to the furnishings but the refrigerated glass case displayed a mouth-watering collection of fresh cakes. I could forgive any odour for good cake.

Nick scrutinised me. 'You're an old-fashioned girl at heart, aren't you, Tara?'

'If you're alluding to the fact that I'm not comfortable having tea dates with a married man then you'd be right.'

It came out a bit waspish, but now I was here with him I was nervous as hell. Thing was, Tozzi was so damn hot that I wanted to melt all over him. He wasn't beautiful in the male model sense like Edouardo, with his dark curly hair, a darling face, killer abs and a fine round bum. Tozzi was a hulking man mountain packing just a teensy bit too much cabernet merlot and brie around his stomach. His face was strong rather than handsome, with a hint of the killer competitiveness that had taken him to the top levels of both sport and business. He had brown hair, brown eyes, and lips that could set in a firm, hard line or curve with sudden humour depending on the moment.

Edouardo had beauty. Tozzi had presence.

'Stop scowling, Tara. My intentions are honourable and harmless. I have a job offer for you. Firstly, what will you have?'

'English Breakfast tea, and orange and almond cake with cream. Please.'

He looked me up and down as if judging where the calories might go. He finished on my breasts.

'And loving it,' I said, doing my best Get Smart impersonation.

When the waitress arrived he ordered for both of us. She flashed him a gorgeous smile and me a quizzical look. That was when I noticed all the heads swivelling our way: Claremont and Euccy Grove mums out for coffee with their toddlers strapped into big-wheeled running strollers. It wasn't idle perving either; more like I-know-him-and-what's-he-doing-out-with-her? kinda scrutiny. I was grateful when the waitress returned and I could dive fork-first into my cake while Tozzi poured milk into his long black.

'I have a work acquaintance who needs help,' he said.

'He's too shy to speak to me himself?'

I smiled as I said it, but truth was I was curious. Tozzi wasn't the kind of guy to act as a go-between.

'I offered to sound you out.'

It crossed my mind that maybe Tozzi was using this job offer as an excuse to spend time with me, then quickly dismissed it.

'He could use your kind of ... talents,' he continued.

My fork stopped in mid-air and I looked across at him. 'What talents would they be?'

'Someone who's curious and ... smart and...'

I straightened up. 'And?'

'Left field,' he finished.

My smile turned to a scowl. 'You mean like ... flaky?'

He took a sip of his coffee to give himself thinking time. 'What I mean is ... someone with a fresh, unique perspective.'

I stared at him suspiciously. He was way too practised at tiptoeing around a woman's sensitive spots. I sighed. Well, he was married.

'And the deal is?'

'He owns a motorcycle racing team.'

'Sweet!'

Next to basketball and fast cars, fast motorbikes were the thing I loved the most. I wasn't stupid enough (or wealthy enough) to own a bike, given my lead-foot tendencies, but I did know how to ride. It was the one useful thing my crazy, bike-obsessed cousin, Crack, had taught me. He owned thirteen bikes in various stages of rebuild and before his girlfriend Sable came along he used to sleep on a mattress in amongst crankshafts and a pile of slicks.

'Not so sweet at the moment. He has a decent rider who should be on track to win the Superbike Moto-GP class—but some things have been happening around the pits: little accidents, delays, parts getting mixed up and putting them behind on their maintenance schedule. Last week, their new tyre order went to Adelaide ... twice. Somehow the paperwork got mixed up.'

'Could just be a run of bad luck.'

'My acquaintance thinks it's meant to look like that—enough to be disruptive, but not enough to be suspicious.'

'Does he have any ideas on who it might be? Or why they're doing it?'

'I think the "why" bit is simple. He's got the final race for the season coming up on Sunday. Someone wants to stop him winning it. As for the rest … you'll have to talk to Bolo.'

I watched Tozzi take the sugar sachets out of their holder and attempt to throw them back in one by one. Old hoopers never die; their rings just get lower.

'Well?' He stopped playing with the sugar and took another sip of his coffee.

It sounded okay and, frankly, Tara Sharp's Paralanguage and Kinesics Agency was in the market for anything investigative that paid, on the basis that I needed to eat, put petrol in Mona and quit living in my parents' garage. Anything except pretending that I knew how to be an escort at Madame Vine's!

I'd actually met Tozzi on a job. He turned out to be a good guy caught up in a bad situation, and I'd switched sides away from consulting for the baddies to try to help him save his business and his reputation. Tozzi kind of owed me a favour. Finding this job was probably his way of saying thank you.

'Did you discuss payment?' I asked baldly. Some things weren't worth beating around the bush about.

Tozzi's caramel aura warmed a little. I'd noticed before that the mention of money did that.

'I believe he's offering fifty bucks an hour spent on the job. Or a retainer of two fifty a day for a week, plus expenses.'

'Which would you take?'

'Both can work for you. I prefer the by-the-hour rate, but then you've usually got to justify it with a lot more paperwork.'

He had a point. Paperwork and I were like oil and water.

'How do I get in touch with him?' I asked.

'I'll have Jenelle get him to contact you.' Tozzi's red-headed PA who had even more of a lead foot than I did.

'Thanks.'

'No problem.'

He gave me one of those irresistable grins that he doled out sparingly. When he smiled like that and his aura went liquid caramel, I seemed to lose control of my spine.

'How's Antonia?' I asked, deliberately dampening his mood—and mine.

His aura blanched and a dark spot above his shoulder, which had been barely visible, enlarged. He frowned, opening his mouth to give me the usual fine-and-mind-your-own-business spiel. Then he seemed to change his mind. 'Actually, she's in rehab.'

'Super!' I said, feeling nothing of the sort. Tozzi's wife had an A-plus cocaine habit and an even worse case of

Material Girl. It was my secret wish that he'd ditch her and drive off with me (and the Reventon) into the sunset.

Nobody, NOBODY, knew about that particular fantasy, especially the man himself. I knew he found me attractive in an opposites-attract or a boy-you're-different-from-every-other-girl-I've-ever-met kind of way, but leaving his socialite wife wasn't part of that equation.

'In rehab in Perth?' I asked politely.

'In Brisbane. She doesn't know anyone much over there; figured that would be best.'

I knew I should have felt all poor-thing-good-for-her but the only thing on my mind was, he's home alone! Did that make me a bad person? In my defence, Toni Tozzi was also a total witch.

'How long for?' I asked.

'Two weeks with an option for three, and a follow-up program once she's home. She's already been there a week. I think she's going to do it this time, Tara. I really do. It was her idea. She wanted it.'

He looked so hopeful, so boyish, that the right words just fell out of my mouth. 'I'm sure she will. It'll be alright.'

The self-assured grin was back. 'Thanks. And a word of advice … the bike-racing crowd—it's serious stuff to them. Lot of ego and money tied up there. Go carefully.'

'Like I wouldn't?'

He raised an eyebrow. 'You want a lift home?'

I nodded. 'Can I drive?'

'Hell, no.'

Chapter 3

Smitty rang as I opened the sliding door to my flat. 'How did it go? Did you wear the white top? What did he want?'

'Fine. Yes. He had a job for me,' I replied.

'Oh.' She sounded profoundly disappointed.

'But there's more.'

'Oh?' An uplift in tone.

'Antonia's gone to rehab in Brisbane. Two weeks, maybe three.'

'And?'

'That's it really. He's hoping they can patch things up.'

'Oh.' Back to the dismal tone.

'Smitts, he's married and he's going to stay married. Besides, I've got a boyfriend.'

'Eddy is divine, I agree. But he's so young, darling. You don't want to be his mother. And Tozzi won't stay married. Can't you tell? No. Well, I suppose you were never a good judge of that sort of thing. It's just going to take a little longer than I thought.' She sighed. 'At least the man's got some staying power. He's trying to make it work with Antonia. He doesn't give up easily. I like that.'

'You are SUCH a romantic. Not everyone has a Henry in their life,' I said.

'Pooh,' she replied airily. 'Now don't forget our date. I'm going to text it to you as well: Thursday 4pm at the Beach Café.'

'Got it,' I said. 'Should I bring pepper spray?'

'No violence, Tara. My six-year-old son is already facing an assault charge,' she said sternly. 'Now, I have errands to run and then I have to take Fridge to the beach for a long walk before he burrows his way through to China.'

Fridge was the Evans' new dog. Bones, the previous incumbent, had shed his last hair a few weeks ago and gone to doggie heaven. The kids were so distraught Henry had gone right out to the pound and returned with a young, exuberant and enormous bitser who, somehow, had developed a strange affinity for me over everyone else. Maybe it was because I shared my sushi with him when I babysat the kids. I mean, the dog could eat anything.

'Fridge is cool,' I said, imitating the kids.

'Raybans are cool,' said Smitty. 'Fridge is impossible.'

I hung up smiling. Smitty always did that to me. In fact, thinking back on our years at school and uni together, I couldn't remember a time that Smitty hadn't made me smile.

My other bestie, Martin Longbok, was another story.

Bok and I had been drawn together by mutual antagonism, and to this day we found sport in pressing each other's buttons; a love-bait kind of arrangement.

I pulled my phone out of my pocket and called him.

'Martin Longbok,' he answered.

'How's my Glossy Guru?' I asked.

Bok was editor of a local fashion mag, which meant he got lots of freebies and had a wardrobe worthy of a Hollywood A-lister. Who'd have thought that skinny little dark-haired boy who used to punch me in the arm at school would become one of the city's foremost fashionistas?

'Aaah, T,' he said. 'Just about to call you. Been looking at some shots of your young beau, Edouardo. I want to use him in a swimsuit shoot but his agency is playing phone tag with me. Think you could let him know? Maybe he can hurry things from his end.'

'Sure,' I said. 'By the way, I've got a job.'

He paused for a second. 'Don't tell me … ummm … snake-catcher. No … no … palm-reader.'

'Witty,' I said. 'And no. I'm investigating some incidents up at Wanneroo Raceway.'

Bok gave a mock gasp. 'You and racing cars! Lordy, lordy! What fool hired you?'

'Motorbikes, actually.' I heard my voice getting proper, like Smitty's—my default tone when Bok started needling me.

'Even better,' he said.

'Well, at least I have a job and a date.'

'Oooh, please don't sting me, Queen Wasp.'

I laughed, not able to stay mad at him for long. 'You don't have any handbags you don't want, do you?' Bok kept a box of supplier gifts in his office.

He gave an exaggerated sigh. 'Let me look... What about Guess?'

'Too flashy,' I said.

'Louis V?'

'Too staid.'

'Picky, picky. What about Miu Miu?'

'A satchel?'

'Uh-huh.'

I gave an excited yelp. 'Yes, please!'

'Well, only if you promise to keep out of trouble. All that recent Johnny Viaspa business gave me grey hairs. Hey, did you see him in the *West Australian* today? He's sponsoring a charity event at Challenge. One hand's giving money for SIDs research while the other's selling drugs to teenagers. How twisted is that?'

My call waiting started up. 'Gotta go. I'll pass the message on to Ed.' I pressed 'accept' and hung up on Bok. ''Lo, Tara Sharp speaking.'

'Ms Sharp, my name is Bolo Ignatius. Nick Tozzi said you might be interested in doing some investigative work for me.'

Bolo Ignatius? Was he kidding me?

'Hello, Mr Ignatius. I certainly am. Where and when can we talk?'

'Call me Bolo. Are you free this evening? I'm keen to keep this investigation discreet so would prefer not to meet at my office.' He spoke quickly, as though he was about to run off somewhere.

'What time and where?' I said.

'Before dinner—say 7PM? At the Cocked Dog?'

'If you want to keep it discreet, may I recommend Sable's?' My cousin Crack and his girlfriend, Sable, had just opened up a bar and drawing a clientele was slow work. 'It's in North Fremantle opposite the Antiques place on the highway.'

'Yes, I know the area. Excellent,' he said. 'See you there at seven.'

My call waiting started bleating again. 'Bye … err … Bolo.' Bolo! Sounded like I was putting out a police alert. 'Tara Sharp speaking.'

'Missy, that you?'

'Mr Hara!'

'You come for dinner tonight?'

'I'd love to,' I sort of fibbed, 'but I have a business appointment at seven. Sorry!'

Mr Hara was my occasional boss and mentor. He'd taught me how to use my … ahem … gift for seeing people's auras and was the reason I now ran Tara Sharp's Paralanguage and Kinesics Agency. Hoshi's wife could cook like an angel, so eating there was food heaven. She also hated me, which meant I worried that I might find slivers of glass in my cannelloni.

'Eight is fine. Bring your friend Bok Choy and some wine,' said Mr Hara, and hung up.

Bok Choy? I couldn't wait to call Bok back and… Someone was knocking at the door. What the…? Suddenly the whole world wanted to talk to me.

I peeked around the curtain, not wanting to be caught out again. To my relief it was JoBob, or one half of them anyway—the vampire half.

My mother, Joanna, had turned 'wounded sensibility' into an art form. She could also out-snob the best of them when she chose to, by using the I'm-the-granddaughter-of-a-former-Lord-Mayor-of-Perth card.

I cracked the door open.

'Tara, darling, we've been invited to dinner over at the Dewars' on Saturday night. Make yourself available, won't you?'

Her requests never really bore any resemblance to … requests.

'Will Phillip be there?' I asked.

She patted her blonde rinse and tried to look at her reflection between the smudges on my window. 'I have no idea. You really must clean this glass—it's appalling. And take the birds out for me. Your father has to go into the city and my hip is aching.'

She left then leaving me in a sweat. The Dewars were one of Perth's Five Families and entrenched Euccy Grove socialites. My mother had been trying to marry me off to their son Phillip for years. Joanna didn't seem to get the fact that he had every chemical addiction you could name and then some. Or that I found him on the low side of repulsive.

I stomped down to the birds' cage, suddenly in a foul mood. Don't ever return home to live with your parents when you've been independent for nearly ten years. The only person who doesn't remember that you're an adult is usually your mother.

When I opened the cage, Hoo jumped obligingly onto my hand. I took the half-dozen steps up to the end of the driveway and popped her down on the lawn. By the time I'd returned for Brains, she was on top of the cage, flapping her wings and playing Superwoman.

'Come on, sweetie,' I cooed, holding my hand out.

She swiped her beak at me.

With one eye on Hoo, now cheerfully demolishing lawn roots, I ducked back into my flat and grabbed an almond from my bribery supply. Brains spotted the offering and hopped onto my hand.

After dumping her on the grass next to Hoo, I sprawled out in the shade of the pepper tree. The birds both gravitated towards me, as usual, and it wasn't long before Brains was perched on my chest and Hoo on the tip of one of my shoes. I tried shooing them off, but galahs know their own mind and they wouldn't budge. I resigned myself to being a human perch and settled in to reflect on the last month.

Things had improved in my life since my former

boyfriend, Pascal, had run off with my furniture and my flatmate. I had my own business and was enjoying the work so far, and I was dating a hot guy. If I could just earn enough money to move out of my parents' garage and into an apartment of my own, I would say things were on the up—

'Uggh! Bad bird,' I said, sitting up abruptly as an enormous runny green dollop spread down my white shirt. Not only that but Hoo, not to be outdone, had chomped a bit off the end of my shoe while I was lost in thought.

'Sharp.'

Swivelling my head, I saw constables Bligh and Barnes standing at the end of the driveway. Bill Barnes was a chunky, chuckly type of cop who liked to wink at you behind his partner's back. Fiona Bligh was by-the-book, chip-on-her-shoulder serious. I'd met them during an encounter with Perth's primo crime lord, Johnny Viaspa— Johnny Vogue to the rest of the city. Things hadn't quite turned out the way Bligh had hoped—Viaspa was still on the loose—and I kinda think she blamed me for it.

I hadn't seen Bligh in over a month. Would have been happy never to see her again. Not that I didn't like her, she was a decent sort, but her visits meant trouble. In fact, any police officer appearing in my parents' driveway was unlikely to be about anything good.

'Constables,' I said without getting up.

'What's that green stuff on your shirt, Sharp?' asked

Bligh. 'Looks like a dog farted on you.'

Barnes laughed.

'The hazard of pet birds,' I sniffed, chin in the air. 'What can I do for you?'

Both their faces lost any trace of humour and their auras contracted into thin lines of colour. Barnes gave me a nod-wink and headed off on a tour of the garden while Bligh squatted close to me.

'You seen John Viaspa lately?' she asked.

'How many times do I have to tell you … I wouldn't spit on him if he was on fire!' I retorted.

'Well, I'd advise you very strongly to keep it that way.'

I stared at her. What the hell was this about?

'Off the record, we've had a body turn up in the river that might be linked to him,' she added.

A cold, wet hand squeezed my heart. 'O-oh?'

'Not that it should alarm you, Sharp. I mean, you just said you don't mix in those circles.'

'No, siree. I do not!' I stood up then to hide the trembling assailing my limbs. 'Johnny Viaspa doesn't even know who I am.' Liar, liar, pants on fire.

Bligh leaned forward to scratch Brains, who faked with a friendly claw and then nipped her. 'Ow!' she said, sucking her finger.

Barnes ambled back from his tour of the yard and squatted down alongside Bligh. His fingers fought their way into the pocket of his overly tight pants and fished out a sandwich crust. Brains lunged for it and gobbled.

When she'd finished, she hopped onto Barnes's foot and began preening herself.

I gave Bligh a sympathetic look. 'It's all about the food.'

She stood up. 'I'll remember that. And you remember what I said. Come on, Bill.'

She strode off, leaving Barnes hostage to Brains. 'Tara,' he said pleadingly, pointing at his foot.

I coaxed Brains off with a grass burr and watched Barnes hurry after his partner.

I put the birds back in the cage and fed them, then headed down to my flat. I knew I should go to the gym, but my motivation had dissolved with the news that the Swan River had coughed up a dead body associated with Johnny Viaspa. Now all I wanted to do was lock the door and hide. I mean, I guess I'd always known that the man was capable of murder. But having a police officer point it out to you, in a way that seemed like a warning, made it real.

I changed my poop-smeared shirt and carted my laptop to bed, then shot Bok a quick text message about dinner while I waited for it to boot up. He came back with a 'no can do'. Seemed my Bok Choy had a date after all. I was tempted to call and demand details but decided to wait him out. If you pressed Bok too closely on anything he delighted in taking the perverse angle and would clam up. Sometimes it was better to let him come to you.

Instead, I checked the local news sites for anything about a dead body floating in the Swan. Nothing.

I Googled Johnny Viaspa as well, and sure enough there he was, large as life, shaking hands with the SIDs charity he'd supported. The photograph didn't reveal the pus colour of his aura or his cold eyes. Nor did the article mention his criminal record or reputation as the biggest illegal drug dispenser in our state. Johnny V, it seemed, was working hard on looking benevolent and law-abiding.

A message from Edouardo popped up on Facebook asking me to have dinner tonight. I was about to reply that I couldn't make it, when I had a brainwave. Mrs Hara loved presentable young men (Bok was her favourite). If I took Ed with me instead of Bok, she might not be so inclined to poison my pasta. I flicked Mr Hara a text asking if it was okay for me to bring a different friend. He replied quickly with aye aye—Hoshi Hara-speak for that's fine.

I sent Ed a message inviting him to dinner at Hara's and he replied with a giant thumbs up.

All goo-oo-ood.

Then my phone rang again. It was Wal.

'Hello?' I said.

'Teach?'

Wallace Grominsky, narcoleptic former roadie and current chief of security at the Tara Sharp Agency called me 'Teach' because I'd met him through a class I'd run from home: 'Improving Your Communication Skills'. Now Wal was having a thing with my Aunt Lavilla. Every time I thought about her and Wal together, I came back to, Da-a-amn, that's just wrong.

'Got some good and bad news for you,' Wal said.

'Good first,' I said, leaning back against the wrought iron of my bedhead.

'I got nowhere to live.'

'Aren't you at Liv's?'

'Need a place of my own.'

'She kicked you out?'

'Yeah.' He sounded forlorn.

'What about the boarding house?'

'Can't go back there on account of having no income. 'Sides, can't work for you over there, got no car. Okay if I doss on your couch for a while till I get myself sorted?'

I opened my mouth to say 'No way in the world' when the call waiting bleep started up.

'Hold on,' I said to Wal, and switched over.

'Tara, darling, you MUST help me.'

'But, Liv, I've—'

'I can't have guns in my house. You MUST take Wallace in while I sort something out for him. He has no money and no family and I won't have him returning to his former life. He's a changed man, and I really must insist that you help him stay that way. I'm setting up something for him but I don't want him knowing. Just a week, darling, I promise. Must rush now. Things to do.' She hung up.

Damn!

I went back to Wal's call with a sinking heart.

'It's me, Wal. Yeah, sure. You can doss on the couch. Just for a bit though.'

'Thanks, Teach. Take the rent out of my wages.'

Wal was on a percentage of my earnings, so the wages thing was an unfunny joke between us.

'Yeah, right. Now what's the bad news?'

'Sam Barbaro turned up floating under the Freo wharves with his eyes missing,' he said as calmly as if he were ordering a bucket of chips at the drive-through.

I suddenly felt sick. This must have been the body Constable Bligh was talking about. Barbaro had bird-napped Brains. He was also a small-town hood who had strong ties with Johnny Viaspa. 'Dead?'

'Dead,' said Wal.

'Who did it?'

'I ain't got speed dial to any murderers' confession booth.'

'Yeah. Sorry. Shit, that's awful. I mean, Barbaro should be in jail, not dead.'

'I got a bad feelin', boss.'

'Yeah. Me too. Hey, I have to go out this evening to meet a client. When do you have to move?'

'Now.'

'Now?'

'Yeah. I'm outside your place.'

'Jeez!' I hung up and bolted out the door and up the driveway. If JoBob saw Wal loitering outside, they'd call the cops. Last thing I needed was another visit from Bligh and Barnes. Or worse, Whitey.

My security chief was leaning against Mona, smoking a rollie, looking like a Russian Mafioso: tatts, tight black jeans, long red hair pulled back in a ponytail, cut-off tee showing brawny arms.

I grabbed the cig from his mouth and crushed it underfoot. 'No smoking in my place and no visitors.'

I trusted Wal, but I didn't trust him. He hadn't let me down—yet—but the truth was, he was a bit psycho. He wasn't a huge guy, but he was stocky and tough and kept a kitbag full of weapons in his cupboard. The scariest thing about Wal, though, was his lack of fear. He reminded me of Mel Gibson in Braveheart—sans the pretty face and shapely legs. Mel acted the half-crazy thing really well. Wal was the half-crazy thing.

Not that you'd know it right now. He picked up his bags and followed me back down the driveway as meek as a lamb.

Inside my flat, I scooped all the clothes off the couch and threw them on my bed. 'Couch is yours.'

Wal slung his bags down on a cushion and then joined them.

Spotting my errant bra hanging from the window rail, I dived over and stuffed it in my jeans pocket.

'I gotta go out now, Wal,' I said. 'I think there's food in the—'

But Wal was asleep; head lolling, lips puttering as he exhaled. He'd only been on his narcolepsy meds a short time and hadn't really stablised.

I shook my head and sighed. This had been one strange day.

Chapter 4

I was a bit early with Bolo Ignatius so I thought I'd drive up to the Burger Bus near the Ocean Beach Hotel for a double meat and bacon burger. Dinner was a couple of hours away and I didn't want my stomach gurgling through the meeting.

The OBH had long been my local pub. I'd met boyfriends there, shot pool with mates, and poured my heart out to Smitty and Bok over many cheap scotch and cokes. Like half the young people of Perth, the OBH held many memories for me, including some I wished I'd forgotten. This evening it was already filling up with its current crop of beautiful young things, and I envied them their eighteen-and-anything-is-possible attitudes. At almost twenty-eight, I was still unfettered and knew I probably shouldn't be. Where was the career? Where was the mortgage? And the life partner? And the kids?

Pushing my momentary life crisis to the side, I paid for the burger and decided to eat in the car park above dog beach. I took the beach road back north a little, and drank in the view.

Like most cities, Perth has different faces. Today, my city was all about business and get on with it. The wind was crisp, turning over neat whitecaps on the Indian Ocean. Days like this infused me with energy and made me think I could take on anyone.

I pulled into a parking bay just above the beach and got out to sit on my bonnet, eat and scout for Smitty and Fridge. They often walked about this time and it was hard to miss them, seeing as Fridge was the size of a Shetland pony. With the brown and white shaggy coat of a Saint Bernard and the square head of a Great Dane, he was also a kind of mutant beast.

I spotted him in the distance bounding crazily about in the sand below, chasing his ball, seagulls, anything that looked like fun.

I waved and shouted out to Smitty. My flailing caught her attention and she threw Fridge's ball back up towards the dunes in my general direction. It landed on the rocks below me.

Fridge bounded across the strip of beach and leaped effortlessly up the jagged outcrop to reclaim it. He paused at the top, his nose pricked up into the wind as he scented my burger. With an excited yelp, he dropped the ball and rushed at me like a Pamplona bull. I reacted too slowly and before I could move, giant paws knocked me on my back, and gobs of stringy saliva slathered my hair. I tried to shout for Smitty, but a dog's tongue the size of an Atlantic salmon muted me.

Then it moved to my hand, licking and gulping my burger down into that giant mouth and gullet.

'Fridge! Fridge!' shouted Smitty, puffing her way up the rocks. 'Bad dog! Get down!'

After a bit more remonstrating, some manoeuvring to attach his lead and some heavy-duty tugging, Fridge withdrew. But not without one final sloppy lick up the side of my neck and into my ear.

Dazed, I sat up.

'Dammit, T, sorry about that, but you know Fridge adores you almost as much as burgers.'

Barely restraining her laughter, Smitty handed her beach towel to me to dry off. Then she tapped Fridge on the haunches with his lead and he sat down, tongue lolling happily. 'What are you doing here anyway? You haven't forgotten tomorrow have you?' she asked.

I scraped bits of beetroot and lettuce off Mona's bonnet and dumped them in a nearby bin.

'Just killing time on my way to Sable's.'

'Say hi to the happy couple for me,' she said smiling.

I rolled my eyes. 'I miss the old Crack.'

'When a guy falls as hard as he did for Sable, he'll do just about anything to please her. I think it's sweet.'

I shrugged and wagged my finger at Fridge. 'The only thing I know is that if you eat my food, we can't be friends.'

He yipped.

'I think you'd better get going before he decides he's coming home with you,' Smitty said.

I nodded. 'Good idea. I'll see you for the showdown.'

Fridge howled as I jumped into Mona and began to reverse out. The last thing I saw was him trying to haul Smitty after me. I planted my foot to make a quick escape.

My cousin Crack and his go-getting girlfriend, Sable, had bought the warehouse lease from a fashion designer wholesaler, and converted it into a slick cocktail bar. The interior was all acid-cleaned walls and plush couches. Sable's dad was a grano-worker who'd scored her a selection of granite slabs for a low price. With the right lighting on them, the bar tops twinkled greens and pinks and reds from their black rock backgrounds.

Crack was behind the bar when I entered and gave me a wave. With his long dark hair tied back in a neat ponytail and a fitted t-shirt and jeans, he looked like a younger version of Christian Kane. The opposite sex had always dug Crack, but he generally only had eyes for girls named Ducati, Aprilia and Honda. Until Sable came along.

Crack's mum, Cynthia (Syn to the family, on account of some of her wild youth), was horrified to see her son change so much. But my mother lauded Crack's new girlfriend as having 'whipped the fellow into shape'. That was, until she and Sable went head to head over the intricacies of making pavlova one family Christmas. Since then Sable had been relegated, along with Syn and Crack, into Joanna's tolerated-because-family basket.

I ducked into the ladies, washed my face and hands, then combed the Fridge-attack out of my hair, before returning to say hello.

'Hey, dude,' I said, plopping myself down on a bar stool. 'How's-it-goin'?'

Crack pulled a dismal face. 'Slow. Sable wants me to sell one of the bikes to pay for next month's rent. Or get a job.'

Until he'd met Sable, Crack had lived in a large room underneath his parents' two-storey home surrounded by the bits and pieces of his thirteen motorbikes. One time, I'd crashed on his couch after a party and stepped in a tub of sump oil trying to find the loo in the middle of the night.

'That bad?' I asked.

He nodded. 'Worse. We had an investor to get us over the opening hump, but they went belly up and we've had to borrow from the bank. Just need a bit of breathing space to get the place happening. Numbers have been pretty good but we're carrying a shitload of bank interest that's eating up our takings.'

My heart went out to him. Crack had never been going to amount to much before he met Sable. He thought the world of her … but selling one of his bikes… Didn't she know he'd rather sell a testicle?

'Wish I had some money to lend you,' I said. 'What're

you gonna do?'

He served me a glass of tequila and lime with a cute strawberry cut into a flower shape clinging to the straw. 'Dunno. Here, it's on the house.'

I reached into my purse and slapped some notes on the bar. 'No way. Not with things the way they are.'

He counted the money into the till appreciatively. 'What's happening, anyway? How're Joanna and Bob?'

'Fine,' I said. 'I'm meeting a guy called Bolo Ignatius here in a minute. He might have some work for me.'

Crack paused mid-count. 'Bolo Ignatius?'

'Yeah. You know him?'

His eye roll told me that I needed to get a brain transplant. 'Moto-Sane Racing. Who doesn't?'

'What have you heard?'

'Moto-Sane's one of the top racing teams in the nation. You need a lot of money for that kinda gig. Good sponsors and a good rider. He's got both. Do me a favour and find a way to mention my name,' he said, pulling a business card from his wallet with his name and number underneath a Sable's logo. 'Or better still, introduce me.'

'Sure, cuz.'

We touched knuckles and he mooched off down the bar to serve someone else. I dropped his card in my bag and munched my strawberry flower as I watched the door.

It wasn't long before a short, balding guy in bike leathers hustled on through. Even in the club lighting his aura was visible as a strong blue with vivid red flashes. He scanned the bar and made a beeline for me.

He hopped up onto the seat next to me and stuck out his hand. 'Tara Sharp? I'm Bolo Ignatius.'

I returned the quick, firm handshake with surprise. 'How did you know me?'

'I saw you in the paper recently. Didn't you help one of the local cops catch a burglar?'

'Errr … yeah … sort of… Actually, it was Nick Tozzi's mother who was burgled. I happened to be in the right place at the right time. Saw the guy getting away.'

'Getting away from Eireen Tozzi? Outstanding!'

Actually, a dead villain now, I thought with a shiver.

'I gather you know her?' I asked.

'Indeed. I'm terrified of the woman.'

'Me too.'

We both smiled.

This was getting off to a good start, so I kept rolling. 'So tell me about your problem.'

He glanced around to make sure no one was close enough to hear. 'I need the utmost discretion on this, Tara. I wouldn't want to see any of this business end up in the papers.'

'Of course not,' I assured him. 'Client confidentiality and discretion are my middle names. If it makes you feel more comfortable I can send over my client agreement.'

I could feel my nose growing from the lie. I didn't even have a letterhead let alone a client agreement.

'Not necessary,' he said, to my relief. 'I want this

informal and off the record. Nick Tozzi recommended you and that's good enough for me.'

'Nick and I have ... worked together recently,' I said.

'He said that you view things differently to most. I'm a businessman, Tara. I know how useful lateral thinking can be.'

'I'll certainly do my best. But go on, please.'

His face fell into an intense arrangement of lines. 'The final qualifier for the National Motorcycle Championships is on next weekend. If my team doesn't get the win we're ... in trouble.'

'What sort of trouble?'

'My sponsors have told me they won't continue to invest if we don't qualify this year.'

'I appreciate the pressure you must be under,' I said. 'But how can I help you?'

'Little accidents kept happening that affected our preparation for the last few races. I want you to help ensure the same thing doesn't happen again.'

'Tell me about these accidents.'

He took a deep breath and his blue aura became agitated. 'Broken levers, bad petrol mixes, electronics malfunctions. Endless little things.'

'And you wouldn't put any of it down to poor maintenance or a run of bad luck?'

He looked annoyed. 'Would I be sitting here talking to you if I thought that? These are NOT coincidences.'

Lesson number one, Sharp—don't disagree with the

client when they're offering you a job.

'Fair enough. Do you have any idea who might be behind it?' I asked.

'Yes and no. Two other teams are on the same points as us at the top of the table. And a third team is only a few points behind.'

'That's tight.'

'One of them has to be responsible, but I don't know which one. I want you to find out.'

'Surely you can eliminate the team behind you if they can't win?'

'Not necessarily,' he said. 'If we have to withdraw for some reason, they'll move up a place.'

'Do you have any history with the owners of the other teams?' I asked.

He shook his head. 'Nothing specific. But it's a very competitive business, Tara.'

Nick had said as much. I got out my phone and tapped in some notes. 'Can you tell me the names of the other teams so I can do some background work?'

'Riley, Chesley, and Bennetts. I assume that means you're happy to take the job?'

'Yes.' My mind was already racing ahead with possibilities as I put in the names. 'Nick said something about your tyre orders going astray?'

'Just another example,' he said. 'We buy our slicks from a supplier in Adelaide.'

'Why there?'

'Personal preference. And so I don't have to deal with Riley's.'

I glanced at my list of team names. 'Is that the same Riley?'

'Riley's Tyres. Team Riley. One and the same. Wouldn't use them if they had the last rubber on earth.' He flushed. 'So to speak.'

So much for no previous history.

'So when can I come out to the track?' I asked.

'Tomorrow. There's an opportunity for you to work in the pits during practice. You'll arouse less suspicion that way.'

Excitement squirted hotly into my stomach. Me. The pits. Hell, yeah.

'In what capacity?' I asked as coolly as I could manage.

'There's a man with a mobile food van who sells lunch on practice days. He's got a bad back and I said I'd find someone who could handle the van this week until he comes back.'

'Cook?' I croaked, my throat suddenly dry.

'No, no. Nothing like that. Just sandwiches and cans of drink. Maybe the odd bucket of hot chips. Here's his address.' He reached into his pocket and pulled out his business card with a name and address handwritten on the back. 'My number's there as well. Can I ring Jim and tell him you'll be at his place at 6AM tomorrow to pick up the van? Track opens at eight.'

I swallowed hard. I eat hot chips; I don't cook them.

'Sure.'

'Now,' he said, 'what pay arrangement would you prefer? Hourly or retainer plus expenses?'

Visions of myself knee-deep in curried egg and lettuce were quickly replaced with the thought of cash flow.

'Retainer. And I'll need … that is … my … errr … terms … are two days in advance when I work on retainer.'

He slipped an envelope out of his pocket and held it just out of my reach. 'There's one stipulation, Miss Sharp. I must find out who's behind this ahead of the race on Sunday. No other option is acceptable.'

'I understand.'

'Fine.' He handed the envelope to me. 'This should be enough.'

I swallowed back a whoop at the sight of several crisp one-hundred-dollar notes.

'I'll write you a receipt now,' I said. 'And send through an invoice for the week.'

'No, no,' he said. 'No paper trail! Your advance can serve as a kill fee if you don't deliver the information I need in time. There'll be some expenses. Keep a handwritten tally that you can destroy afterwards. You'll get the balance of payment plus expenses next Monday.'

It sounded fair enough.

Crack mooched back along the bar. 'Ahem, can I get you two any drinks?' he asked, giving me the stare.

'I'm right, thanks, but, Bolo, I'd like you to meet my cousin, Crack. Crack's one of your kind. He's been sleeping with his motorbike since he was nine years old.'

Crack leaned over the bar. 'That your Ducati out by the door?'

Bolo nodded without turning his head.

'Limited edition 1198 R Corse,' said Crack, as though talking to himself. 'I'd have to give her my bed.'

Bolo laughed. 'You know bikes?'

Crack's eyebrows shot up so high they almost touched his hairline. 'Know bikes! I can put anything back together. No formal training though. Dad wanted me to be a dentist.'

Crack's dad had more of a thing about professionals than Joanna did. Crack's mum, on the other hand, had wanted him to join the circus. How his parents' marriage had ever survived as long as it had was one of life's seven wonders.

Bolo pulled a card from his wallet. 'Come have a look around the pits sometime.'

Crack's mouth hung wide open long after Bolo had roared off into the night on his Ducati. When he finally closed it, he took off his apron, ducked under the bar and gave me a hug.

'Jeez?' I said, squirming in his embrace. Crack hadn't hugged me since I'd pushed over the Laidley twins for bullying him when we were ten.

'Things always happen around you, T. It's your karma,

I swear.'

'Is that like … karma … or Karma?'

'Both,' he said. 'You're fucking amazing, I swear.'

He laughed and tried to pick me up, but I weighed over eighty kilos and was half a head taller than him, so my feet barely left the ground.

'Crack!' Sable's voice cut through the air like a sharpened machete.

I elbowed Crack off me and threw the apron at him. 'Get back to work, cuz.'

He slung the apron over his shoulder and hustled back behind the bar.

Sable appeared next to him. 'Hello, Tara. Here by yourself?'

Sable was like her name: a dark, brown-haired beauty who moved with an animal grace. She favoured bangles, tiny little tank tops, tight pants and high heels. Next to her I felt enormous and awkward. It didn't help that she treated me with suspicion. Aside from Bok, Crack was the person I'd gotten into the most trouble with over the years, and we'd made the mistake of reminiscing once too often around Sable. She saw me as a bad influence and was more than a little disapproving of my single status.

To my relief, Edouardo walked in the door on cue.

'No, actually, I'm meeting someone,' I said, and waved madly at my gorgeous date.

There were only a few customers in the bar this early but all of them turned to look at him—guys included.

I didn't really focus on the slim hips and ripped torso that was evident beneath his thin t-shirt. To me, Ed was distinguished by his startling aquamarine aura, which flowed around him day and night like a slice of the Coral Sea—clear and bright and healthy.

'He's with you?' Sable didn't even bother to keep the disbelief from her voice.

I didn't answer, waiting for Ed to come close enough to slip his arm around me. He dropped a light kiss on my head and flashed Crack and Sable a stunning smile.

'Ed, meet my cousin Crack and his partner, Sable,' I said.

I took a long slurp of my drink while Sable gaped and Ed muttered an appropriate hello. Before Sable could recover enough to start the inquisition, I put the glass back on the bar and stood up.

'Better dash or we'll be late for dinner. Catch you soon, guys.'

With that we left.

Doncha love a grand exit?

Chapter 5

'You're driving,' said Ed as we stepped into the dark car park. 'I caught a lift down here with Vonny.'

'Okay,' I said, letting the 'Vonny' reference go.

Ed and I had only been dating for a month. He was younger than me, fairly new to town and very beautiful. I was expecting him to find his city legs soon and move on.

We climbed into Mona and headed back up the highway towards Mr Hara's. Ed put his arm along the back of my seat rest as we drove and massaged my shoulder.

'Did you get the job?' he asked.

'Yeah,' I said. 'I'm going to be selling sandwiches.'

He stopped rubbing my shoulder for a second. 'What?'

'It's my cover,' I added. 'While I'm investigating for my client.'

My phone beeped with a message as I slowed for a red light. I slipped it out of my jeans pocket and passed it to Ed. 'Can you read it, please?'

I glanced into the rear-view mirror as Ed squinted at

the screen and noticed a dark sedan that had been behind me since leaving Sable's parking area.

'It's from Wal. He says, *Keep a watch out for anyone tailing y*—'

I planted the accelerator and ran the red light, ripping a sharp left off the highway soon after.

'—*ou*,' Ed oophed out. He fell hard against his door and yelped with pain but I didn't have time for apologies. In fact, I didn't say a word for half-a-dozen more hairpin turns and a backtrack around the water tank on top of the Mosman Park hill.

Ed rubbed his shoulder. 'What the—'

'I thought someone was following me,' I explained as I turned down Mr Hara's driveway, then veered off into the garden so I could park Mona behind a large lavender bush.

My heart was pitter-pattering and I fussed with my beach bag to hide the slight shake in my hands.

'Who?' Ed asked. 'I mean … what the…?'

Hoshi's verandah light flooded into the car and I could see Ed looking at me oddly. I gave him a broad smile and played for distraction. 'By the way, Bok wants you to do a swimsuit spread for his magazine.'

Ed stared hard at me, then got out of the car and came around to my side. Before I knew it, he'd opened the door, clicked open my seatbelt and pulled me out. My legs were still a little weak and I buckled, trembling.

He caught me and held me close. 'Tara, are you going to tell me what's going on?'

I sighed and said softly, 'The police came to see me. They found a guy floating near the wharves in Fremantle.'

'And?'

'He was involved in my last job. Reading between the lines, there might be some 'cleaning up' going on. So, I'm just being … careful.'

'Wha-at? You mean the guy's dead?'

Ed's voice could get quite high when he was suprised.

The front door was flung open, saving me from further explanations.

'We'll talk about this later,' whispered Ed, as Mrs Hara huffed out onto the verandah.

'Tara Sharp, why are you parking in my lavender bush? Tell me why I should not chop your tyres into little pieces,' she demanded.

Crap. I grabbed Ed by the hand and dragged him over to her, positioning him so she got a full view of his beautiful face.

'Sorry, Mrs Hara, I need to keep my car out of sight for the moment. But I brought my friend Edouardo for dinner. I hope that's okay. You met him at my Aunt Liv's a while ago.'

Her thunderous expression changed into a smile as blinding as a lighthouse beam. 'Aaah, Edouardo, from the old country. *Si*. Are you Italian?'

'Spanish,' he said apologetically. 'Half.'

'Never mind, you still like to eat,' she said, crooking a finger and waddling off into the house.

Mrs Hara's waddle was deceptive. For a large woman she was nimble on her feet when she needed to be, and silent. A large Italian ninja. One time she'd caught Hoshi and me eating chocolate bikkies and emptied out all his sake bottles as punishment.

Eireen Tozzi scared me to death, but Mrs Hara turned my brain to brine.

Hand in hand, Ed and I followed her down the hall of their modest cottage in a not-so-modest suburb. Not that the Haras didn't have money. They just didn't like the tax man to know about it.

The kitchen was a homey room, ordered yet bursting with furniture, utensils and delicious aromas. My mouth watered at the smell of lasagna and garlic bread. The walls were apple green and the window ledge had been given over to a row of blue and white china ducks; not Mrs Hara's favoured Wembley Ware, but nearly as ghastly. The collectable marron plate that had cost me my Mandarina Duck handbag to buy, sat in pride of place on a lace doily in the centre of the kitchen table. Seeing as I'd just endangered Mrs Hara's lavender, it was probably the only thing standing between her butcher's knife and me.

Oh, and Ed, of course. Beautiful young men always put Mrs Hara in a better mood.

Mr Hara sat at the kitchen table flicking channels on the TV hanging on the wall near the fridge. 'What put the wind up you, Missy?' he asked without taking his eyes off the news.

'Hi, Hoshi.' I sat down on the chair next to him.

He turned his face to me and gave a smile. 'Your aura's all messed up.'

'You remember Edouardo?' I said brightly.

The almond eyes slid over Ed and back to the TV. 'Sure, sure. The young one.'

I felt a hot flush begin at my belly button and work its way up to my face. It was true, Ed was younger, but I didn't need it pointed out quite so baldly.

'Hoshi, turn that thing off,' said Mrs Hara.

She slammed a huge dish of lasagna down on the wooden table already set for dinner, following it with a plate of hand-sized slabs of homemade garlic bread, Greek and French salads and a dish of baked eggplant drizzled in herbs and oil.

Ed couldn't help an involuntary gasp of pleasure.

Mrs Hara's frown shifted to a smile and I breathed out in relief.

We made companionable small talk and ate until I could no longer convince my stomach it had any space. While Ed and Mrs Hara cleared the table, Hoshi tapped my hand.

'You do me a favour, Tara?'

'Sure,' I said, drunk with pasta and garlic love.

'I gotta nightclub job on Friday night. Boss wants me to go watch the crowd. Been having some trouble there. Need to see who.'

Should be simple enough, I thought. Even though auras

could be a bit indistinct at night, there was usually enough aura movement and glow in a crowd to see disturbances.

'Mrs Hara doesn't like me to go out so late. I'm thinking maybe you take the job, get the money?' he added.

'How much?'

Hoshi and I were always very direct about money. It was one of the reasons I liked working for him. That and the fact that he'd helped me turn my curse into something that could almost earn me a living.

When I'd met Hoshi, I'd been about to commit myself to psychiatric care. Seeing auras and being hypersensitive to people's body language had been driving me totally bonkers. I hadn't been able to keep a decent relationship or a job. My life was crap. And lonely. Bok understood about the aura stuff, but dear Smitty just thought I was 'different'.

Since learning I wasn't the only one who could see such things, and finding out how to better manage my gift, I'd gained a semblance of control over my life. Bottom line: Hoshi had saved me from myself. I could never say no to him if he asked for a favour; the money thing was just a formality.

'Fifty dollars to turn up. Three hundred dollars if you find who cause trouble.'

Wow, things were looking up in my finances department. 'Sounds okay. Now I need to ask you for something in return.'

His eyes narrowed. 'Speak.'

'Can you teach me some self-defence?'

'You mean fight-fight?' He made punching movements with his fists. 'Takes many years to learn my stuff. Much discipline.'

I sighed and lowered my voice so that Mrs Hara and Ed couldn't hear me from where they were standing looking lovingly into the pot of custard she was stirring. 'I know that, but Sammy Barbaro's been found floating under a Freo jetty. I'm feeling a little insecure.'

'You think it's John Viaspa?' he asked.

'I'm guessing so.'

He got up and went over to a narrow sideboard. From inside the carved doors, he produced a tall narrow-necked bottle of clear fluid and two shot glasses.

'Some things can be taught quick. You come soon, and we practise.'

I nodded and lifted the shot glass he handed me to my lips. 'Scull!'

'Kanpai!' he replied.

Chapter 6

Ed drove me home, on account of Mr Hara breaking out the Sambuca and me being such an obliging guest. Thing was, Sambuca made me horny as hell and by the time Ed pulled up outside Lilac Street, the idea that he'd drive home and come back with the car in the morning seemed to have been forgotten.

We canoodled down the driveway, past the sleeping, covered galahs and paused near the pool gate. Things got hot and heavy pretty quickly from there. I began to pull Ed down onto the grass but he resisted.

'What about your parents?' he muttered.

The thought of JoBob flashing a torch on Ed's shapely naked butt penetrated my Sambuca haze and I lurched towards the door of my flat instead.

While I scrabbled around in my beach bag for my key, Ed's hands began to wander to places they'd hereto never ventured. For a young guy he seemed to know exactly what was where. Overcome by a wave of pure lust, I left the key in the lock and turned back to those warm, insistent fingers. I swear I couldn't help myself when I pulled Ed's shirt over his head and unzipped his jeans. The jeans slid down his legs, leaving him naked apart from a pair of moonlight-enhanced Hello Kitty briefs.

I began to purr. And then giggle.

'Tara, let's get inside,' he said helplessly. 'Remember. Inside.'

I saluted and giggled again. 'Yes, sireee, Captain Ed.'

Then I ran my fingers down his muscled torso. He sucked in his stomach and Hello Kitty grew.

'Tara,' he said more urgently. 'In!'

Before I could turn back towards the door, it slid open and a body barrelled out, taking us down like a pair of bowling pins. I landed on Ed, and another body landed on me. A cool hard object dug into my neck.

'Freeze,' said a familiar voice.

I did just what the man said, sobering up in less than a gulp.

'Wal,' I whispered. 'It's Tara and Ed. Put the gun down.'

'Fuckin' wankers. Sneakin' up on a man when he's sleepin'.'

'Wal,' I said. 'It's Tara. I'm coming home. Into my flat. You're staying with me. Remember?'

The pressure on my neck eased a fraction. 'Teach?'

'Yeah. That's right.'

Wal began to mumble: a slur of disjointed words I couldn't understand. Something about his voice sounded odd, like he was half-drugged or dreaming.

Jeez! Wal was sleep-assaulting.

'Tara?'

Ed quivered underneath me. I could sense his urge to try to fling both Wal and me off. He was big and strong enough to do it, but Wal knew how to handle himself. And he had a gun.

'Don't move!' I whispered in Ed's ear. 'He's on medication and he's sleepwalking. God knows what he'll do. Let me try to wake him up first.'

We lay there, the three of us, in an unpleasant human sandwich. All the warm fuzzy sensations brought on by a good meal, a little too much golden liquid and some tantalising foreplay drained away. They were replaced by a knot in my gut, a pounding heart and an unwelcome desire to pee.

'Wal,' I said more firmly, 'it's Tara Sharp. Put the gun down and get off me.'

'Dirtbag!' he growled in response and dug the muzzle deeper into the back of my skull. 'Gonna blow your brains to shit kingdom.'

'Tar-ah!' Ed sounded a tad hysterical.

I didn't blame him. Our dates never seemed to go well. I remembered how the first one had ended in us nearly being caught in a police bust. I wanted to say I was sorry but a sudden cold wet sensation kept my apology unspoken. Water spray drummed into my side and splattered my face.

Wal, shocked out of his sleepwalking mind-state, shifted his weight.

Ed and I rolled, tossing him sideways. I dived for his shoulders and Ed crashed across his legs. As I dropped my bulk onto Wal's forearm, a heeled boot stomped on his hand, forcing him to release the pistol with a yelp of pain.

I grabbed the weapon and leaped away.

The light from a mobile phone flicked on, showing me the owner of the boot: a dark-clad figure with a pale face and heavily made-up eyes. Who the hell...?

'Cass? Is that you?'

'Yeah. Sorry about the water. Thought you could use some help.'

I took care to point the pistol at the ground while I grappled for something sensible to say in the circumstances. Cass was a kid who'd helped me out when I was doing some undercover work in the Bunkas, a less than salubrious area of Perth. I'd told her to contact me if she ever needed help, but I never expected to see her in my backyard in the middle of the night.

'Teach?' That came from Wal, along with a groan. 'Whass goin' on?'

Cass directed her phone light at the tangle of arms and legs that was Wal and Ed.

'You've been sleepwalking,' I told Wal. 'You tackled Ed and me when we were coming in. Lucky Cass here turned the water on you. Woke you up.'

'That my piece you got?'

I nodded. Water dripped from my chin and nose. I really wanted to wipe my face but I wasn't letting go of the pistol until I was sure Wal was properly with us.

'You awake?' I said.

He shook his head like a dog shedding water and extricated himself from underneath Ed. Then he stood up and reached out his hand in apology.

'Sorry, man. Musta been them sleepin' pills the doc gave me.'

Ed got to his feet and accepted the handshake. 'S-sure, Wal. Wouldn't be taking them again though.'

A light came on along the back of the house, flooding the swimming pool but leaving us still in the dark.

'Tara? Is that you?' called my dad.

Crap.

'Inside. Quick!' I hissed at the others.

Half-naked Ed moved quicker than anyone else, scooping up his shirt and pulling up his pants as he went.

Wal was next, grabbing his piece off me as he scuttled past.

I bent down and seized the snaking hose and jerked my head at Cass. She dipped around behind me and did a fierce scramble through the sliding door just as the garden light went on. This one bathed me with its fluorescence.

My father stood there in a dressing gown and slippers, clutching a metal garden rake.

'It's okay, Dad. I was watering the garden and I slipped over in the dark.'

His shoulders hunched in irritation. 'What in God's name are you watering the garden for at 1am? You scared your mother to death.'

'I … errr … couldn't sleep. Just trying to help out a bit.'

I tried to beam with reassurance, but my dad had seen that before.

'Have you been drinking?'

'No, Dad,' I said meekly.

'Then turn the hose off and go to bed, Tara. We'll speak in the morning.'

'Sorry I woke you.' I suddenly felt seventeen again: well-chastised and guilty.

The lights went off abruptly, leaving me to find the tap in the dark. Hose duly turned off, I entered my flat wet, dirty and agitated.

Ed, Wal and Cass were towelling off. Four mugs were already set out on the sink next to a tin of Milo and the kettle was on. So was my bedside lamp, giving a soft focus to the mud and grass stains on the lino floor.

I was about to demand that no one stood on my clothes when I suddenly realised they weren't strewn about. In fact, the flat was neater than a pin, clothes folded over the hanging frame and the bed made. A whiff of Jif assailed my nostrils. I stared at the sink; it gleamed in the lamplight.

'Has my mother been in here?' I asked suspiciously.

Wal went over and poured hot water into the mugs. 'I tidied it. There was nowhere to sit.'

I couldn't argue with that so I just took the Milo he

offered.

Ed got up nervously as Wal settled himself back on the couch and promptly closed his eyes. I had an insane desire to giggle but swallowed it. We sipped our drinks in silence for a moment and listened to Wal's tiny snores.

'I guess Wal heard us and thought I was in trouble,' I said.

Ed opened his mouth to say something, glanced at Cass, and didn't.

Cass seemed a little uncomfortable now things had settled down. I got the feeling she wasn't going to tell me why she was in my garden in the middle of the night in front of Ed, so I called him a taxi when we'd finished our drinks and walked him out to the kerb to wait for it.

'Sorry about tonight,' I ventured.

He didn't laugh, or make a cheerful comment about not being bored. He just said goodbye, squeezed my arm and got in the taxi. Damn!

He's too young for me anyway, I reasoned as I walked back to my flat. But that didn't stop me feeling tired and pissed off.

Cass was rinsing the cups when I got inside. Wal had settled into louder snores but was still sitting upright on the couch.

'Cass?' I said.

She put the last cup down and came over to where

I'd flopped on my bed. I tapped the end with my foot and she sat down in the appointed spot. Her make-up had smudged halfway down her cheeks and one leg of her stockings had torn right through and was wrinkled around her ankle. She looked like a punk reject.

'My mum and I had a fight. She chucked me out,' she said, fiddling with the arsenal of jewellery along her cheek, nose and lip.

'Why?'

"Cos she's a crazy bitch,' she said with a shrug.

Her pale face was made paler by the black shift she wore and I noticed some purple bruising on her neck that looked suspiciously like fingermarks.

'How did you get those?'

'She wanted to watch something else on television.'

'Your mother tried to strangle you because you couldn't agree on a TV station?'

A shrug. 'Shit happens. Jus' need a place to stay for a few days while I get some money from Centrelink. I had nowhere to go that she wouldn't find me and you said you'd help me if I ever needed it.'

'How did you find me?'

'White Pages.'

'But there's a ton of Sharps. And the house's not even under my initial.'

Another shrug. 'Picked the the poshest suburb, caught the train here. Walked down the street and waited. Saw your car pull up. Followed you down.'

'How long have you been sitting outside there?'

'Since dark.'

'You had any food?'

She shook her head.

I glanced at Wal then walked over to the fridge and looked inside. I retrieved a packet of Tim Tams and brought them back over to her.

She took them and ripped the packet open.

I watched her dip one of them into her Milo.

'Look, I haven't got much room here, Cass. You got other family?' I asked.

'Lily's in Bandyup prison and Danny-boy's gone up north. We kinda split up.'

'Lily's your sister, right?'

Nod.

I sighed. 'Look, it's really late. Let's get some sleep and talk about it in the morning.'

I dragged the spare doona under the couch, taking care to avoid Wal's feet, and spread it on onto the floor. Then dropped couch cushions and one of my pillows on it.

She rubbed her eyes and nodded. 'Thanks,' she said, and without another word collapsed onto the cushioned-doona and curled up.

I turned the light out, remembering at the last minute to set the alarm for my early start as a sandwich maker at Wanneroo, hoping that this whole evening would fade from my memory soon.

But it wasn't quite over.

My phone rang just as I fell into a dream that involved butter icing and Edouardo. I ignored it, too comfortable and sleepy to wake up. On the third go around, I roused myself to answer. The caller ID wasn't familiar.

''lo,' I croaked.

'Ms Sharp?' a distant voice whispered.

'Hmmmm?'

'Ms Sharp, it's Lena Vine.'

I didn't say anything for a moment while my brain fired the necessary neurons to register that a brothel madam was ringing me after 1AM.

'I need your help, Ms Sharp. It's Audrey.' Her voice was so quiet I could hardly hear her.

'What? How can I help you?'

'It's... I... Audrey's dead. Can you come over straight away?'

Chapter 7

By the time I dressed and made it over to Leederville, it was nearly 2AM. I took Wal with me but left Cass soundly asleep on the floor.

Madame Vine's front yard was already crawling with police and plastered with crimescene tape. Every nook and cranny of the garden was lit by portable lamps. Whitey stood at the front door, dressed in civvies and talking to my other least favourite constables, Cravich and Blake. A partially covered body lay not far from their feet. Even from where I stood I recognised the to-die-for heels peeking out from the bottom of the sheet. To-die-for. I wished to hell I'd never had that thought.

One of Audrey's arms was outflung and twisted and the dark shadow around her head had to be a pool of blood. I was glad I wasn't any closer.

Whitey saw Wal and me and came straight over. 'What are you doing here, Sharp? Showing up for work?'

'Yes, but not the way you think. Madame Vine called

me to help with the investigation.'

'You got a PI's licence?'

I shook my head.

'Then I suggest you go home to bed.'

'What happened?'

'This is a police matter,' said Whitey officiously. 'I can't discuss it.'

My hands went to my hips. 'I'd like to see my client.'

'Your client,' he said, wiggling his fingers in the air to indicate inverted commas, 'is busy talking to police. Now you and your boyfriend need to beat it.' He scowled openly at Wal.

Wal made a noise in the back of his throat that could have been a cough. Or maybe a growl. He didn't like being called my boyfriend. I felt the same way.

'Boss?' he said under his breath.

I shook my head the tiniest bit, meaning 'let it go', and turned back to Whitey. It was hard to believe this arrogant git was the same sleazeball who'd called me out of the blue a month or so ago on the off-chance I might want to have an affair with him. Or maybe it wasn't. Two sides of the same coin.

'Please tell Madame Vine I'm here.' My voice rose an octave. It was two in the morning; I didn't need this shit.

'Problem, Detective Whitehead?' called out Cravich.

Oh my God! Whitey had been promoted to detective, which meant he might have been undercover when I'd seen him here before—not just a client!

Fortunately, before he could reply, a white government truck pulled up in the street. Forensics, I guessed.

'Don't move,' Whitey ordered. He ran over to the truck, leaving Wal and me standing by the gate.

I got out my phone and called Madame Vine's number. She answered in a second.

'I'm outside,' I said. 'The police won't let me in.'

'I'm coming.'

At first glance, she seemed composed: still in work attire and full make-up, which hid her extreme pallor and bloodshot eyes. Once she was closer, though, I could see her trembling. Her expression was dazed.

'Can you tell me what happened?' I asked gently.

While she gathered her thoughts, I watched Constable Blake shepherd a half-dozen very embarrassed men out onto the verandah for questioning. I wondered how many of them would be recognised by the curious neighbours peering out their windows at the disturbance.

I scanned the line. No one I knew except for the guy I recognised from my previous visit. Mr Zegna Suit looked particularly embrassed and annoyed.

A few moments later, the men were joined by Madame Vine's girls. The police made them sit a distance from the men.

Madame Vine cleared her throat and took a breath. 'I was in my office. Audrey went out and answered the door to a caller. From what the police have said, there was probably no one there so she stepped out on the verandah to look into the garden.' She gave me an imploring look. 'I've told her not to do that. We get a lot of pranksters. More of late, since the threats started. I've told her to open the door on the chain then shut it if no one's there.'

'Do you have security?'

Madame Vine nodded. 'Leonard had heard a noise in the back garden. He was out there looking into it because the security camera was down. Audrey answered the door instead, and when she stepped out someone … shot her … from the street.'

'Were they in a car?'

She shook her head. 'I don't know. No one saw it.'

She began to shiver in the uncontrollable way people did when suffering deep shock.

'Madame Vine, you need to sit down. We can talk tomorrow.'

'No. Now. While it's fresh,' she insisted. 'Tomorrow…'

Tomorrow would be all police and newspapers. Tomorrow she'd begin mourning her lover.

'Okay.' I opened a memo on my phone. 'What happened this evening? Anything unusual?'

'No. It was quiet.'

'No prank calls earlier?'

'No.'

'Do you have any idea why someone would … m-murder … Audrey?' I'd never dealt with this kind of thing before and it was hard to say the word. 'Do you think the killer was after her, or could it have been a random event?'

'I really don't know.' Her voice began to sound faint again. 'Tara, you can see things others can't. Tell me, please, do you notice anything here amongst the clients? Or the girls?'

I didn't have the heart to tell her it was hard to read auras at night, so I made a show of scanning the customers, the girls and the police. From across the garden, I could only see a smudge of distortion around their bodies: their energy heat. The customers were giving up a lot of that, while the police were cooler and less disturbed. The girls were the most interesting: two of them had barely visible energy lines, almost as if the event hadn't stirred any emotion in them at all.

'Who are the two girls at the end?' I asked.

She looked over. 'Kate is the blonde, and Louise.'

'What were they doing … err … at the time … of the … shooting?'

Madame Vine pressed her fingers to her forehead. 'They were in the lounge, I believe. Neither of them had a customer.'

I typed their names into my phone. 'I'd like to talk to them both tomorrow. Could you arrange it?'

'Of course. Do you sense something?'

'I can't say yet. I'll know more when I've spoken to them. Is there anything else you can think of that might be a clue?'

Whitey came back before she could answer. 'You'll

have to move on, Sharp. We're extending the crimescene to include the street. Miss Vine, would you please go inside? One of the detectives is waiting to speak to you.'

Another profound fit of shivering shook the woman's body. I reached out and patted her hand. 'I'll call you tomorrow.'

She nodded and walked unsteadily back to the house.

'She needs medical attention,' I hissed at Whitey.

'Don't tell me my job,' he snarled back, and began widening the taped-off area so that I had to step back.

'Freakin' idiot,' I muttered over my shoulder to Wal as I backed away.

But Wal didn't reply. In fact, when I looked, he wasn't even there.

I walked back to my car to wait for him, and watched the forensics guy donning his bootees and coat. Wouldn't be much evidence left with all those cops stomping around!

Wal returned a few minutes later, sliding quietly into the passenger seat.

'Where the hell did you go?' I felt tired and shaken.

'Bin talkin' to Leonard Roc.'

'The security guy?'

He nodded. 'We used to work a band together.'

'He tell you anything?'

'Didn't see nothin' of the shooting. First he knew was one of the girls screaming.'

'He didn't hear the gunshot?'

Wal shook his head. 'Must have used a silencer. Lennie

was out back checking the security cameras. One had stopped working.'

'So it was planned maybe?'

Wal nodded. 'I reckon.'

'I wonder if it's got anything to do with the problems she's been having.'

'Which are?' asked Wal.

'That's why she originally called me. She thinks one of her employees is pissed off. Someone's been leaving dead animals on the doorstep and sending nuisance texts.'

'Sounds more like someone's trying to scare her.'

'Did your friend Leonard mention anything about it?'

'Nah,' said Wal. 'Probably too freaked himself to be thinkin' straight.'

'I suppose.' I wasn't feeling too good about being here. A murder investigation was way out of my league.

'Have to say, it's a big step up from shitty texts to a drive-by shooting,' commented Wal.

As usual, he was right on the money.

Chapter 8

Sleep amounted to three hours. When my alarm went off, Cass was still snuggled into my spare doona and Wal was stretched out on the couch, fully clothed. Neither of them stirred.

Crap. That's how I felt. And now I had to make sandwiches all day.

'Urrrr!' I sat up and scrubbed my face.

Cass opened a make-up-smudged eye. She looked disoriented.

'You're on my floor because you got kicked out of home,' I said.

A little nod. She licked her lips. 'Why are you up? It's still night-time.'

'No,' I corrected, 'it's morning and I have to go to work.'

With that, I set my jaw and planted my feet on the floor. Grabbing my towel, I headed for the shower. When I got back, fully awake and fully cranky, Cass was up and rooting through the kitchenette cupboards.

'You've got no food here,' she said.

'I eat out a lot,' I said, thumbing the clothes rack. 'There's bread in the freezer.'

What did you wear to work in a sandwich van? Jeans and a white t-shirt seemed right. I assembled what I needed and pulled the screen across between me and Wal to dress. Not that I should have worried—his face was buried deep in the couch, a cushion resting on the back of his head.

'Where are ya working?' Cass asked.

I stood on my tiptoes and peered over the screen. She had the kettle on, and was spreading jam on toast and cutting it into unbelievably neat triangles.

'Hey, can you make sandwiches?' I asked.

She stared at me in surprise. 'Who can't?'

I pulled a face, grabbed a spare towel off my rack and hurled it across the room at her. 'Shower's outside in the pool house. You got any clothes?'

She shook her head. 'Mum wouldn't let me take anything.'

I rifled through the drawer at the bottom of the rack and found a t-shirt. 'Wear this over your dress,' I said, passing it out from behind the screen. 'And here...' I threw her a hair band. 'Tie your hair back.'

Her expression turned stubborn, like she might argue or tell me to piss off, but I wasn't going to have any of it.

'Look, I'm working on a case, which means I have to disguise myself as a sandwich-seller. I need help with the food while I get around and ask some questions. Think you can do that?'

Her mouth snapped shut, cutting off whatever she'd been thinking of saying, and she nodded.

'Good. I'll give you forty per day.'

Her scowl disappeared altogether. 'Dollars?'

I stepped out from behind the screen. 'Yeah. If you pull your weight. Now hurry up.'

We drove through Perky's Pies for a second breakfast: two custard tarts, one vanilla milkshake and one chocolate.

Cass didn't have much to say until she'd finished her custard tart. She gave her mouth a refined dab with a paper napkin. JoBob would approve. Then she burped long and loud.

Maybe not.

'What's the job?' she asked.

'My client owns a bike-racing team. Someone's been causing trouble. Probably one of the other teams. He's got an important event coming up on Sunday that he can't afford to lose. So just keep your eyes and ears open for anything.'

I got a nod. Without her Goth make-up on and with her hair scraped back, Cass looked younger than her sixteen years—and sweeter. Her eyes were a soft green and her aura was like a cinnamon sprinkle. But that was all a bit misleading. I knew that Cass's idea of a good time was throwing beer bottles at the railway tracks. 'Sweet' probably didn't work as a description for her; 'tough and resourceful with attitude' seemed better. She'd showed me those traits when I was out chasing a lead in the Bunkas. I hadn't forgotten.

Nor had she.

Whatever happened at home must have been bad. I'd bet money that Cass had a high tolerance for dysfunction.

I took the Coast Road up towards Karrinyup, drank in the white-topped ocean waves and glancing sun: air clean and cool. Perth really was the most beautiful city in the world and the best-kept secret.

The food van owner lived in a salmon-brick duplex not far from Observation City in Scarborough. The rest of the street was full of mansions. He was tinkering under the hood of the van when we pulled up, and straightened up with difficulty, hands pressing into his lower back.

'I'm Tara Sharp,' I called out. 'Bolo Ignatius asked me to run your van while you're recuperating this week.'

He nodded and we got out.

'This is my ... err ... assistant, Cass.'

'Jim,' said the sandwich man proffering his hand. 'Thanks fer doin' this. Bolo says you've bin in caterin'.'

'Ahh. Yeah. Sure.'

'Jus' bring her back here when you've finished. I'll restock each day and the missus will clean her down.'

I liked the sound of that.

He opened the van door and beckoned us in. 'She's got

everything you need. Grill runs on gas, so don't forget to turn the valve off when you've finished. Menu and price list here.'

I stared at the well-scrubbed hot plate and deep fryer alongside. How did that work, I wondered.

Jim's forehead creased with doubt as he saw my expression. 'There're two five-kilo bags of chips in the freezer, above the meat patties and the dooper dogs.'

My stomach heaved at the thought of battered sausages.

No such problem for Cass. 'Cool,' she said. 'Milkshakes?'

Jim pointed to an appliance with a silver swizzle. 'Three flavours. Choc, vanilla and strawberry. Ice cream's an extra fifty cents.'

Cass nodded, casting a critical eye over everything. 'Looks easy enough. Sandwich filling in the fridge?'

'Yep.' Jim seemed happier then. 'The security guard at the gate'll show you where to park and hook up to the mains power. There's a list of instructions in the drawer under the cutlery. Call me if you need to know anything else.'

He handed me a bright yellow card with a tiny image of a BLT in one corner and his name and number in the middle.

'Thanks.'

He dangled the keys in front of me. 'Look after my girl.' He clearly didn't mean his wife.

I injected some assurance into my smile. 'Of course.

What time do you normally close?'

'Around 2PM. Unless a late order comes in.'

'Then we'll see you about two forty-five. Mind if I leave my car parked here?'

Jim stared at Mona. 'I guess so. What's the story with the paintwork?'

I stared at the flames on the side of my car, courtesy of a cheap paint job from a majorly dodgy spray painter named Bog in the Bunkas. The colour had been bad enough—orange—but he'd got creative and thrown in some black flame transfers for free. I now officially drove the she-beast from hell. 'A friend did it.'

'You need some new friends. Pull her into the driveway when you drive the van out.'

'Cheers.'

I performed the car manoeuvring, then jumped back into the van. With only a minor gear-crunch or two we were off and headed up the coast road again.

Wanneroo Raceway nestled amongst the coastal dunes fifty clicks north of the city. In the late seventies it was renamed Barbagallo Raceway but most people still called it Wanneroo Raceway or Wanneroo Park. I'd been there a few times, usually on V8 race day, but never for the bikes. Despite the thought of frying chips and buttering bread rolls all morning, I felt excited. The smell of fuel had the same effect on me as the leather seats in the Lambo.

We pulled into the visitors' car park thirty minutes later, and I left Cass unpacking Styrofoam containers while I went for a reccy.

The place was pretty much how I remembered it, apart from the new clubhouse at the back. The track was on the east side of the pits, and on the west side was Bron's Service Centre, a workshop that ran all year round servicing cars and bikes and no doubt supplying suddenly-needed parts. I did a walk around the entire pit area and hung over the railing at the finish line, drinking in the smell of burnt fuel as several bikes buzzed past. Then I wandered up to the information booth and asked where I'd find the security guard.

The girl in the booth tucked the gum in one side of her mouth and said, 'He should be at the gate. He must have gone to the office. You in Jim's van?' She pointed to the visitors' car park.

'Yeah. Just covering for him until his back is better.'

'Lemme give you my order now then. Jim knows I can't leave the booth for too long so he always has it ready for me.'

'Sure. You been working here a while?' I asked casually.

'Five years. Best job I've ever had. Booth's air-conditioned and I'm allowed to read magazines when it's quiet.' She scribbled something on a Post-it note and slid it across the counter.

'Chicken and lettuce on a white poppy-seed roll,

no butter. Can of Diet Coke. Strawberry muffin. For Sharee,' I read aloud.

'That's me.' She gave me a white-toothed smile and jangled her earrings, which were two cute black and white sheep with goggly eyes.

'I'm Tara,' I said. 'What time do you want your order?'

'Eleven forty-five, please. I like to get in before the wrenches. You won't have to worry about the Chesley team though. They bring their own caterer.' She flicked the tip of her nose and lifted it in the air. Her aura bubbled with energy.

'Guess you know everybody here?'

'Yeah,' she said brightly. 'That's part of my job.'

'Great.' I smiled back just as brightly. 'See you soon.'

I made a mental note to tell Cass to put extra chicken in Sharee's roll. She'd likely be a great source of information.

Cass! I hurried back to the van, where I found my homeless teenager in a heated discussion with the security guard.

'You have to move now,' the guard was saying.

Cass's face was set in obstinate mode and her aura had turned a dense brown.

'What's the problem?' I asked, turning my smile wattage up a notch.

The security guard and his milky-red aura shrank a bit at the sight of me. Some people reacted like that to my size

90

and my direct manner.

'I was just looking for you to find out where I should park,' I added apologetically.

'Refreshments have a designated area and a dedicated power outlet,' he said.

'Thanks … errr…?'

'Jase.' He proffered his hand in a friendlier manner. 'Your spot's right over there, alongside the toilet block.'

Next to the loo? Choice! 'Okay.'

'I'll follow you up there to make sure you settle in,' he said.

I transcribed this as "to keep an eye on you". 'Great.'

'So where's Jim?' he asked.

'He's got a bad back,' I answered, climbing into the driver's seat. 'Cass!'

But she'd walked off and was talking to a young guy in overalls.

With Jase leading the van as if it were a hearse and he was a funeral director, I drove to my allocated spot. By the time I'd parked and plugged into the power to Jase's arm-waving satisfaction, and written down his special order, most of the people in the pits area had come out to watch and smirk. When Cass caught up with me, my cheeks were flaming hot with annoyance.

'What have you been doing?' I snapped.

She gave me a hooded-eyed look. 'I've been investigating like you said to. The guy I just talked to told me who's racing here today and a bit about them.'

My temper cooled a little. 'He did?'

'Yeah. Then he asked me out.' She seemed surprised.

'On a date? What did you say?'

'What do you think I said?'

'What did you learn?'

'He works for the track owner. 'Parently there're four local teams up here practising today—Riley, Moto-Sane, Bennett and Chesley something or other. Like you said, there's some big race coming up on Sunday that they all want to win.'

'That's right. The final qualifier for the National Championships. Anything else?'

'He thinks that Moto-Sane should win—they've got the best bike and rider—but they probably won't get it together on the day. Team Riley's his favourite to win. He reckons there's a thing going on between those two teams.'

Funny that Bolo hadn't mentioned that. 'He say why?'

She shook her head. 'I didn't ask. Didn't want to seem too nosy straight up.'

'Fair enough.' I reached into my bag and brought out my phone. After touching open the notes section I handed it to her. 'We'd better get to work. But first, type all that in so we don't forget it?'

She shook her head. 'I'll remember.'

'But you might not,' I insisted.

She put her hands behind her back like a little kid. 'Yes, I will.' The freckly spots in her cinnamon aura became pronounced.

I was about to push the issue when I remembered her reaction when I'd given her my card after she'd helped me out with some surveillance at Burnside Station. I'd thought then that maybe she couldn't read all that well, but I'd forgotten it until now. And if she couldn't, maybe she couldn't write confidently either.

'Make sure you do,' I grumped to cover my realisation.

Cass got to work buttering rolls, chopping lettuce and filling the bain-marie. She seemed right at home preparing food. Meanwhile, I made an awful mess practising how to use the milkshake maker.

'Don't put so much milk in it,' she suggested.

I bit back a retort because she was right. 'You worked in a restaurant before?' I asked.

She shrugged. 'Maccas for a while. I did the cooking at home too. Mum doesn't do food.'

I eyed her with growing respect. 'You wanna make up Jase's and Sharee's orders?'

'Sure.'

I read them out aloud as if I needed to hear them myself.

As she got to work stuffing chicken into rolls, I put some notes on my phone, including the problems between Riley and Moto-Sane. 'Did your new friend say anything else about the teams?'

She resealed the lettuce container and shoved it in the fridge. 'He's not my friend.'

I made face at her. 'I mean your beau?'

She stared at me mystified. 'Are you for real?'

I grinned. 'No really … what did he say?'

'He wishes he was working for Moto-Sane. Apparently they pay really good.'

'Well,' I corrected automatically. Maybe there was a little of my mother in me after all. 'Has he got a name?'

'T-Dog.'

I shot her a look. 'T-Dog?'

She shrugged. 'That's what he said. He's on a job-skills scheme. Apprentice mechanical assistant class two or somethin'. Means he gets to clean the oil trays and sweep the pits.'

'Okay. Moto-Sane pays well,' I said, typing. 'That's good work, Cass.'

She flushed.

'Now I need to find out all the names of the people working for the teams and do some digging.' That probably amounted to about twelve or fifteen people. I was beginning to wish I'd taken the hourly rate.

I slipped my phone back in my pocket and ripped open a packet of potato gems, tipping them into the simmering deep fryer. Oil spat everywhere and the whole van quickly filled with smoke.

'Turn it down!' Cass coughed.

By the time I'd found the knob, the gems had crisped into little black nuggets. I scooped them out and revved the exhaust fan to max.

We waited for the van to clear of smoke then Cass offered to take over the chip-making.

After a couple of practise runs we worked out a system for dividing the tasks. Cass toook over everything that required cooking or electrical appliances and I manned the sandwiches and rolls.

Sharee came for her food right on time and we had it waiting for her. She peered inside the paper bag and gave a slight nod of approval.

Whew.

Jase followed a few minutes later. He handed me two pit passes with his cash payment. 'You'll need them to get inside the pits.'

I thanked him, and then suddenly we had a queue.

Whenever we got a short break, I washed up while Cass chopped more lettuce and tomatoes. By the time most of the lunch rush had been and gone, I hoped I never saw another deep-fried potato cake again.

So why then was I scarfing down a chiko roll?

Suddenly the memory of Audrey dead under a sheet on Madame Vine's verandah floated into my consciousness. I threw the chiko roll away, got a bottle of water from the fridge and opened the door, gulping in fresh air.

'Tara?' asked Cass.

'I'm okay,' I said. 'Just need some sleep.'

She nodded, accepting my explanation, the way teenagers do when they have other things on their mind.

We began cleaning up and I had just switched off the bain-marie when Bolo and another short guy turned up at the serving window. Bolo glanced at Cass while I looked over the short guy. He was wearing tight jeans that showed off his lean butt and legs, a t-shirt that had iron creases along the shoulder, and clean boots. His nose was large in his sharp-angled face.

If he was wearing an ironed tee, then he had to be married or in a steady relationship. I couldn't think of any single man that I knew who ironed his t-shirts—even the gay guys.

'You new here?' asked Bolo.

I followed his lead, pretending that we didn't know each other. 'Yeah. My name's Tara and this is my ... err ... Cass. We're going to be filling in for Jim until he gets over his bad back.'

'Bolo,' he said. 'I run one of the teams here. This is Lu Red. He rides for me.'

'Hi,' I said. 'Well, what can I get you, Bolo and Lu?'

As I copied down their order, I checked out Lu a bit more. Drivers and riders were all, without exception, risk junkies. Mostly they tended to be small. Didn't work so well if you were too big for your bike or had trouble fitting your legs behind the steering wheel of your racing car. Intense personalites were common too. Lu had a wound-up expression like he might pop a spring and bounce right on out of here at any moment.

Bolo clearly didn't want anyone, even his own rider, knowing what I was doing, so I served them up their two beef rolls with mustard and two cans of Coke and they went on their way. I watched them walk back to the rollerdoor lock-up garage section in the pits. There were only a handful of those, the rest were mesh cages. Looked like Bolo could afford the best.

'All done?' asked Cass.

I heaved a sigh. 'Yeah. I'll disconnect the power and meet you at the gate. Why don't you go and say goodbye to T-Dog? See if you can find out anything else.'

Cass nodded, slipped the apron over her head and ducked out the door.

I locked up the van and went to do a bit of my own snooping around the pits.

Not much was happening behind the stall sign that said Team Chesley; just a mechanic curled up asleep on a pile of rags next to a Kawasaki.

Two stalls down, Team Bennett was all locked up. But further along, Team Riley was in a small group meeting, all gathered close, sitting on upturned crates and drums. Two bikes sat beside them, one of them covered. The uncovered one was a Suzuki.

I walked straight on in without hesitation. Surprise was often a good way to get involuntary reactions and see auras.

'Hi,' I said brightly. 'I'm from Jim's Food Van. You want to get any early orders in for tomorrow?'

Of the four guys at the meeting, three of them responded with mild surprise and not much else. But the aura of the fourth guy, the one talking, flared sulphur yellow. I swear I could almost smell rotten eggs. I took a step back. Mr

Hara always said sulphur yellow was an aura to run from.

'What the fuck are you doing just walking in here unannounced?' the sulphur man demanded.

The others looked uncomfortable but nobody spoke up. I figured he must be the boss. That and the fact that he wore a casual suit and expensive shoes while the rest were dressed in jeans and grease-stained tees.

'Like I said, I came to offer an early-bird discount on lunches, but the deal just got cancelled on account of the potential customer being an arsehole.'

Not my best customer service move. Or a great way to go about gathering intel, but I hadn't bargained on being verbally attacked. Tozzi had been right: these guys were deadly serious.

I eyeballed the suited guy and backed out until I was standing in the daylight again. Then I turned and strode back to the van. By the time I'd unhooked the power and driven over to the gate, Cass was waiting for me.

'I didn't talk to T-Dog—he's over the other side of the track spreading sand.'

Job-skilling AKA slave labour, I thought.

'Check in with him tomorrow,' I said. 'We've made a start here.'

Tonight, though, I had homework to do on Bolo's problems and some hard thinking about how I might help Madame Vine.

Chapter 9

We exchanged vehicles at Jim's place and I gave him the takings. After a quick debrief, we were on our way home. It was 3.45PM and the seabreeze was howling in. Crisp cool mornings in Perth were heavenly; cool windy arvos were a plague.

Cass had the window down. She'd taken the elastic band out of her hair and it flew around her face, reminding me of Fridge with his nose into the breeze.

I put up with the cool, buffeting wind because it made it hard to talk and I was beat. All I could think of was having my place back to myself.

And sleeping.

Wal was waiting for us when we got back to the flat, sitting on the couch, his backpack at his feet. I sniffed the air. At least he hadn't been smoking, and the flat was even more spotless than yesterday. I'd never find anything!

Cass crawled onto the couch next to him and closed her eyes. I badly wanted to do the same but Wal had news.

'Boss, I got a place to stay. Wondering if you could drop me there.'

'Oh?' I tried not to sound too pleased. 'Where?'

'Liv's got a friend who needs a caretaker for his building. It's down on the highway on the corner of Glyde Street.'

Bless you, Liv!

Glyde Street was five minute away and right near my gym. 'No problem,' I said. 'Just let me change.'

I dived behind the screen and switched out of my cooking oil-spattered clothes into shorts and a gym top. Then I grabbed a pair of odd socks and my sneakers, and Wal and I were out the door.

'I'll bring dinner home,' I called out to Cass as I left.

She waved a hand but never opened her eyes.

The flat was above an antiques shop on the highway. Wal sent Liv a text to say we were on our way and when we got there she was waiting outside.

'Liv!' I enveloped her in a bear-sized hug and whispered 'Thank you' in her ear.

My dear eccentric aunt looked unbelievably hot in white bootleg jeans and a layered but fitted top that showed off her still-flat stomach. Her heels were teetering high and see-through with a gold trim, her hair was piled high and secured loosely with gold combs. She looked like an advertisement for brunch on the Mediterranean. As usual, Wal's eyes popped.

I totally got Wal's attraction to Liv. I mean, she was gorgeous and smart as well as elegantly offbeat.

I totally did not get her attraction to Wal.

Liv had left a string of broken hearts all over the world: businessmen, politicans, and artists. She'd been a muse for more than one famous writer. But this thing with Wal just didn't make sense to me. Although they did both love heavy metal music and Monopoly.

Common interests were strange beasties. I thought about Edouardo and me: we both dug Indian food, Mui Mui handbags, and Flaming Drambuies. Tozzi and I were both basketball and car addicts. And I suppose in a way, I was pleased Liv had someone to fuss over—other than me.

Liv got the key from the shop assistant and we went up the stairs at the back of the building. The key opened a large open-plan room with a sink and kitchenette in one corner, a big old couch in the centre, and a once splendid, now tarnished, brass double bed over near the window.

'Shit,' said Wal with open-mouthed appreciation.

'Where's the toilet?' I asked.

'Downstairs. So is the shower. Not ideal,' said Liv. 'I've brought you some food, Wallace, and some old linen I had lying around in the cupboard.' She nodded towards the pile on the bed.

Wal flushed and licked his lips as if he was thinking something unseemly. I took that as my cue to leave them to it.

Ten minutes later I was at my gym, chit-chatting with Craigo, my muscled-up personal trainer, in his office. Craigo and I had become pretty friendly since winning a triathlon together. He was already talking about entering another one.

Rather Be Dead? was a small gym with a pretty select clientele. Dad had given me a membership in the hope that I might meet someone 'suitable' there. My instructor, Craigo, was a doll—and they sold the best muesli slice. As it turned out, the place was useful for more than just food and fitness. I'd once seen a photo on the noticeboard here which had helped me solve a previous case. It also allowed me to blackmail Johnny Viaspa into leaving Nick Tozzi and me alone.

Being a small establishment, you sometimes had to wait for the equipment, but the waiting itself was pretty cool given the excellent air-conditioning and the numerous widescreen TVs and the eye candy. I caught up on the week's gossip with Craigo until a Stairmaster was free. As I dived forward, a guy got to it before me—just. He saw my disappointment and laughed.

'You take it,' he said. 'I was waiting for the bench press machine anyway.'

'Are you sure?' I said, hoping he was. If I didn't get on the machine now I was going to curl up on one of Craigo's funky couches and pass out.

'Yeah.' Another friendly smile.

My tired brain began to register him properly. He was

attractive in a short-haired, well-built, decent-faced kind of way. Not outstanding like Ed, or Mr Charisma Tozzi, but just … nice.

I mustered a semi-decent grin. 'I owe you.'

'I'll hold you to that.' He tossed his towel over his shoulder and headed to the bench press.

I exercised until I'd exorcised cooking oil and chiko roll from my pores, then dragged my spent carcass via the Vege Express back to Lilac Street. At the drive-through, I got vegetarian cannelloni and vegetarian lasagna; not because I didn't like meat, but because I felt like pasta and I was too tired to get out of my car and go in search of anything else. A quick trip through the local bottle-o added a six pack of Crown Lager and a two-litre bottle of ginger ale, all thanks to Bolo's advance.

The birds hung upside down and squawked for attention as I staggered past but I didn't stop to play with them. Dinner was calling.

Cass was sound asleep.

I dropped the hot food on her lap. 'Half each,' I said before trooping back out to the shower.

Cass had the plates and cutlery out by the time I returned. I unearthed my sleep-shirt from a neatly folded pile beneath the clothes rack courtesy of Wal the neat-freak. Two beers and a huge plate of veggie lasagne later, I was able to speak again.

'Thanks for helping out today,' I said.

Instead of my comment making her smile, it seemed

to unsettle her. Her aura deepened from cinnamon to a burnt colour, and her mouth pinched into a line as though she was worried about what was coming next.

To give her a moment, I leaned over and retrieved my laptop from under the couch where Wal had put it. We sat in silence while it booted up.

'Look, do you want to help me for the rest of the week?' I said. 'You'll get your forty bucks and I'll make sure you get fed as well.'

She nodded but still no smile.

'You do need to ring your mum and tell her where you are though,' I added.

'No way.' She almost spat it out.

'How old are you?'

'Sixteen.'

As far as I knew, it was legal to leave home at sixteen but I'd Google it to double check.

'Staying with me isn't a permanent thing, right, Cass. Just until we can find you somewhere else,' I said.

Her frown deepened, and I saw rebellious anger flicker in her eyes.

I rubbed my forehead. I was dead tired and suddenly not at all sure I wanted responsibility for a homeless teen who I barely knew. Worst of all, I was going to have to tell JoBob I had a homeless kid from the Bunkas sleeping on my floor before they caught sight of Cass and her piercings and rang the cops. Both those thoughts conspired to make me even more direct than usual.

'Listen. You came to me, remember. I'll help you to find a place and some work if I can. If you don't like that idea, you'll have to find someone else to doss with. And lose the sulk. If you like what I'm saying, good. If you don't like it, speak up, or use the door.'

Listen to me. What a hard-arse!

Cass's aura roiled around her and it looked as if she might be preparing to spit out a mouthful of abuse, but then suddenly she settled back into the couch, shoulders relaxing.

'Okay,' she said finally.

Crisis averted.

'Right. Now I'm going to find you some more clothes and you can have a shower. Then you're going to meet my parents. This is their house—and garage. It needs to be okay with them.'

'How come you're still living at home at your age?'

'Circumstances.' I tried to keep the grim look off my face.

I put my laptop on the couch and went behind the screen to rummage for clothes. Wal's epic tidying feat was quickly coming undone. Emerging, I handed Cass a skirt I'd shrunk in the dryer, and one of my more figure-hugging t-shirts. She was well covered but she was still smaller than me. I sent her off to get clean.

While she was occupied, I opened my phone notes and transferred the information to a computer file. Then I added everything I could think of about our day at the race track, including the names of the people we'd met: Jase, T-Dog, Sharee and Lu Red. After that, I used Google to help me gather info on the four racing teams and their owners.

Team Bennett was owned by Tony Bennett of Bennett's Hardware chain.

Team Chesley was owned by two local business identities: George Shakes, the diamond specialist jeweller, and Frosty Hardwick, proprietor of Steel Engineering. Apparently the team had been named after their favourite country and western singer.

Team Riley was owned by Robert Riley, the tyre mini-tycoon.

Moto-Sane was owned by Bolo Ignatius, sporting goods wholesaler. Bolo's business had to be his connection with Nick Tozzi.

I yawned. This was boring but necessary groundwork. Reading auras could only tell me so much. I had to be looking in the right direction in the first place.

That made me think of Madame Vine and the two women I'd promised to speak to: Kate and Louise. I searched the news sites for reports on the murder but it was all international news. A quick check of the West Australian newspaper online didn't reveal much either. So far it had been kept out of the media, which meant Madame Vine had some decent media contacts keeping it quiet. Or the cops were sitting on it.

Cass returned with her hair wet and her face scrubbed.

Aside from the piercings in her ears and nose, she looked sweet and innocent. I needed to introduce her to JoBob now before the scowl returned!

'Right,' I said, offloading the laptop again and picking up a full basket of washing. 'Come on.'

She trailed me out of the flat, up around the pool and in through JoBob's back door.

'It's Mr and Mrs Sharp,' I whispered to her as we stepped inside.

Dad was at his favourite post in the family room: recliner rocker, feet up, Fox Sports News on and the paper handy. When he saw I had company, he dropped the footrest and stood up. 'Tara?'

'Dad, this is a … friend of mine, Cass. She's staying on my couch for a few days.' I felt like a kid asking permission to have a friend sleep over.

'The couch?'

This came from Joanna, aka Mommie Dearest, aka Commandant-General of Manners and the Proper Way Things Should Be Done. I turned and saw her poking her head around from the laundry where she was probably ironing starch into Dad's jocks. I led Cass across the room to meet her.

'Hi, Mum. This is my friend Cass. She's … err … in between places at the moment. Thought she might sleep on the couch in the flat for a few days.'

I waited for the raised eyebrow and icy disapproval as Joanna eyed Cass off.

Cass sniffed the air. 'That casserole smells great. Is that turmeric and coriander in it?'

Joanna's eyebrow, which had begun its ascension to great heights, dropped back into place. 'Yes. A Moroccan mix,' she said. 'Tomorrow night's dinner. Do you like to cook, Cassandra?'

I had no idea if Cass was short for Cassandra, but from here on in it would be. I could just hear Joanna: Tara's young friend Cassandra from the east. Not the eastern suburbs!

Surprisingly, Cass didn't seem to mind the longer use of her name. In fact, her cheeks warmed and her aura expanded. 'I don't know much about it but I sometimes create my own dishes,' she said shyly.

My mother had a two-toned turquoise and red aura that ran around her body in defined streams. The turquoise signified her energy and presence and the red showed her predilection for material things. When I was younger, the streams were vivid and fierce, like bright rings of light. The last few years, though, I'd noticed a mellowing of their intensity, which made it easier for me to be around her. On some days I even saw flashes of yellow, which, according to Mr Hara's aura charts, suggested Mum was changing a little, allowing some joy into her life. Dad was semi-retired now, so maybe that explained the yellow. Certainly right now her aura was shooting out bolts of it. Here was the woman who'd made me wear gloves to church as a teenager, asking a Goth girl with multiple piercings and purple hair about cooking!

'I wish Tara would take an interest in food,' Joanna said with a sigh.

'I like to eat it,' I said quickly.

Unbelievably, both of them rolled their eyes at me.

I didn't like the way this was going at all.

'Why don't you come for dinner tomorrow night, Cassandra? I'll copy out the recipe and give it to you. It's one from Masterchef.'

'I love that show,' said Cass. 'Especially the celebrity one.'

Joanna beamed approval.

And there it was—a meeting of minds. Just like Liv and Wal had connected over heavy metal and Monopoly.

'Tara, get some fresh sheets. Your father will get the fold-out bed from the closet and carry it down for Cassandra,' Joanna said.

Dad and I looked at each other in astonishment, then, with only the faintest shrug of his shoulders, he went off to do as he was bid.

While Cassandra and Mum talked about their current favourite Masterchef contestants, I snaffled some sheets from the linen closet and some food from the fridge. Cheese, yoghurt, bread and half a deep-dish apple pie would do it nicely.

Dad came back rolling the fold-out bed and the three of us trooped back down to the flat. When the bed was set up and made, Dad waved good night and left us to it.

'Your mum's fully sick, eh?' said Cass.

I paused mid-forkful of apple pie. 'That's one way of putting it. So you really dig cooking, huh?'

Cass shrugged. 'Yeah. Like I said before, I used to do it at home for Lily. Mum doesn't eat much.'

'Lily's your sister. The one who's in jail?'

Cass began to pick ferociously at her fingernails. 'She was clean for a whole year. Her loser boyfriend got her using again. One day I'm gonna make him pay for that.' She looked like she wanted to cry but she fought it back. 'Are we starting early again tomorrow morning?'

I nodded. 'I have to check out the rest of the team members. You can do the van preparation while I snoop around.'

'Right.' She lay down on the fold-out bed and rolled onto her side away from me. 'Night.'

'Night,' I replied, turning off the overhead light and switching on my bed lamp. When I'd finished wolfing down the remains of the apple pie, I dragged my arse off to the bathroom to brush my teeth.

My reflection told me I was looking a bit rough, but not nearly as rough as Madame Vine had looked. I wasn't sure how I was going to do it, but somehow I had to help the poor woman.

Chapter 10

We managed to make it to Jim's for the van handover by seven fifteen the next morning. Seven hours' sleep beat the heck out of three, so I felt marginally better. A Perky's hot danish each and two large takeaway coffees helped.

By Scarborough, my mind had begun to multiply questions. I hadn't heard from Ed since the other night—what did that mean? How was Wal settling into the new flat? Who killed Audrey, for chrissakes. And how the hell was I going to find out before Sunday who was sabotaging Bolo's team?

In fact, so many things were bothering me, once we'd parked the van and I'd plugged in the power, I went for a walk to calm down. Cass seemed happy to chop lettuce and onion without me, so I headed down to the track.

Sharee wasn't at work yet and the booth was closed. I read some of the posters stuck to the outside. Most of them advertised upcoming events: Formula Ford and the return of the V8s. There was a poster for a circus, and a couple of handwritten ads—one selling second-hand furniture because the owner was leaving town before the end of the year, offering a bargain on a plush sofa and a Balinese-style queen bed. I liked the price but the ad was dated August, which probably meant they had been sold already.

My phone rang. 'It's Nick, Tara.'

My heart and insides did their usual flip-flop at the sound of his voice. 'Hi. I was going to call you today.'

'You first then,' he said.

'Wondered if you had time to talk to me? About the Bolo case, I mean.'

'What about dinner tonight?' he said after a pause.

'Fine.' I felt instantly nervous. I enjoyed being around Tozzi but I didn't want him thinking I might be a quick fix of 'whatever' while his wife was away. The fine line we were treading between work, friendship and flirtation needed to be directed back towards the work end. 'Business, of course,' I added.

'Of course. Why would it be anything else?' he said in a deeper voice.

'Yes. Your turn.'

'Mine was a personal question. Now that we're catching up later, I'll ask you then.'

'Oh, okay.' No! The waiting would kill me!

'I'll pick you up at seven thirty,' he said.

'Let me pick you up.' Antonia was away so there'd be no chance of running into her if I went to Tozzi's house.

'Okay. But I'll be at Eireen's. I have to go over and hang a picture for her.'

Eireen—Nick's tiny but terrifying mother—and I got on well, in a pour me another sherry, young lady kind of way.

'Sure,' I said, turning away from the booth to walk back towards the pits.

Nick hung up without saying goodbye. Almost immediately my phone rang again.

'Tara?'

'Ed?'

'Yeah. Who else?'

Apprehension twisted my insides. 'I thought maybe you'd put me on your Dangerous Hazards list,' I said lightly.

'Well, yeah. But that was a while ago.'

We both laughed. That was good.

'Martin's got me that swimwear job and I was wondering if you'd come with me?'

Me. At a male swimwear shoot? My mind boggled. 'Sure, but, uh, why?'

'Sounds pathetic, I know,' he said, 'but it's my first one. I've done underwear before, but that was in a studio. This is at the beach. I just wanted some moral suppport.'

'I'm working up at the racetrack all week,' I said, trying not to show how pleased I was.

'The shoot's Friday afternoon at four.'

'Should be fine. I can finish here early enough to be there.'

We chatted about a few more details and he hung up just as I got to the occupied garages in the pit lane.

This time I began with the Moto-Sane team. Bolo stood anxiously inside the rollerdoor, watching over his mechanic's shoulder as the guy peered into the petrol tank of a black Honda CBR 1000cc street-legal sexy beast. Lu Red stood on the far side next to an attractive blonde.

'I think there's something in there,' said the mechanic.

Red and the woman exchanged looks while the guy continued prodding about inside the tank.

'Got it,' said the mechanic, carefully retracting a pair of long-nosed pliers. Clamped between their ends was a piece of fuel-drenched rag.

'What the fuck!' said Lu Red. 'For shit's sake, Clem. How did you manage that?'

The mechanic straightened up, his face flushed. His tan aura flattened into a hard brown. 'You think I did this? What do you think I am—a fucking idiot?'

He thrust the pliers forward and dropped the rag onto Red's sneakered foot. Fuel splashed onto the woman's sandal and she gave a little squeal.

'You fuckin'—' began Red.

'Hi,' I said.

They all froze and turned around.

'Anyone like to put in an order for food from the van?'

Bolo gave me a strained smile and nodded. 'C-come in. It's Tara, isn't it?'

I pulled my phone from my pocket and stepped up

close to the bike. Red kicked the soaked rag away with his foot and the mechanic retreated to the back of the garage and began clanging tools around.

'Would you like something too?' I asked the woman brightly.

Up close she was beautiful. Her face was flawless, except for a thin scar that tapered from one corner of her mouth down and under her chin. She had straight, silky blonde hair, a tiny waist and killer nails. And the way her aura was interacting with Lu Red's, it seemed the pair had something going on.

'No. My man might, though,' she purred, putting a possessive hand on Red's arm.

Red was staring at Clem with an expression sourer than one of JoBob's prize lemons. 'Uh, yeah. Chicken and mayo on wholemeal. No butter,' he said without even a glance at me.

'Drinks?'

'Coke.'

'Righto. What time did you want to pick it up?'

He flicked to his watch. 'Looks like I might make it out to practice after all. So I'll take it early. Eleven thirty.'

I nodded and turned to Bolo.

'No, thanks,' he said.

I gave Clem another quick look. He had his back to us, his head buried in a large crate looking for something.

'It'll be waiting for you,' I said to Red.

After leaving the stall, I took a couple of steps around

the corner and stopped. Within seconds their voices were raised again and the argument continued. Red blamed Clem for being lazy and useless. Clem came back at him saying that Red was too busy sniffing after her to know what was going on. Bolo chimed in with some 'calm downs' and a promise to get to the bottom of it, then it all quietened down.

By the time I got back to the van, Cass was leaning on the serving window bench, chin resting on her palm, having a D&M with a scruffy teenager wearing a dusty uniform.

'Hi, Cass,' I said. 'Hi, T-Dog.'

The boy's mouth sagged open. 'How'd you know my name?'

'You just look like a T-Dog.'

He gave me a suspicious look, mumbled something about having to sweep the pit office and scarpered.

Cass screwed her face up at me. 'You scared him off.'

'Faint heart never won fair lady,' I countered, but she didn't seem to have a clue what that meant.

We got into the van and did the rest of the food prep while I told Cass about the argument I'd overheard at Moto-Sane.

'So the rider's blaming the mechanic for putting a rag in the petrol tank?' she said.

'Yeah.'

'Maybe it was an accident?'

'Try telling Bolo that.'

'He's your client, right?'

I nodded.

Sharee appeared to drop in her order, interrupting our discussion. She was wearing a bright-red t-shirt that said 'Bike Me'. Today's earrings were red electric guitars.

'How're you settling in?' she asked us.

'Fine. Other than the fact that some of the natives aren't all that friendly,' I said. 'Or happy.'

'Oh?'

'Just walked in on a big argument in the Moto-Sane stall.'

'Don't tell me!' She slapped her hand to her forehead. 'Lu and Clem going at it again? It's been like that all season. Someone needs to bang their heads together.'

'What's the problem?' I asked.

She glanced around to make sure no one was listening. 'I think Clem's got a thing for Lu's woman, and Lu knows it.'

Behind me, Cass gave soft derisive grunt, which thankfully Sharee didn't hear.

'Really?' I said.

'Lu is so besotted with her. He'd fall apart if she left him.'

'Is that likely?'

Sharee thought about it for a moment. 'She wouldn't leave him for Clem, I don't think.'

'For someone else?'

She shrugged. 'Dunno. Maybe. Hey, I better get back.'

Cass and I exchanged looks after she'd gone and I

added some more notes into my phone.

From then on, orders trickled in. Jase did a couple of passes to check on us; and Red came by to pick up his order right on the dot of eleven thirty—without a thank you.

As rush hour approached, Cass started to take control. 'Everything's ready to go. You wanna do the deep-frying?' she said.

I sighed. 'If I must.'

'I've set the oil to the right temperature,' she said, like a mother encouraging her ten-year-old to cook.

Tentatively I dropped half a packet of straight-cut fries into the bubbling oil.

'Take them out now!' Cass said from behind me a few minutes later.

I lifted the drainer up and the chips, amazingly, appeared golden brown and appetising. 'I did it!'

Cass held out a metal tray. 'See, you can cook.'

'They look good. I'll have a large serve of those,' said a deep voice from the queue building outside the van window.

Feeling ridiculously pleased, I scooped some into a paper cup and salted them.

From then on, Cass and I didn't get a chance to speak other than passing food to and fro. We fell into a rhythm where I took the orders and gave change while Cass made up the food. I repeated each order out loud as she was about to make it so she didn't have to read it from the pad.

When Jase came for his lunch, I added a freebie bucket of chips. His aura brightened in gratitude, so I took the opportunity to fish a bit.

'These bike racers are pretty intense. Heard a bunch of arguments while I was taking orders this morning,' I said, poking the chiko rolls and potato cake with tongs as I talked. 'Guess there's a fair bit at stake. Money and all.'

'Tempers run hot in the pits. On the track too. Seen some crazy stuff. Nothing like the fight the other night, though.'

'Oh?' I said, r-e-a-l casual.

'Had to call the cops in and all.'

'True story?'

His chest expanded a little with a willing audience. 'Yeah. I mean, I coulda handled it, but the track owner likes to have everything done by the book.'

I gave him an admiring look. 'A smart person knows when to fold. So who was fighting?'

Cass stopped washing up and listened as well.

'That mechanic from Moto-Sane,' said Jase.

'Clem? Wow, he doesn't look like the type.' I thought about his angry reaction to Lu Red's needling. 'Who did he have a beef with?'

'One of Riley's wrenches. Claimed the guy had been interfering with Lu Red's bike. Like I said, things get heated before a big meet.'

'Do you reckon it was true?'

Jase ate a couple more chips and thought about it.

'Guess it's possible. Everyone knows Moto-Sane's been having problems. But it's not real likely. They lock the garages when they're not there. And we're always around checking.'

'At night too?'

'Yeah. Twenty-four seven.'

'That's a pretty serious thing to accuse someone of. What did the cops reckon?'

'Fight was all over by the time they got here.' Jase pursed his lips.

'What?'

'Was a funny thing, though: Clem never told the cops what it was about. He just made out like it was an argument over nothing.'

'Maybe it was?'

Jase nodded, crushed his empty chips container and tossed it into the nearby petrol drum bin. 'Yeah. Probably. Better get back to work.'

After Cass and I had finished cleaning up, she went to find T-Dog to say goodbye while I wandered down to the track to watch practice. Lu Red was out on the black Honda CBR 1000. He sped past, leaving a cloud of four-stroke vapour in the air.

I saw Bolo leaning against the fence near the start/finish line with a board and pen in hand. Seemed like an opportunity to ask him a few things but I hesitated. It might seem suspicious, him talking to the sandwich girl. Maybe I'd call him later.

I settled for a visit to Sharee at the information booth.

'Did you see Lu?' she asked excitedly.

I noticed she had a stopwatch in her hand. 'You timing him?'

She put her fingers to her lips. 'Don't tell anyone. Not much else to do on practice days. Race day, well, that's something else.'

'Is he fast? Lu Red?'

'Fifty-six seconds flat last practice. He's real fast when the bike's working. Had a fair bit of bad luck lately though. Gig Riley's getting real close. Fifty-six-oh-three this morning. Gig's been getting in a bunch of practice. And the Suzuki's going like a dream.'

'You know a bit about bikes?'

'Bikes, cars, sidecars, motocross. I've got four brothers and they're all petrolheads. Besides, it's my job.' She clicked the stopwatch as Red came past the post. 'Fifty-five-ninety-eight. Oh my God, that's close to the lap record.'

I glanced over at Bolo. Red's girlfriend had joined him. Bolo wasn't watching the track anymore and their conversation looked heated.

I nodded towards them. 'You'd think they'd be happy about it.'

Sharee finished writing the time in a little pink notebook and looked up. 'Lu deserves better than her. She's so, like … controlling'

'How do you mean?'

'Makes all his decisions for him. You know ... how high and when. Have you seen his t-shirts?'

I thought about the ironed-in creases. 'Yeah, I noticed that. What's her name anyway? No one bothered to introduce me.'

'Sally. From some rich family over east. They own some fashion line or something. No ... wait ... handbags and shit. Accessories.'

'Does she like him racing?'

Sharee shrugged. 'Never talked to her. Only know what I've heard from ... you know ... around.'

'And?'

Sharee gave me a conspiratorial look. 'She and Mr Ignatius don't see eye to eye on most things. I heard she handled all Lu's contract negotiations and it got pretty heated.'

'Like ... she's his manager then?'

'With benefits!'

I pulled a face and laughed. 'Anyway, time I got going,' I said. 'See you tomorrow.'

She nodded. 'Yeah. Good lunch by the way. Jim always puts too much salt on it.'

'I'll tell Cass. Thanks.'

And I did, on the way home. For a moment she almost looked pleased, but that could have just been her face muscles getting tired of scowling.

Chapter 11

Cass had first shower, then went off to retrieve the washing from JoBob. While she was doing that, I lay on the bed thinking about what I now knew.

For starters, the owner of Team Riley was an arsehole. Then there was the Lu Red-Clem thing happening over the blonde woman, Sally, who I'd also seen arguing with Bolo. And the fight between the two mechanics: Clem and Riley's guy. The latter definitely sounded worthwhile investigating. Then another thought occurred to me.

I called Wal and he answered quickly. 'Yeah, Teach?'

'Please don't call me that, Wal,' I said. 'Makes me feel older than you.'

'Sure, boss.'

I swallowed a sigh. 'Listen, your friend, Leonard, can you check him out? See if you can find out what he's been doing since you last worked together.'

'He's cool, boss, I tell ya.'

'Will you do it, Wal?'

He grunted his agreement and hung up.

Cass returned with a basket of folded clothes and two cookbooks. 'Your mum says hello.'

'Is that all?' I asked suspiciously.

'Ummm, she also said to remind you about Saturday night. Dinner with Phillip something?'

Uggh. Somehow I needed to find a way out of that one.

Cass curled up on the fold-out bed and began browsing the cookbooks. I knew she couldn't read well but there were plenty of glossy pictures. I went back to thinking about the things I had to do. Talking to Nick was number one. Kate and Louise at Madame Vine's next. I included Crack on my list—he might know something useful now I had a better idea what questions to ask. Tomorrow I had to meet Smitty and Rampant Kindy Mum, and the next day I was babysitting Ed at his photo shoot. When that was finished, there was the nightclub gig for Mr Hara.

I couldn't see much in the way of sleep over the next few days so made a mental note to get to bed early tonight. Not a bad thing to have in mind given I was having dinner with Tozzi.

I thought about ringing Smitty for clothes advice for my dinner date, but it was acid hour at her place. I settled for Bok instead, calling him from the garden so that Cass didn't hear my tragic wardrobe dependency problem.

'Darling,' he said. 'Thanks for sorting it with Ed.'

'He wants me to come to the shoot with him. That okay with you?'

Silence.

'Bok?'

'Sure. That is … well…'

Bok never hedged with me. It was always straight to the point like a well-thrown dagger. 'Wassup, man?'

'You're welcome to come. But you should know that he's shooting with Jenny Munro.'

Jenny Munro!

'Bok! How could you? The bitch from hell with Ed!'

'Now, T, be nice. It's an article on some of our elite sportspeople. Each one's partnered with a model.'

'But why Ed?' I moaned.

'Jenny's pretty tall. I had to put her with one of the bigger guys.'

'Bok. How could you do this to me?'

'Stop being so dramatic,' he snapped, much more like his regular self. 'Come to the shoot, behave, and I'll bring some Louis Roederer to cheer you up.'

Champagne could cure most of the world's ills—but NOT, I was pretty sure, having your boyfriend rubbing up against Jenny Munro. Last time I'd seen Munro, we'd competed against each other in the running section of a team triathlon. Jenny's an Ironwoman and pro athlete. She should have taken out line honours, but I was being chased by two of Johnny Vogue's hoods (one of them the recently departed Sammy Barbaro) and beat her across the line. She went down in a screaming heap of recriminations but I was too busy running for safety to bother with it.

Besides, I owed her one. She broke my nose with a deliberate elbow in a basketball final when we were juniors. Not something you forget in hurry. Or ever. Evil bitch.

'Alright,' I said. 'But if she baits me…'

'If she baits you, you'll behave like the perfect lady that you are and ignore her. This shoot is excellent exposure for your boyfriend, T. You wouldn't want to spoil it, would you?'

Exposure was right!

Bok's always been talented at working me. We've been friends ever since he hit me on the head with a ruler in primary school and I repaid the compliment by tipping him off his chair. We knew each other inside out and back to front, and he wasn't above playing dirty to get me to do what he wanted. But he was also always there for me.

'I'm having dinner with Nick Tozzi tonight. Strictly business,' I added, quickly 'What should I wear?'

'Remember you have a boyfriend, Tara Sharp.'

Bok was gaining ground on Joanna as guilt-meister!

'Nick's got me a job. I'm just meeting him about it.'

'Then why are you worried about what you're wearing?'

'Just tell me!'

'Well … black is back … as long as it's red.'

It took me a second to realise he was slinging me a ridiculous fashion-speak line.

'Loser,' I said.

I heard him laughing as I hung up.

I took a deep breath. Now it was time for the thing I really couldn't put off any longer. I rang Madame Vine.

'Yes?' she answered quietly.

'Madame Vine. It's Tara Sharp. H-how are you going?'

'I'm … coping, thank you, Tara.'

'I'm … err … glad. Have the police made any progress on finding out who … did it?'

'They tell me it will take time but they're confident of a result. I'm not so sure, though.' She was silent for a moment. When she finally spoke, her voice had become thinner, more strangled. 'I must find Audrey's killer, Tara. I'll do anything to find him. You understand. Please, help me.'

I had to be honest with her. 'Madame Vine, I'm happy to help you, but you realise that I'm not a trained private investigator? The police aren't going to share any information with me. They're much more likely to succeed than I am. In fact, I'm not sure what I can really do.'

'The truth is, Tara, the police have been keeping the place under surveillance since the threats started. But I'm not happy with their results. It couldn't hurt to have you asking questions as well,' she said.

I thought about Whitey's attitude towards me and wondered. 'Do you mind if I ask why you want me involved?'

Another silence. This one shorter, though. 'Like I said, I'll do anything. And people I trust recommend you.'

'Oh. Okay. But no promises.' It was my turn to hesitate. What did I do now? Go with the only idea I had. 'The two women, Kate and—'

'Louise.'

'Yes. When could I speak to them?'

'They're at work now.'

I glanced at my watch. 'I'll be over as soon as I can then.'

'Thank you, Tara. I can pay you well.'

'It's not the money, Madame Vine. I prefer to only take jobs I think I can be effective on.'

'Please, call me Lena.'

'I'll see you soon ... Lena.'

I went back inside and told Cass I was going out. She nodded vaguely, engrossed in the cookbooks.

'You're having dinner with Mum and Dad, aren't you?' I checked.

Another nod.

'Right. Well, I have to see another ... client, then I have a business dinner. Lock the door when you go to bed, I'll take my key.'

Nothing.

I sighed. Teenagers.

I wouldn't have time to come back home so I needed to dress for dinner now. Ransacking my wardrobe, I found the only red thing I owned: a dress I'd bought for Smitty's birthday party the previous year.

Three minutes in the shower and out and I slipped it

on. It still fitted—a little snugger perhaps—but I was too preoccupied with thoughts of Madame Vine to take much notice. I couldn't get rid of the image of Audrey's stilettos as she lay dead on the verandah.

'You look like you're going to puke,' Cass observed from behind her cookery book.

'Errr … sure. I'll see you later.'

I grabbed my beach bag, car keys and a light wrap, and slipped on my black heels. Cass's eyes widened and she looked like she might say something, then thought better of it.

'What?' I asked.

'All good,' she said and buried her head in the book again.

I called Wal and arranged to pick him up on the way to Leederville. He was at Liv's apartment, having dinner, so I took a detour through Claremont. When he got into the front passenger seat, I noticed gravy stains on his shirt and wine on his breath.

'Sorry to drag you away from dinner,' I said. 'Did you find out anything about your mate Leonard?'

'I asked around,' he said slowly.

'And?'

'Seems he got out of the can a while back for pushing.'

'Pushing what?'

'Coke. Whatever. They reckon he's clean now though.'

'Okay. Thanks. Maybe you could suss him out some more while I'm talking to Madame Vine. Good job, Wal.'

'No sweat, boss. It's my job. Nice dress.'

I gave him a sideways look to see if he was joking, but his expression seemed perfectly serious.

On the drive over, I brought him up to speed on the ins and outs of the Bolo Ignatius job.

'Two gigs at once, boss. We must be getting a good reputayshun,' he said.

We? I swallowed to moisten my suddenly dry mouth.

'Maybe. Look, I'm going to talk to two of Lena Vine's girls, Kate and Louise. I want you to poke around while I do.'

'Gotcha!'

'Be subtle.'

'My first name. Subtle Wal.' He burped for emphasis.

I parked outside the brothel and slung my wrap across the front of my dress to tone it down a bit. The police tape was gone from the street, but a section of the garden was still cordoned off and a police officer stood by the door. We skirted the tape and told the policeman that we had an appointment.

Leonard, Madame Vine's security guard, answered the bell and he and Wal low-fived each other.

'This is my boss, Tara Sharp,' said Wal by way of introduction. 'Boss, meet Leonard Roc.'

Leonard was a big, muscled guy with a jaw thick enough to chop wood on. Hello, HGH! He held out a hand as big as a shovel to shake mine. 'G'day, love.'

His aura had thin streaks of white snaking through it like cracks. He wasn't long away from a major illness. It hadn't reached the *no* aura stage that, in my experience, meant he was dying, but he was on that path. Part of me wanted to say something but I'd learned that lesson a while ago. Stay out of strangers' lives.

'Hi, Mr Roc,' I said.

He found that amusing.

Lena Vine came up behind him and he stepped out of her way. Only a day had passed since I'd seen her and yet she seemed to have lost kilos. Her eyes were bloodshot from sleeplessness and trauma and her aura boiled unhappily.

'Come this way, Tara,' she said.

I followed her to a room opposite her office, which turned out to be the staff lounge. Not as opulent as the front lounge where the clients waited, but comfortable and clean. A pretty, fair-headed girl around my age sat in one of the chairs, flicking through a magazine. I could see immediately that she wasn't really paying attention to it.

'This is Kate,' Lena said. 'I'll close the door and make sure you're not disturbed. When you've finished, open the door and I'll bring Louise in.'

I parked my butt opposite Kate and sucked in her ambience. That turned out not to be the best idea. I got hit with an unpleasantly sticky sensation.

'Thanks for talking to me, Kate. Madame ... Lena is

very anxious to find Audrey's … you know.'

Kate lifted her eyes to meet mine. Her gaze was uninterested and slightly out of focus. 'Whatever. Why are you asking me anyway?'

I sucked in a breath. 'Can you tell me what you remember about the evening?'

She rolled her eyes. 'Like I haven't told the police a hundred times already.'

'Yeah. But I'm not the police, so just tell it like it was.'

'Who are you? A PI?' She showed a flicker of interest.

'Just a friend of a … friend of Lena's.'

'Oh.' Boredom returned. 'Well, I was in the lounge … doing my nails. I saw Audy go past and open the door. She didn't come back in. Then someone else went out. Then everyone started screaming.'

'What did you do?'

She stared at me, as if struggling to understand my question.

'What—did—you—do?' I repeated.

'Nothing. The others were all doing it. Poor old Audy.'

She licked her lips and tried to express some emotion but couldn't seem to sustain it. It was like talking to a rag doll. Ten minutes later I hadn't got much further and called it quits. Her answers had gotten more and more vague. I took another look at her aura. In the artificial light the other night, I'd thought it missing altogether, but could now see it was just so diluted it was almost invisible.

She drew a handkerchief from her sleeve and wiped her

nose. Suddenly, I knew what was wrong. Kate was stoned. Not obvious, incapable stoned. More like practised and still functioning—just.

I got up abruptly and opened the door. 'Thanks.'

She seemed mildly surprised and then shrugged. 'Whatever.'

Louise replaced her on the couch within moments. She was as fidgety and tense as Kate had been chemically flattened, her aura running in a tight grey bead around her body.

'Hi, Louise, I have some questions about the other night.'

'I've told the police what I know,' she said flatly.

'I'm a friend of Lena's, not a cop. So please, just tell me again.'

She hunched over defensively. 'I was in the lounge with Kate. Audrey went past to open the door and didn't come back.'

'Didn't you think that was strange?'

'Why should I?'

'The door was left open. Did you hear her fall?'

'I was listening to my iPod.'

'Uh-huh.' I took a stab at being a bit more provocative. 'How did you get on with Audrey?'

'Fine.' Her aura stayed tight and hard.

'What about Lena?'

'Fine.'

'Can you think of anyone who might want to hurt

either of them?'

'No.' This time sulphur sparks ignited in her aura like a match had been lit.

'Okay, thanks.'

'That all?'

'Yes.'

She gave me a suspicious look then got up and left.

Lena appeared almost immediately at the door, as if she'd been hovering.

'Could I speak to you privately?' I said.

'Certainly, come to the office.'

I followed her the short distance down the corridor and stayed standing when she closed the door and sat at her desk. Audrey's adjoining office door was open, her things still in place.

'What do you know about Louise's background?' I asked.

She thought for a moment, pressing her temples as if to relieve a headache. 'She's from Victoria, a student who found she couldn't live on her allowance. Many of my girls come to me because of that problem. She's been here nearly two years and I've never had any problems with her. Her other details are on file. Was there something in particular?'

'Could I review the file, particularly her previous job history? And, if you have it, a list of her clients since she's been here.'

She raised an eyebrow. 'Fortunately, I actually keep

those sorts of records. Not all establishments do.'

'Wonderful. I have to run to an appointment. Could you email them to me?' I gave her my address. 'I'll be in touch soon.'

'Do you think Louise is involved in what happened?'

'I'm not saying that. I just need to check some things out. In the meantime, don't treat her any differently to anyone else. By the way, do you have a "no drugs" policy among your employees?'

She frowned. 'A very strict one. It's one of my criteria for job selection.'

'And your security guard, Leonard Roc, how did he end up working here?'

'Leonard was trained by Instant Security. He came very highly recommended.'

'I assume they run background checks?'

'Scrupulous. I've used them before and always been very pleased with their standards.'

'So you know he had a previous drug conviction?'

'Leonard is quite reformed. I believe in giving people a chance to change their lives.'

'Fair enough. But on that note, you might want to have a word with Kate about changing hers.'

She pursed her lips and nodded. 'Thank you.'

Wal and I swapped stories on the way back to Liv's.

'Len reckons it hadta be someone who's been there,' he

told me. 'You know, with the girls. Someone who knew to get him out the back so they could get a clear shot on Audrey. Someone who knew she'd be the one to answer the door.'

'Sure seems that way,' I said. 'I need you to check out a company called Instant Security for me. See what you can find out about them—who the owner is, what their reputation is like.'

'That where Len came from?'

I nodded.

He chewed his lip but gave his begrudging grunt of agreement. 'Still think you're barking up the wrong tree, boss.'

'We'll see,' I said. 'Meanwhile, I'm going to do digging on one of the girls there. Got a feeling about her.'

Wal gave me a sideways glance. 'You got more than that, doncha?'

'What do you mean?'

''Bin talking to Liv about you. She reckons you've got second sight or somethin'.'

I almost ran Mona off the highway. 'What?'

'She reckons you don't just read folks' body language, you see things about them as well. Colours and shit.'

How the hell did Liv know that? It wasn't something I'd ever talked to her about. I mean, she knew I was a bit erratic sometimes but...

'And you believe that?' I asked, stalling.

'Yeah, reckon I do. Seen you react real quick sometimes,

like you can tell shit's gonna happen before it does.'

I bit my lip. The only people who knew I could see auras were Bok, Mr Hara and the psychiatrist. Should I add Wal to that exclusive list? He and I weren't exactly friends. Wal was psycho, and yet … he was kinda growing on me.

'Maybe,' I said carefully. 'Sometimes.'

I waited for his reaction.

'Cool.' He nodded his approval.

He left it at that and so did I.

Chapter 12

I dropped Wal at Liv's and sped on to Eireen Tozzi's mansion in Euccy Grove. Scrambling out of the car, I discarded my wrap on the back seat and smoothed my hair before pressing the doorbell.

Eireen answered dressed in a pink satin dressing gown and black pumps. Her hair was dyed a violent red; quite a change from the lacquered black beehive she'd had last time.

'Oh, it's Joanna's girl,' she said, as if speaking to someone else.

'Tara,' I reminded her.

'Yes.' She gave my outfit the once-over with pursed, disapproving lips.

Suddenly, I felt horribly self-conscious. What was wrong with my dress? As soon as Eireen had trotted down the hall to get Nick, I fished through my bag for my phone and speed dialled Smitty.

'I'm at Eireen Tozzi's picking Nick up for dinner,' I

whispered. 'Bok told me to wear red.'

'Red? But you hardly have any red in your…' Suddenly her intimate knowledge of my wardrobe clicked in. 'Tara. Please tell me you're not wearing the dress you bought for my Pimps and Hos party?'

'Um … well … yes. Bok told me to wear red. It's all I have?'

'Do you have a coat? Or a wrap?'

'A wrap,' I wailed.

'Put it on.'

'It's in the car.'

'Darling. This is bad. Flee now. Run out the door—'

'Tara?'

Too late. Tozzi had appeared.

'Darling. Brazen it out,' were Smitty's last words before I hung up on her.

I straightened my shoulders and lifted my chin. 'Sorry, just got a call.'

Nick's eyes bugged a little and he bit his lip. His caramel aura seemed to get thicker, like he was coated by chocolate. 'Where did you want to eat?' he asked.

When I shrugged, he said, 'What about Freo?'

Fremantle was a little out of our way but a good option if we didn't want to be seen together. Right then, I'd have settled for takeaway fish and chips in front of the TV. But Smitty had said to brazen it out, so I did.

'So what was it that you wanted to ask me?' I asked as we walked out to the car.

'I … err … needed some advice. Wanted to get Antonia a gift for, you know, getting through rehab. Thought you might be able to suggest something.'

'Oh.' I tried really hard not to sound disappointed. 'Um… I'm not good on presents. Sorry.'

He shrugged. 'Okay.'

'So how's the job going?' he asked as I swirled Mona past the Lambo and out of the white-stoned driveway.

'That's what I wanted to talk to you about. Bolo asked me to go out to the track undercover and observe the other teams. Well, I'm doing that but now I need some background.'

'You think I can help?'

'Maybe. The owners of the teams are all prominent local businessmen. I figured you might have heard things about them.'

I accelerated onto the highway and headed south to Freo. The moon looked way romantic against the cloudy, dark sky.

'There are four of them,' I went on. 'Tony Bennett, from the hardware chain; George Shakes and Frosty Hardwick, who own Team Chesley; Robert Riley from Riley's Tyres; and then Bolo.'

Tozzi nodded. 'I hear Bennett's pretty straight, but there've been whispers that the chain's going broke. Hardware's a pretty tough game when you're an independent. Chesley … well, I'm surprised Shakes and Hardwick could agree even to buy a team, let alone

141

operate one. Never go into business with family, Tara.'

'No danger of that,' I said, shuddering at the very thought of JoBob and me working together. 'How are they related?'

'Shakes and Hardwick married each other's sisters.'

'Oh?' When you lived in a small, isolated city you tended to accumulate general knowledge and scuttlebutt about people you'd never met. George Shakes and Frosty Hardwick had been on my social radar for years—I'd even been to one of Shakes' jewellery soirées. But I'd never known he and Hardwick had a family connection. Joanna, on the other hand, knew everything and more about Perth genealogy. I made a mental note to ask her for more info.

'Riley, though…' Tozzi trailed off.

'What?'

'Let's just say he's on the tough side of ruthless.'

Mr Rotten Egg, Sulphur Aura, Arsehole Riley? Quelle surprise! 'Do you think he'd do anything to make sure his son won the championship?' I asked.

'Yes. In fact, I could almost guarantee it.'

It fitted but it seemed too obvious.

'What about Bolo's team?' I asked. 'Do you know much about them? His rider? Mechanic?'

Tozzi shook his head. 'Not really. I mean, I hear that Lu Red's fast. Bolo found him racing country-circuit speedway in Victoria. Had a talent for speed but had never ridden a bike before. Bolo brought him back here and taught him how to ride a four-stroke. He owes Bolo a lot. So Bolo says, anyway.'

'Have you ever met Red's girlfriend?'

'You're testing me now. I meet a lot of people.' He screwed up his face. 'Maybe once or twice. Great legs. Slim. That's about all I remember.'

Great legs. I switched lanes in irritation, causing an eruption of horn-tooting.

'Bolo's never mentioned her to you?'

'What are you getting at, Tara?'

'Nothing. Just fitting pieces together.'

Glancing in my rear-view mirror, I caught a glimpse of a dark car behind me. It was identical to the one I'd thought was following me the other night.

'Hold tight,' I said, toeing the accelerator.

Tozzi was smart enough to grab for the ceiling grip before I swerved off the highway towards the beach. The road was deserted, so I floored it all the way to Port Beach before doubling back to the highway and turning right onto the Freo bridge. Neither of us spoke until I'd found a park on the west side of the CBD near the old warehouses.

'You going to tell me what that was about?' asked Tozzi, when I turned the engine off.

I thought about lying, but he probably needed to know.

'I had an off-the-record visit from the local cops warning me to keep clear of John Viaspa,' I told him, and rolled my eyes. 'Like I needed that! Anyway, then I heard that Sammy Barbaro turned up doing a dead puffer fish impersonation under the Freo wharves. Minus his eyes. It's making me a bit nervous. I've seen the same car behind me a couple of times.'

Tozzi gave a low whistle. 'I hadn't heard about Barbaro. You think Viaspa did it?'

I shrugged and unbelted. 'Sammy knew a lot of stuff that could connect him to that mining scam they had going on. The only other people that know about it is us.'

'You should've gone to the police at the time.'

'No.'

'You still could.'

'I told you. I don't want to spend the next twenty years in some witness-protection program. I'd rather take my chances my way.'

Tozzi sighed. 'I feel responsible for this.'

'Then you shouldn't,' I said firmly. 'I make my own choices.'

'And we all know where that gets you.'

'Well, I chose not to sleep with you,' I said tartly. 'That was smart.'

He reddened then laughed. 'You did. But if you wear that dress for much longer...'

My hand crept to my neck. 'What's wrong with my dress?'

'Have you looked in the mirror?'

'I didn't have time,' I said. 'And Cass is staying with me. It would have been weird.'

'Cass?'

'Remember the kid from the Bunkas? The one I gave my handbag to?'

'Vividly,' he said. 'How could I forget someone whose boyfriend threw bottles at my car?'

'Not your car. At the train. Or the train track at least.'

'At least.'

'Well, anyway, she's staying with me.'

'Why?'

'Her mum threw her out of home. She's got bruises around her neck—I think her mum tried to choke her. That's actually the other reason I wanted to catch up with you.'

He leaned back against the headrest and stared through the windscreen as if bracing himself. 'Yes?'

I swallowed. 'I was hoping you might be able to find her a job.'

'A job? Are you crazy?'

'No. Just a bit left field,' I said sarcastically, grabbing my wrap and getting out of the car.

I walked quickly towards High Street. Nick caught me just before we reached the brightly lit main thoroughfare. He took my arm and we stopped and faced each other.

'Look, saying you are left field wasn't meant as an insult, Tara.'

'Right. Sure.'

'I meant it as a compliment,' he persisted.

I fidgeted, suddenly nervous about a bunch of things—

Tozzi using his serious tone; whether I'd lost the person tailing me; whether there'd been a person tailing me.

As well as feeling jumpy, I was starving.

'Then why are you always laughing at me?' I said.

'Because you amuse me.'

'How condescendingly sweet of you!'

He made an exasperated noise and grabbed my shoulders. 'Tara, why do you turn everything I say into a personal attack?'

'Because that's what it is. Have you ever listened to yourself speak? People either irritate or amuse you. Like pets.'

As his hands tightened on me, I got an odd sensation in my stomach. I glanced down and saw a bright energy cord running between us, belly button to belly button. It had happened twice before, and this time was no less unnerving. Maybe that's why I couldn't let go of the Nick Tozzi attraction. The cord pulsed like a high pressure hose whenever we got close.

I looked up to see him staring at the place where my red dress crossed over my breasts. His breathing pattern had changed and his aura was beginning to swamp me. I knew I had to get out of there. Something was about to happen that I'd really regret.

'Um … look… I think dinner was a bad idea,' I said, stepping back, shrugging off his grip. 'Thanks for your help, though. I have to go now. You don't mind catching a taxi home, do you?'

Not waiting for a reply, I wrenched myself out of his grip and ran like hell.

As I passed through North Freo on my way home, the neon sign advertising Sable's caught my eye. I veered left and pulled into the car park. I needed to talk to Crack. And besides, I didn't want to go home to my flat and sit there thinking about what had just happened.

Soon, I was perched at the bar, sipping a soda. Things were quiet, and Sable was out the back Facetiming with her cousin in Spain, so Crack was happy to plant himself opposite me with only the occasional nervous glance over at the staff room.

'How's the job going?' he asked.

'Slowly,' I said. 'I was kinda hoping you could give me some background on a few things.'

His eyes took on the shine that told me he'd happily talk about bike racing well into his next life. 'What did you want to know?'

'You heard about any problems between Team Riley and Moto-Sane? Or between the mechanics? Apparently they had a fight out at the track. Cops got called in.'

'Yeah? Well, I don't know either of the wrenches, but I've heard they both came from the same works team in Europe. Maybe it's a long running thing?'

He poured himself a glass of lemonade. I was pleased to see it. Crack had a penchant for rum, and rum had a penchant for Crack. Together, they got a bit crazy. One time after a rum-and-cola night, Crack tried to jump off a flyover bridge in Claremont, just to see if he could. I tied him to the railing with his belt until we both sobered up. I guess drinking was another thing Sable had saved him from.

'Which team?' I asked.

'Aprilia, I think.'

'So they have a history?'

'Could do.'

'What about Gig Riley?'

'Gig's a pretty fine rider, but he's not a natural like Bolo's guy.'

'What do you mean?'

'It's kinda hard to explain. Lemme think... You know how in basketball you get those players who can just do things without thinking? It's like they see the gaps on the court. The really good billiards players are the same—they reckon they see the lines on the table. Well, bikes are no different. You can be technically good but not have the feel.'

I raised an eyebrow. 'When you're "one with the machine"?'

'Sounds corny, I know, but it's actually true.'

I understood what he meant. 'So what about the father?'

'Riley senior's a hard bastard. Not someone you wanna cross from what I hear.'

'And the other two? Bennett and Chesley?'

'Chesley's a partnership. You know Shakes the jeweller?'

I nodded.

'It's kind of a hobby for him. Same for the engineer guy, Hardwick. Fair bit of internal politics, so I hear.'

'And Bennett?'

'Honest-to-goodness racing family. Been doing it for years. The father used to race cars and the uncle was into speedway. They say the youngest Bennett girl is mad keen on drifting.'

I grunted with disapproval. As far as I could tell, the motorsport of drifting was like skydiving without a parachute.

'Thanks, Crack,' I said. Pretty much everything he'd said confirmed what I'd learnt so far and I now had a lead on the fight between the mechanics. I drained my soda.

'You want a real drink, T?' he asked.

It was tempting. For once I had some money in my pocket and I could taxi home. Then I thought of Lena Vine. I still had to check through her files on Louise.

'Nah, got some work to do.'

He looked a bit disappointed.

'Let's have a night out soon,' I added. 'Bok too.'

He grinned at that idea.

The three of us could take the town apart together—just so long as we kept away from bridges.

On the way home, I stopped in Bayview for a consolation chocolate caramel cone at the ice creamery opposite Latte Ole. Patrons were bursting out of the café doors onto the sidewalk as the place did its evening transformation into a bar. I wondered how many people I knew were in there, and for a second considered going in.

Go home, Tara, I told myself sternly. Do your work.

Then I saw Ed stumbling out.

I opened my mouth to call to him, but shut it when a slim girl in a low cut LBD detached from a group near the door and snuggled in under his arm. They kissed briefly on the lips and walked off together, heads bent in deep conversation. My heart contracted into a hard, unhappy lump. Was that Vonny, the girl he'd mentioned?

I wanted to follow them but gave myself a lecture about having some pride. Instead I drove home licking my ice cream and feeling miserable.

Chapter 13

Cass was already asleep, so I tiptoed around for a bit then climbed into bed with my laptop. First I checked the Aprilia site. There were a couple of dealers listed, of which the closest was in Fremantle. I'd swing by there tomorrow and see what I could find out about Clem and Riley's wrench.

Next, I dug around for anything on Bennett's Hardware being in financial trouble. Sure enough, there were rumours about it on some of the financial forums. They'd also dropped off the latest Australia's Top Companies list, but I noticed that Riley's Tyres had snuck in at ninety-nine. If the rumours were true about an imminent collapse, Team Bennett might be riding in their last race.

I opened my email and clicked on the attachment Lena Vine had sent me. It contained her files on both Louise and Kate. I only gave Kate's a cursory glance; I hadn't asked for it, and wasn't really interested in junkies. According to the file, Kate was a home-grown girl from Bunbury who'd worked in various cafés, restaurants and clubs around Perth. The reason she'd given Madame Vine for wishing to become a 'team member' was her desire to save money to go on an overseas holiday.

I closed her file and opened Louise's. Her real name was Lexi Clarke. She'd transferred her university course from Ballarat to Western Australia and was living in a share house near Broadway Fair. I scanned her list of clients. No one jumped out at me, so I started the arduous job of Googling each one. A few turned out to be lawyers or doctors or mining execs, but I couldn't see any obvious connections with anyone unsavoury—not that bad guys tended to advertise on the Internet. I wasn't sure who I'd been hoping to see on the list. Johnny Viaspa, perhaps?

I cut and pasted both girls' client lists into another email and sent it to Mr Hara. He might notice something I hadn't. *PS*, I added to the message, *I'll be around for my first self-defence lesson tomorrow night.*

Shutting down my computer, I leaned over and put it on the floor beside me.

I was asleep before it switched off.

My phone rang at five the next morning. 'Yes?' I yawned into the mouthpiece.

'Tara? It's Bolo Ignatius. Sorry for the early call. I wanted to catch you before you head up to the raceway this morning. Something's happened.' He sounded upset.

I sat up in bed and rubbed my eyes. 'What?'

'I've had a … errr … death threat.'

'Wha-a-t?' I stiffened. 'How?'

'A text message telling me to pull my team out of the last round or else.'

'Or else what?'

'The message had a picture attached. I've sent it to you already.'

'Hold on,' I said. 'I'll check.'

I hung up and saw I had a message waiting. It wasn't nice, unless you went for pictures of a man hanging from a rope. I felt a bit sick as I called him back.

'You should go to the police. They might be able to track who sent it,' I said.

'No.'

'Well, let it be on the record that I am advising you to do so,' I said.

'Have you found out anything yet?'

'I should have some feedback for you soon. Can you meet me this evening?'

'When?' he asked.

I was accompanying Smitty to her meeting with Rampant Kindy Mum this afternoon, but I could catch up with Bolo afterwards.

'How about 5PM in the car park at Cott Beach?' I said. 'I drive a Monaro.'

'The one with flames?'

'You've seen it?'

'Heard about it.'

'Great,' I said. 'See you there. Mean time, think about the police.'

I hung up and sat for a moment. Death threat? My pulse accelerated. Something that serious and he didn't want to go to the cops. Now why would that be?

'Who was that?' asked a sleepy voice from the fold-out bed.

'Our client.

'Mr Ignatius?'

'Uhuh.'

'It didn't sound good.'

'It isn't,' I said grimly. 'Someone's threatening him. Sent him a nasty picture. I'm going to the gym, Cass. Back in an hour. We'll head off then—grab some breakfast on the way.'

'No need,' said Cass sleepily. 'Your mum sent down eggs and bacon. I'll cook while you're at the gym.'

My mother had sent down food? It'd been hard enough believing the vampire lady had taken to Cass. Now, this! My mother allowed me to raid her fridge with a slightly disapproving frown. But providing food for me … that hadn't happened since school lunches stopped when I was sixteen.

Within ten minutes I was at the gym. Craigo was fiddling with the cappuccino machine as I strolled past the counter.

There were already a few people there on the walking machines.

He looked up. 'Tara! You just coming home from a night out?'

'No. Why?' Did I look that bad? Actually, I felt pretty tragic to tell the truth.

'Actually, I meant … you don't do this, remember?'

'Do what?'

'Sweat in the morning.'

Craigo and I had had many a conversation about the merits and demerits of early morning exercise. I swore it endangered my biorhythms.

'I've got a job,' I said mournfully. 'It's the only time I can get here.'

'Poor darling. I'll have a hot chocolate ready to go for afterwards.'

'Make it two,' I said, thinking of Cass.

I did a walk and slow jog warm-up for about twenty minutes on the running machine and mulled over a heap of things. Audrey's murder and Bolo's death threat should have been at the forefront of my mind, but the truth was, a third thing was crowding in. I couldn't stop thinking about Edouardo cheating on me.

By the time I moved onto the stair and weights machines, I'd decided he was.

More people arrived in the gym as I moved onto the rowing machine, and when I looked up towards the end of my set, I found myself staring straight at Nice Guy's legs.

He was looking a bit rough himself, standing in the aisle as if not knowing where to start. He saw me and flashed a grin. I noticed his aura for the first time. It was a colour I'd never really seen before: a grey-green. Grey usually meant something dark or unhappy was going on in the person's life. Tozzi had a darkish grey spot, which I imagined had something to do with his cokehead wife. But generally people with green auras were calm and rejuvenating to be around.

I took another look at Nice Guy. 'You want this one?' I asked. 'I owe you.'

'I'm right, thanks.'

He folded his arms and spread his shapely legs, watching me. I finished my set a little more flushed than normal due to his scrutiny. It wasn't often an attractive guy watched me work out. And he was attractive: legs, arse and torso toned without being overdone; not a spare ounce on him.

I wiped my face with my towel and reached for my water bottle, all under Nice Guy's calm gaze.

'All yours,' I said cheerfully. 'Gotta run.'

He shot out a hand to help me up. 'Josh,' he said.

I took it. 'Tara.'

His touch was like plunging my hand into cool water. His aura darkened momentarily then settled back into a beautiful green.

'See you again,' I added and got the hell out of there.

I collected my hot chocolates from Craigo and paid

him. 'Who's the new guy?'

'Cute, huh?' said Craigo. 'Just in town for a week on work. You should see him in kickboxing class. Un-be-liev-able. And h-o-t.' He waved his fingers as if they were on fire and blew on them.

I headed out to Mona, balancing the drinks and feeling my ego soothed a little. Ed wasn't the only one who could pull the opposite sex.

I scoffed down Cass's eggs, bacon and toast in record time. 'D'lish. What's the sauce?'

She grinned. 'Hollandaise. Joanna makes it.'

'Really?'

Joanna makes it. Why was the vampire lady chumming up to Cass?

'What are you going to do about the threats?' she asked.

I shrugged. 'Bolo doesn't want the police involved.'

'Sounds suspect.' Her tone suggested she was a connoisseur of such things.

'Not necessarily,' I said, thinking about my own reluctance to get the police involved in my problems. 'Sometimes it just gets too messy.'

She shook her head. 'Suspect.'

I swallowed my annoyance at being contradicted. 'Whatever. Let's go.'

After swapping Mona for the van at Jim's place, we headed for the track.

'So how was dinner last night?' I asked.

'Great. Actually, your mum and dad are pretty cool.'

'You are kidding?' I said.

'No.' She scowled at me and stared moodily out the window.

'How are my parents possibly cool?' I asked, when it became obvious she was sulking.

'Well, they eat their meals together. And they talk to each other without shouting. Your dad washes up for your mum. Just cool stuff. Okay?'

I suddenly felt bad for not appreciating all the blessings in my life; and for wanting to have my flat-stroke-garage back to myself.

'I guess that is pretty cool,' I admitted. Then I tackled the so-far unspoken thing. 'Look, it's been great having you help me out, but the job will only last a few more days. Bolo wants a result before the race. So we should talk about what you're going to do next, where you can live, you know, long term.'

'I'm not going home.'

I thought of the ring of bruises around her neck. 'Fair enough.'

'You want me out.' It was a statement.

'No, Cass. But it's a small flat and I'm busy doing stuff. I don't want you being lonely and not having things of your own to do.'

She stayed silent.

'I'm asking around for a job for you,' I added.

'Can't I just work for you? Like Wal does.'

It took me two sets of traffic lights to think of a reply. 'Err … well … that's sweet of you … but … thing is, a lot of the time I don't make enough to be able to pay you. I can barely pay Wal. And here's the thing…'

She tilted her face towards me, listening intently.

I didn't know how to say this delicately, so I opted for the direct approach. 'To be any kind of investigator you need to be over eighteen and able to read.'

A few more traffic lights passed.

It was another bright-sunshine-with-cool-wind kind of day; the type that makes you feel you can move mountains. There was energy in the air.

Since working with Hoshi and learning more about my gift/curse, I'd realised my sensitivity to the weather. When the pressure dropped, I felt like a slug on Valium. On days like this, I usually felt charged, but today too many things were weighing on me.

I'd turned right off the Coast Road towards Wanneroo before Cass spoke again.

'So … you sayin' if I could read better, you'd let me work for you?'

Damn!

'If you were older and well … yeah… I guess so … but I'd also have to be making enough to pay you, you know, long term, which I'm not at the moment.'

She nodded absently, as if the idea of payment was of little or no consequence. I didn't push it any further and we moved on to talking about Bolo and the death threat.

She looked at the picture on my phone and pulled a face. 'Looks like it came off a porn site,' she said with authority.

I didn't like to ask her how she'd know.

Chapter 14

After a wave to Jase on the way through the gates, I parked the van in the allotted place and hooked up to the power.

'You alright to set up while I do a circuit?' I asked Cass.

She nodded and climbed into the back of the van.

I headed down to Sharee's booth but she wasn't in. There were a few new posters pasted to the message board; I noticed the advert for the furniture was still there.

Checking I had my phone, I moseyed over to the pits.

This time Team Bennett's rollerdoor was open and the cover was off the blue and red Yamaha inside. I couldn't see a mechanic, but a guy in clean jeans and a dark blue t-shirt was crouched down examining the tyres.

'Hi,' I said. 'I'm Tara from the food van. Do you want to put in a food order for lunch?'

The guy stood up and it was clear immediately that he was the rider. They tended to be the same build—lightweight but strong, and small to medium in height.

There was usually something intense going on with them too. With Lu Red it was the fist-clenching. With this guy it was his brilliant green cat's eyes.

'Tara-from-the-food-van. Is that like Jenny-from-the-block?' he joked.

'Sure. I guess.' I wiggled a few steps in my best J-Lo imitation.

'I like big girls. Especially big girls who make me sandwiches.'

My expression switched from smiling to stony. 'And I like tall guys with manners.'

He looked crestfallen briefly then laughed. 'Guess I deserved that.'

'Uh-huh.'

'Will you forgive me if I order some food?'

'Sure.' I pulled my phone from my pocket. 'Shoot.'

'Meatballs and tomato with mayo on a white roll. And a 7Up.'

Uggh. I'd learnt a lot about people's tastes, or lack thereof, in the last few days. 'Got it. You riding in the race on Sunday?'

'That's why I'm here.'

'You gonna win?'

His effervescent blue aura contracted as if someone had pinched it. 'Maybe. Depends, I guess.'

'On what?'

'You know. The usual. Who rides well. Who rides smart.'

'There's a difference?'

'Yup.'

'You look like you're smart,' I said.

'Every dog has his day,' he shot back.

'Okay. Well, good luck … err … can I have your name?' I added, waving my phone. 'For the order.'

'Frank Farina.' He seemed disappointed that I'd had to ask.

'What time would you like to pick it up?'

'Midday,' he said. 'Practice starts at 2PM. I need time to digest.'

'I'll see you soon then.'

That comment seemed to brighten his ego and his aura flooded back to its full sparkling-blue strength. Men!

I walked on past the Chesley garage. A bike revved inside and a pall of blue smoke blew out the door. Inside, people were shouting over the noise. Didn't seem like the right time to pay a visit, so I moved on to Riley's.

Neither Riley senior nor junior was there, so I grabbed the opportunity to talk to the mechanic. I cleared my throat and he looked up, wiped his hands on a rag and strolled over.

'You want a lunch order?' I asked.

'Didn't you come around here the other day?' he said.

'Yeah. Got chewed out by your boss.'

'Old Man Riley can be a bit of a wanker. Sorry about that. I'm Dave.'

'Tara,' I said. 'No sweat. Pretty tense time leading up

to a race, I guess.'

'Particularly this one.'

Dave seemed almost to be talking to himself. His aura churned with dark, unhappy, brownish colours with some purple flecks. I'd learnt from Hoshi that purple indicated passion, but whatever good things this guy had going on were currently being swamped by the negative browns. I felt a sudden desire to touch his aura to encourage the purple to expand. I hooked my hands behind my back so as not to do something freaky.

'I've heard your rider's pretty good,' I said.

'It's not all about the rider,' he said abruptly, then gave me his order. 'I've got to get back to work.'

So much for squeezing information out of him. I keyed his name into my phone and moved on to Moto-Sane.

Lu Red was half dressed in his racing leathers—the bottom half—revealing a lean and lightly muscled torso. He was staring at the shelves cluttered with cans of oil and containers of nuts and washers, while Clem, Bolo's mechanic, drained oil from one container into another. Red's girlfriend was nowhere to be seen.

'Orders?' I sang out.

Red nodded, then gave me his—exactly the same as last time.

'You want something?' I asked Clem.

'Sure,' he said. 'Two sausage rolls, a donut and a can of Coke.'

And I thought I ate badly!

The energy bouncing between the two men seemed less volatile today, though Clem still wasn't overly friendly.

'Your girlfriend want something?' I asked Red, glancing around for her.

He gave me an odd look. 'Maybe she would, if she was here. She's at work.'

'Just thinking ahead,' I said.

'An enterprising sandwich vendor. Outstanding!'

It was a condescending, arrogant comment but I let it slide. I said goodbye and hustled back to Cass.

She had the whole thing under control: deep fryer bubbling, the salads cut, and a thick brown sauce cooking in a saucepan on the hotplate.

'What's that?'

'Beef gravy. I thought it'd be nice for the chips.'

I stuck a finger in it and slurped a taste. 'Yum.'

'Find out anything new?' she asked.

'All riders are jerks,' I said as I squeezed into the van. Mobile cafés were like European dress sizes—not designed for big people.

The rush came, and lasted until just after 2PM. I buttered, served and splashed oil and salt around until the last customer walked away. Then I left Cass cleaning up and went to watch the start of practice.

Frank Farina was on the grid alongside Gig Riley. I recognised both bikes. Lu Red's Honda grumbled down the pit lane to join them.

Sharee was hanging out of her booth with her timer in her hand. As I got closer I saw that her face was flushed and her white skeleton earrings were jiggling. If I didn't know better I'd say she had a guy in the bottom of the booth doing unseemly things to her. Watching bikes race clearly got her all hot and sweaty.

'Don't block my view,' she said, waving me to the side. 'This is gonna be good.'

A small crowd had gathered near the finish line, including Jase the security guard and Cass's skinny apprentice friend, T-Dog. Riley senior bore down on the observers and they automatically parted to let him through, his aura slicing ahead of him like a sharp knife cutting soft cheese.

Further along the railing was another smaller group. Clem and … *Crack*? It looked like my cousin had taken Bolo up on his offer.

'They usually come out at different times. You know, avoid each other. This is a mind game, going up against each other in practice.'

'Uh-huh.'

I watched Lu Red line up next to the other two.

The practice marshal gave them the all-clear signal and the three bikes were at the end of the straight before I could cough out their exhaust smoke.

'You bet on the races?' I asked Sharee.

She shrugged. 'Sometimes. Not this one, though. Could

go any way.'

'I thought Red was the fastest?'

'Yes, but he's been a bit unsettled,' she said, sounding like she was talking about one of her pets. 'And Gig's got major incentive.'

'How so?'

'He's been offered a huge bonus by his dad if he wins.'

'What kind of bonus?'

'Big.' She rolled her eyes. 'Like a house. And you can't write Frank off. He's a crafty bugger, you know. Anything goes wrong and he's there waiting to pounce.'

'What about Chesley??'

She shook her head. 'Not this year. Bike's a dud.'

I let her chatter on until the bikes sounded at the back of the home straight. Gig came through the line first, followed by Frank. The Honda was nowhere to be seen. Glancing over at Clem, I saw him barking into a two-way radio. Soon after, the marshal came past and picked him up.

'Not again,' groaned Sharee. 'What's wrong now?'

My phone rang. I stepped away from the booth to answer it and noticed the time. I had to hurry if I was going to make my parent-intervention meeting with Smitty.

The call was from Tozzi so I let it ring out. I wasn't ready to talk to him yet. My missed calls showed one from Ed as well. He could wait too, until I knew what I was going to say.

Cass was waiting for me in the front seat of the truck, eyes already closed. I unhooked us from the power outlet and hit the road.

I fished in my bag for my wallet when I stopped at a set of traffic lights. 'Here.' I slapped a hundred and twenty dollars of Bolo's retainer on Cass's lap. 'Thanks for your help. You'll get another forty tomorrow.'

She turned the notes over carefully in her hand as though they might bite her.

'They're your wages. I've got a meeting at four at one of the beach cafés with a friend, and then another one straight afterwards with Bolo. Why don't I drop you at the shops on the way there and pick you up on the way back? You might want to buy yourself some t-shirts and undies. And a toothbrush.'

There was an ominous silence. Cass didn't like being told what to do.

'You can't keep washing the same pair every day,' I added more gently.

A sigh escaped her lips. 'Yeah. I guess.'

'Maybe you should call your mum too?'

That got no answer at all.

Chapter 15

We got back to Lilac Street with enough time for me to shower and change into a pair of fresh jeans and a halter top. At the last second I grabbed a short jacket in case Smitty thought I was showing too much skin.

I dropped Cass off at the Napoleon Street lights with a promise that I'd be back to pick her up. She didn't have a phone, which made it all a bit tricky, but we agreed on a time and place. Ten minutes later, I was walking into the Beach Café, scoping for Smitts.

She was at a table on the beach side, wearing pearls and a cherry red aura, sitting ramrod straight. As I got closer, I saw that her hair was styled to within an inch of its life and her make-up was Clarins perfect. Smitts' aura was normally a lovely halo that was restful on my psyche, but today it was swirling like suds down a drain.

When she saw me, it slowed a little and her face lit up. 'T. So glad you made it before she did. Sit here.' She beckoned me to her side of the table.

'You don't think it looks a bit intimidating? Like we're ganging up?'

'Yes,' she said firmly. 'And we are.'

The waiter came past and I ordered cheesecake and a milkshake.

'What do you want me to do?' I asked when he'd gone. 'Threaten to take her out the back and smack her around with my beach bag?'

'Not yet,' she said slowly, as if considering it.

'Hey!' I punched her arm. 'I was joking.'

'Of course you were.' She fanned her cheeks with a serviette.

Smitts was right off her game. Normally, witty repartee rolled from her lips. She was always the one with the comeback when I got mad and tongue-tied.

'Smitty,' I said, 'chill.'

'Crap, she's here.' Smitts took a deep breath. 'As you'd say, T, game on.'

I looked up and saw the cheesecake and the demented parent arriving at the table at the same time.

The cheesecake was strawberry. The demented parent was well-fleshed and well-dressed, a matronly type in a tailored suit and understated expensive flats. Her hair sat in a bob and she wore minimal make-up. The diamond rock on her ring finger, however, belied the whole subtle look, flashing enough ker-ching for a Hollywood premiere. Her aura was a thick red-brown that made me think of raw chocolate-cake mix—without the yumminess. I guessed we were all around the same age but she made me feel ten years younger.

'Jane,' she said and sat down.

Her voice was so plummy I swear I could taste the syrup.

'Victoria Tarrant. This is Tara Sharp.' Smitty pronounced it Tar-ah.

'Hi, Vicky,' I said, blithely shortening her name.

The stare she gave me could have stripped paint. I suddenly felt like a twelve-year-old schoolgirl about to be chastised by my most loathed teacher, Mrs Rolly. Victoria's jowls even wobbled the same way. That wasn't a good thing. Mrs Rolly had always brought out my worst side.

'Now, what are you going to do about your son, Jane?' she said, leaning her forearms on the table.

'I won't apologise for Joe's behaviour,' said Smitty in a cool voice. 'He was thoroughly provoked by your son. He tells me that Reece peed on his shoe in the toilets and then called him "piss foot".'

Nothing like private-school kids for excelling in crass. The burden of guilt I'd been carrying around about teaching Joe to punch disappeared.

'Gross,' I said. 'Sounds to me like Reece got his just desserts.'

'Reece would never say or do something so disgusting,' Victoria responded haughtily. 'I demand an apology or I'll seek to have your child removed from the school.'

Smitty's hair just about straightened out of its blow-wave in anger. 'I will not apologise.'

'Then I'll have my husband speak with the board. John is a close personal friend of the chairman. He'll be here any moment,' said Victoria.

Just as she finished speaking, a man walked into the café. He was balding and middle-aged with the sort of paunch that came from too many business lunches and airplane flights.

Victoria waved and he wound through the tables to reach us. It wasn't until he got closer that I recognised the Zegna suit.

He didn't really look at me until he'd sat down next to his wife. Then the irritated and slightly pompous look on his face gave way to sweaty alarm as recognition hit him. He cleared his throat in a choking kind of way.

'John, darling, this is Jane Evans and her … friend Tara Sharp,' said Victoria as she slipped a possessive hand onto his shoulder and dusted invisible specks from his coat. 'I've just explained to them how you're close friends with the chairman of the school board.'

'Oh, no need for introductions, Vicky, John and I have seen each other around. In fact, quite recently, I think,' I said, smiling innocently at her husband.

Victoria shot John darling a questioning look.

'Now John is here, I'm sure he'll agree this is just a storm in a teacup and that the best idea would be to talk to your son about his bullying,' I added.

I made sure my expression told him everything he

needed to know: that I would totally spill about seeing him at Madame Vine's.

'Our son's bullying?' spluttered Victoria.

'It seems your boy urinated on our boy's foot and then teased him.'

John flushed then grabbed his wife's flailing hand and covered it with his own. 'Perhaps Ms Sharp is right, Victoria. I do think this has been blown out of proportion. Why don't we just agree that it was an unfortunate incident and put it behind us? We'll speak to Reece, and I'm sure Mrs Evans will speak to her son, and nothing like this will happen again.'

'But … but…' Victoria never got to finish because John gently pulled her to her feet and led his dazed wife away from the table.

Smitty watched them walk through the door, then turned, grabbed my face in her hands and yanked me forward for a kiss on the cheek.

'What the fuck just happened?' she asked.

'Just another example of why you love me. I saw him twice at a brothel in Leederville earlier in the week.'

Smitts' face went from puzzlement, to comprehension, to pure glee. 'I won't even ask what you were doing in a brothel.' She beckoned the waiter. 'Another slice of cheesecake for my friend.'

By the time I met up with Bolo in the car park overlooking Cottesloe Beach, I felt nauseous. A bucket of chips for lunch and two whacking big slices of cheesecake with Smitty for afternoon tea had sent my calorie intake stratospheric and my liver into contortions.

'Tara?'

Bolo was standing at my driver's window, so I beckoned him around to the passenger side. He got in and stared out over the Indian Ocean while I swept pie crumbs off the section of seat between us and threw them out to the seagulls.

'I have some feedback for you,' I said.

He nodded. 'Shoot.'

His aura was acting weird, buffeting into me as if it were stormy waves and I was the beach. He was clearly stressed. I put it down to the death threat.

'Found out a few interesting things about the other teams. Riley senior is so dead set on winning that he's bribing his son with a house.'

'Really?'

'And Bennett Hardware is minutes away from going into liquidation.'

His eyebrows lifted. 'I didn't know that. Tony always plays things very close to the chest.'

'Desperation's a good motive,' I went on, 'but from what I can see, I think winning this race and keeping the sponsors on board will be too little too late for Bennett's. I'd be inclined to count them out. They're about to crash and burn.'

He nodded again, grinning at my choice of expression. 'What about Chesley?' he asked.

'Still working on that one. Can you tell me what the fight between Clem and Riley's wrench, Dave, was about?'

'You know about that?' He ran a hand over his bald head. 'The two of them used to work together. There's some bad blood between them from back then.'

'Did you check out Clem's background before you hired him?'

He shrugged. 'He's good at what he does. That's all I needed to know.'

That didn't seem right. Bolo was a businessman. I couldn't imagine he wouldn't do a reference check.

'Is there a problem between you and Red's girlfriend?' I asked. 'I saw you arguing at the track.'

His face reddened. 'No problem really. She's just … a nuisance. She distracts him. I was asking her to keep her distance when he's at practice.'

'You can do that?'

He gave a rueful smile. 'Not according to her, hence the argument. I figure I'm paying him top dollar to perform. Track practice is just like working in an office. You don't get to hang out with your partner at the office all day, do you?'

'Not normally,' I said, thinking of hanging out with Ed at the photo shoot.

'Thanks for the Bennett information. I need to know

about Chesley asap,' he said.

'Working on it. I'll call you tomorrow. The other thing is, I've got a guy who can be your bodyguard if you're worried about the death threat.'

'Thanks. I'll think about it.'

His aura was still restless but it had stopped crashing into mine. He got out of Mona and hustled back to his BMW 6 Series. With a quiet purr of engine ignition, he was gone.

I glanced in the rear-view, preparing to pull out, when I noticed that the dark sedan that had spooked me twice before was parked only a couple of lengths behind me.

This time I made an impulsive decision not to run away and did a quick one-eighty turn out of my parking bay, heading straight at the suspicious car. The driver, who was hunkered down behind the wheel and wearing a cap, saw my intention and screeched out of his spot, accelerating south down the beach road.

I chased after him, but got caught behind an old Kombi van. With traffic coming the other way, I couldn't overtake.

The sedan turned left into the road that ran through the middle of Cottesloe golf course. Not prepared to lose him, I overtook the Kombi on the left side and pulled a sudden left-hander. Seconds later, a police siren went off.

Crap! I pulled over feeling absolutely pissed off. Not only had I lost my tail, I was about to get booked.

The officer who climbed out of the squad car and

walked up to my window was an all-too-familiar figure.

'Hello, Constable Bligh.'

'Tara.'

We stared at each other in a weird kind of stalemate.

'You were speeding and overtaking dangerously,' she said finally, and pulled her biro from her top pocket. 'Can you tell me why?'

I glanced in my mirror. Bill Barnes was sitting in the car with his head bent over a packet of fries. 'Umm…' I had nothing. 'I was … in a … hurry?'

'You appeared to be chasing that dark sedan.'

'What sedan?'

'The one that was speeding down this road ahead of you.'

'Another car was speeding? Why did you let them go and stop me?'

We eyed each other steadily. I sensed she wanted to say a whole lot more. Instead, she wrote me a ticket.

Thrusting the fine in the window, she leaned in close. 'I've already given you a friendly warning, Tara. Don't get mixed up in this stuff.'

With that, she turned on her heel and stalked off back to her car.

I got a nasty feeling right below my two serves of cheesecake. Who the hell was driving the sedan? And what was Bligh holding out on me about?

Chapter 16

I was a few minutes late to pick up Cass but she was too excited about her new purchases to care. I dropped her at Lilac Street and changed into some gym gear, heading straight back out again to Rather Be Dead?

Plenty of nervous-glances-over-my-shoulder-looking-for-dark-sedans later, I parked in the underground car park and went upstairs to the gym. It took me forty minutes into the toughest level on the bike before I began to settle. When the program finished, I wobbled my way over to the bench press with a severe case of jelly legs.

'Whoa there, Tara,' came a deep voice from behind me and a strong hand steadied my swaying gait. Nice Guy, his palm cool on my back.

'Hi, Josh,' I said. 'Thanks.'

'You okay?'

'Jelly legs from the bike,' I explained. 'Had a weird day. Needed to work some of it out of my system.'

His green aura expanded a little and the greyness

shrank. He was in a pair of track pants and a tight tee. Okay, I couldn't help but notice. He had a man's physique without Tozzi's extra kilos. Ed was muscled but barely out of his teens. Nice Guy was kinda perfectly in the middle of them.

'Snap,' he said, nodding in sympathy. 'You want me to spot your weights for you?'

I gave a tentative smile. 'Sure.'

We didn't talk much while I grunted my way through three sets but I got an eyeful of his chest as he bent down to help me rest the weights. When I'd finished, I towelled off while he leaned against the bar rest.

'You want to catch a bite sometime soon? I could cook for you,' he said.

I froze mid-wipe. The question was totally unexpected and I had more than enough on my plate right now without contemplating a date with another guy. Still, I thought about it for a moment. I mean, it looked like Ed wasn't being exclusive, so why should I be? And part of me wanted to get closer to Nice Guy's calm green aura.

'Um ... maybe. Yes. Err... I don't know. No.'

Instead of being offended by my indecision, he laughed. 'Ah well, I'll be here for a few more days if you change your mind.'

I gave him a smile and stood up. 'Thanks for spotting for me, Josh. See you next time.'

My legs got me outside with some decorum, which was just as well because he watched me all the way.

. . .

Cass was in bed flicking through the cookbooks when I got home.

'Dinner's in the fridge,' she said without looking up.

I peered into the cold cavern that normally only housed dried-up cheese and soured milk and saw a cling-wrapped plate of a delicious-looking chicken salad. My cheesecake over-indulgence had long worn off and my mouth watering so I hurried to have a quick shower.

When I returned, I grabbed my plate and settled on the couch. 'You make this?' I asked.

She nodded. 'Joanna showed me how. I never thought about putting meat in a salad before. Joanna says it's all about the dressing. This one's orange and pecan.'

I shook my head in wonder. Joanna's interest in Cass was unnerving me. What could the vampire lady be planning?

Once the food hit my stomach, fatigue followed, making it too hard to worry much about Joanna. I checked my phone. Two missed calls from Nick Tozzi now. I contemplated ringing him back then dropped the idea. He'd just try to make me explain something I couldn't.

'Same again tomorrow?' asked Cass.

'Tomorrow I need to concentrate on Team Chesley. They use their own caterer, so they won't come by the van.'

'I can ask T-Dog.'

'Yeah, do that. And I'll talk to Sharee again. We'll need

to finish on time though. I have to get to the Aprilia office in Fremantle before 4PM, see what I can find out about Clem's and Dave's backgrounds. Then I've got some other things to do.'

It was kinda weird having to share my schedule with a sixteen-year-old.

Cass looked a bit down in the mouth.

'I'm going to a friend's to get some self-defence lessons. Why don't you come along?'

Her face sparked up. 'Cool.'

We arrived at Hoshi Hara's a little after seven-thirty. I'd lent Cass some exercise gear, but my spare sneakers were way too big so she'd settled for bare feet.

After the introductions, Hoshi took us to the sleep-out, which he'd decked out with rubber mats and a boxing bag.

'You stand there.' He positioned us opposite him. 'Now watch. I teach from gendai budo. Today, judo kata.'

He proceeded to demonstrate a range of quick movements like a strange dance.

Cass looked unimpressed.

'Now you grab me, Missy. Grab me hard from behind like an attacker,' Hoshi told me.

He turned around and showed me his back, hobbling a few steps like a little old man. I did as asked, lunging forward to envelop him in a bear hug. The next thing I knew I was upside down and looking at his crotch.

He peered down at me. 'Easy peasy.'

Cass burst out laughing.

The evening progressed from there. I learned two important things before we headed home: how to break a grip, and to never let a fourth-dan judo black belt use you as his throwing partner. Cass acquitted herself better than me, showing good intincts and balance.

When were were done, she led the way out to the car and I limped after her.

'I look through that list you sent, Missy,' Mr Hara told me before I closed the door. 'Nothing for girl Louise. For girl Kate, though, there was one name I knew.'

'Oh? Who?'

'Fat Frog.'

'Fat Frog?'

'Yeah. Fat Frog gave me the nightclub job you're doing tomorrow night.'

'He's the owner of the club? And his name's really Fat Frog?'

'Yeah, yeah,' said Hoshi. 'Funny coincidence.'

On TV police shows they didn't believe in coincidences and neither did I. 'Do you have the list?'

He disappeared inside for a moment and then returned with a sheet of paper.

I read the name he pointed to. 'Vatroque.'

'That's what I say. Fat Frog.'

My phone woke me in the wee hours again, right in the middle of a dream where Hoshi was throwing me off the Freo bridge.

'What?' I whispered hoarsely.

'Tara, it's Bolo Ignatius. I'd like to use your bodyguard.'

Adrenaline coursed into my sleepiness. 'Problem?'

'Someone tried to break into my house while I was asleep.'

'Tried?'

'My burglar alarm tripped.' He sounded rattled.

I took a deep breath. 'Give me your address and I'll get my guy over there right away.'

'Thanks. Money isn't a problem, you understand. But I don't want the police involved.'

'Got it.'

But I didn't really. What possible reason did Bolo have for keeping the police out of the picture if his life was being threatened? I was starting to have some doubts about my client.

I tried Wal. No answer.

Dragging myself out of bed, I pulled on jeans and put a track top over my pyjama t-shirt.

'Tara?' said Cass sleepily.

'Won't be long. Go back to sleep.'

Wal's new place was only a few minutes away so I was banging on his door before my brain was properly awake. He opened up dressed in jocks and socks and holding a pistol. Nothing about his manner suggested he'd been asleep.

'You didn't answer your phone,' I said.

'Turned it off when I was trying to get to sleep.'

'Doesn't look like it worked.'

'Nah. Freakin' medicine. Can't get it right,' he growled. 'One minute I can't stay awake, the next I can't sleep.'

I glanced down nervously at the gun. 'Can you put that damn thing away?'

He shrugged and stepped aside to let me in. 'Wassup?'

Even in the dim light of his bedside lamp, I could see Liv's finishing touches around the room: a bedspread, a new blind at the window.

'Bolo just called me,' I said. 'He wants protection against some death threats he's been getting. Someone's been at his house tonight. Can you stay with him for a few days?'

Wal immediately pulled some clothes on—jeans, a t-shirt and a pair of running sneakers without socks. Then he went to the narrow cupboard, unlocked it and lifted out a familiar kitbag. 'How serious are the threats?'

'Not sure,' I said. 'They might just be trying to scare him. But they might not.'

I showed him the picture Bolo had sent me of the man hanging from a noose. He nodded as if drawing a silent conclusion and removed a couple of objects from the bag.

I glanced away. Best not to know too much about Wal's weapons' stash. I assumed he had a gun licence but I didn't know for sure. As for his knives…

Satisfied that he had what he needed, he locked up, zipped the bag and walked to the door. 'Let's ride.'

I stopped outside Bolo's place—a mansion a couple of streets away from Millionaires Row, and also uncomfortably close to Johnny Viaspa's house. We walked up to the elaborate front door and knocked. Bolo peered out of a nearby window, then I heard the beep as he cancelled the alarm and opened the door.

I did the intros and reassured my client that he was in good hands. And he was, now that Wal couldn't go to sleep.

The two men shook hands and went back inside together. I heard another set of beeps as Bolo reset the alarm.

On my way home, I did a spur-of-the-moment dogleg so I could drive past Viaspa's house on Coke Road. I'd been keeping my distance from this area lately, having no desire to run into Viaspa, and even less desire for the cops to see me in the vicinity of his house. Fiona Bligh and Bill Barnes were decent, fair-minded cops, but Cravich and Blake—the pair who'd wanted to stripsearch me on one particular occasion—were looking for any excuse to cause me grief. But at 3AM, with no one on the roads, one little peek wouldn't hurt.

I slowed down as I passed Viaspa's wrought-iron gates. The ambient street light and my speed afforded me only a quick glimpse down the long driveway to his house, but I managed to identify two of the three cars parked there. One was the jumped-up limo Viaspa liked to be driven around the city in. The other one, tucked down the side, sent my heart skittering. It looked identical to the sedan that had been tailing me.

All sense of caution flew out the window into the night. Taking a right-hand turn at the next intersecting street, I parked around the corner and slipped my self-defence spray into my pocket. I couldn't afford pepper spray, so I was making do with good old-fashioned olive oil. It only stung a little but it made everything damn hard to see.

Walking back down the road towards Viaspa's house, I realised I probably looked like I'd just escaped from an institution: bare feet, pyjamas barely disguised under crumpled jeans, and a track top with a hole in one elbow. I pulled the hood around my face and hugged the shadows.

One pass of the front gate revealed a blinking security system and a wall that was over three metres high. Luckily there was a side gate in line with the sedan. I'd have to trespass onto next-door's property to peek through it. From what I could see, the neighbour didn't have garden alarms. I didn't give myself more than a second to think about whether it was a good idea or not before I was over the neighbour's low front fence and feeling my way along their side wall.

Oww. Something spiky jabbed my butt through my jeans. Cactus. I moved back to avoid it and stepped into another plant. Jeesus, what was this? The Arizona desert?

I flashed my phone light and realised the whole garden was devoted to spiky succulents and tacky garden ornaments—namely gnomes and fat toads. Money clearly did not buy taste.

Using my phone to guide me, I practised my best minefield walk, but by the time I reached the gate in the wall, I was scratched all over. To make matters worse, though the gate was wrought iron, this side of it was patched over with timber. Johnny Viaspa's neighbours clearly didn't like having a view into his yard.

Flashing my phone light around to try to find an easier path back, I noticed a large empty plastic water container lying on its side next to the house's air-conditioning unit. If I stood on it, I might be able to see over the wall to check the sedan's licence plate. I had to know if it was the same car that had been following me. If it was, I'd call Fiona Bligh. I still had her mobile number from the last time a crazy was stalking me.

Getting the container over near the wall quietly was one thing, getting up on it was another. On its side, it was too uneven to balance on; on its end, it was too tall for me to climb up. I circled around a cactus and picked up one of the toads. It was damn heavy, but just big enough to get me up onto the container. Once there, I was able to touch the top of the brick wall but not see over it.

So close.

I wiggled a bit. The container seemed steady enough so I jumped, managing to get my torso over the edge of the wall. I balanced there for a second before I heard a soft clunk. Crap! That couldn't be good. The container had fallen over when I kicked off it.

I managed to get my knee up, and levered myself around until I was lying along the top of the wall like a lizard on a rock. In the soft driveway light I could just make out the licence plate: UBE 610. I committed it to memory and squinted harder.

Now what?

I surveyed my options. Jumping down into the neighbour's garden meant a high probability of landing in a cactus or on a gnome. That left jumping down on Johnny Viaspa's side. The voice of reason agreed that was not a smart idea.

Instead, I began crawling along the top of the wall towards the front gate. The wall was only half as wide as me, so each forward movement was a feat of balance.

When I was only a metre from the main gate, Viaspa's front door opened and light flooded a large section of the yard. I flattened myself along the wall and tried to make like a statue.

Johnny Viaspa stood silhouetted against the light, hair untied and loose around his shoulders. An overweight retriever sniffed around his feet.

I could smell his sulphurous aura even from across the yard and it brought back memories of his viciousness that got me shivering. I held my breath, praying he didn't come right outside. Thankfully, he shoved the retriever out with his foot, and shut the door again.

This action also had its pros and cons. On the positive side, I got a better look at the car, the number plate and the Hertz rental sticker on the front window. On the down side, the dog was now sniffing along the bottom of the wall, looking for a good spot to do its business.

I waited until it started to dig, then wriggled the last section along the wall, trying to ignore the brick-burn on my stomach.

The dog looked up and growled.

I swiped for the iron upright on the gate, overstretched and missed it. The momentum caught me and I started to fall. A last desperate lunge brought me back in contact with the gate. The next sensation should have been the smack of my face meeting the pavement but a rough jerk brought me up short. My t-shirt had hooked on the crown-tip of one of the iron poles.

I was hanging from the gate, staring out to the street. Thank God it was 3.30AM.

The dog growled again and began tugging at the back of my jeans through the gaps. It could smell the muesli bar I had crumpled in my back pocket. I prised it out and threw it to the dog. Then I swung my feet forward and fumbled in my front pocket for my phone to speed dial Bok. It went to message bank.

I couldn't ring Ed—not after the Wal sleep-tackling episode and seeing him with another girl.

Smitty couldn't shift my weight.

Wal might be able to help out, but he was protecting Bolo, and I didn't want my most lucrative client yet seeing me in this situation.

That left only one alternative—Tozzi.

He answered in a few rings with only a slight croak in his throat. 'Tar-ah?'

'Nick,' I whispered. 'I've got a problem.'

Chapter 17

'What's going on?' Tozzi said.

'I'm stuck on the front gate at Viaspa's place.'

'Stuck?'

'Hanging. I fell off the wall and the iron post has hooked up my pyjamas.'

'Your pyjamas? What the—'

'Please. Come and help me off before someone sees me. The dog's been let out to pee.'

If it hadn't been Johnny Viaspa's place, Tozzi might have laughed at me, possibly even told me it served me right. But he said, 'I'll be there as soon as I can. Do you have any protection?'

'Only my olive oil spray,' I whispered.

'What are you planning to do with that? Cook someone' His voice was muffled.

'I couldn't afford pepper spray,' I snapped. 'Olive oil in the eye makes everything blurry.'

'Listen. If he finds you, start screaming. Better the

neighbours hear and come out to see than you ending up at the bottom of the Swan in concrete boots.'

'Please hurry.'

He hung up.

The dog growled again and gave a short bark. It was up on its front paws, dangerously close to my bum, like it was building up to bite right through my bum cheek. I wiggled one way and then the other, trying to get out of reach. But that got it antsy and it gave a loud yip.

'Shhhh, doggy,' I said.

The only other consumable thing around—other than me—was the olive oil.

Keeping my legs out of reach, I unscrewed the nozzle and reached behind me to drip some out. The yip stopped in favour of a snuffle and some noisy licking at my ankles.

I kept the drip, drip going until a pair of headlights turned onto the street and drove past.

Please let it be Nick. Please let it be Nick.

Finally, I caught a break. Tozzi parked the Lambo out of sight of the gate and came back for me. He tossed something over the fence.

'What's that?' I asked.

'Dog biscuits.'

In a matter of a few seconds, he'd lifted me bodily off the two-and-a-half metre high pole. Not many men could do that. I weigh eighty kilos for a start. But Tozzi's a two-metre giant who once played in the NBA.

'How did you get here,' he said quietly in my ear.

'Car's around the corner.'

'Get in it and follow me.'

I didn't dare disagree, considering the tone in his voice, so I ran to Mona and trailed him down Queenslea Drive towards the highway. Then he suddenly swerved into the car park of the church on the corner. I pulled in next to him and saw his head resting on the Lambo's steering wheel.

I got out of Mona and ran to the passenger side, letting myself in.

'Are you okay?' I asked.

He sat up and stared ahead. 'Why did you do it?'

'I had to,' I said.

'What? Trespass on the property of the one guy in this city who'd happily ghost you?'

'No. Feed the dog olive oil.'

He half-turned his face towards me, though he kept his eyes on the road. 'Are you speaking some strange dialect?'

'I had to do something to stop the dog barking. It liked the olive oil, so I dripped it down onto its nose, only...'

'Only what?'

I noticed his hands tighten on the wheel, but I'd gone too far with my confession to stop now.

'Most of it spilled onto my butt and now I'm sitting on your leather seat.'

He smacked the steering wheel with both hands.

'Get out,' he ordered.

I did as I was told. The tone of his voice made me want to rush inside the church and hide under a pew.

He stormed around to my side of the car to examine the oil damage. Peering through the gap under his arm, I saw two dark stains on the leather in the perfect shape of my bum.

He straightened and turned on me.

My mouth started to run in place of my frozen legs. 'I'm so sorry, Nick. I'll buy you a new seat cover, I promise. And what I meant to say was … that the car was following me again today. It parked behind me down in front of Cott beach—'

'Slow down. I can't understand you.'

I took a breath and tried to settle my heartbeat. 'I took Wal over to Bolo's at 3AM—he needs a bodyguard because of the death threat he got. I drove past Viaspa's and saw the car that's been following me. At least, I think it's the same one. I had to get closer to read the number plate. So I walked through the next-door neighbour's cactus garden and climbed the wall, and then the dog came out and I fell onto the gate.'

'Was it the same car?'

I nodded, suddenly all out of words.

Tozzi grabbed me with one giant paw and pulled me into his arms. There was nothing sexy about it. He was hugging me out of fear … and concern. I felt my aching muscles melt into his body warmth.

'Nick,' I said, 'you shouldn't do this. Besides, I'm all

oily, and I'm bleeding too. From the cactus.'

He hugged me closer. 'I know,' he said into the top of my head. 'You and I need to have a long talk.'

We did, over hot chocolate and raisin toast at the all-night café in Subiaco. The only other people there was a couple cuddling in the window seat. We sipped our drinks and looked the other way.

Eventually, I put my mug down and sighed. 'Thanks for coming to get me. Especially after I … left … you the other night.'

He nodded and leaned closer so he could speak quietly. His caramel aura swamped mine like a hot lava flow.

'Until today I didn't really know if I was being followed or I was just imagining it. Now I have proof,' I said.

'I think you should talk to the police.'

'I will.' Maybe Tozzi was right. Maybe I should say something to Constable Bligh. I had a licence plate number now. But what if I had to tell Bligh more than I wanted to? Like how I'd blackmailed Viaspa into leaving Nick and me alone after finding out he was behind a big mineral-leasing scam? Might be I was the one who ended up in jail. 'I … I… How's Antonia?' I asked, pointedly changing the subject.

His face tightened. 'She's doing well. She's decided to stay until the end of this week.'

'That's good to hear.'

'You know, I think she's beaten it this time.'

I wasn't sure if he was trying to convince me or himself. Either way, the glimmer of hope in his eyes depressed me a little. He still had strong feelings for his wife.

As if sensing my thoughts, he said, 'Look, about the other night... I'm sorry... That damn dress you were wearing just... I'm not trying to come on to you. What I mean is ... it's not my intention to ... it just keeps happening.' He stuffed his hands in his coat pockets and leaned back in his chair. 'Sometimes when I'm near you I feel like I've just stuck my finger in a power socket.'

It was a blunt and surprising admission that I didn't know how to answer. Eventually I decided to respond in kind—honestly.

'You're a married man trying to keep his marriage on track, Nick. You're the last person I'd consider seeing. But...'

'But what?'

'But yes, there's something there. I mean ... an attraction. Maybe if we "out" it, it'll go away.'

Fat chance on my part, I knew.

He thought about what I'd just said. 'Acknowledgment of a problem is usually the first step to solving it.'

I frowned, not liking being referred to as 'a problem'. 'Yeah, I guess.'

He beamed as if I'd just solved an epic puzzle for him. 'Okay then. Eat up and we'll call it a night.'

As we walked back to our cars Tozzi said, 'I have someone who could keep an eye on you.'

I shook my head. 'I've got my own security guy.'

'What? You mean that red-headed roadie who keeps falling asleep?'

'Wal knows what he's doing,' I said defensively. 'And he's getting treatment.'

'You said he was watching out for Bolo.'

'Only for a few days.'

'Well, the offer's there. We're friends, Tara, aren't we?'

I nodded, albeit a bit miserably.

'Please let me have someone watch your back.'

I shook my head stubbornly. 'You helped me out tonight. That's enough.'

He clenched his fists in frustration. 'Fine. Good night.'

I slid into my car, kicked it over and headed home for bed.

Chapter 18

The discovery that I really did have someone following me weighed heavily all the next morning. Suddenly, I couldn't wait to get to Hoshi Hara's for another lesson in self-defence. I also wanted to hole up at home with Tim Tams, but this was my last chance to nose around Team Chesley to see if I could get any feel for trouble.

'Cass,' I said as I pulled food containers from the van fridge, 'I've got to do a lot of digging around today. Can you hold the fort? I'll be back to drop in the orders.'

'Sure.'

She was already engrossed in chopping salad and prepping the deep fryer, so I left her to it and hurried straight to the Chesley bay.

The rollerdoor was up, and a Kawasaki was out the front, being washed down by a skinny young guy who could have been T-Dog's brother. George Shakes—jeweller and international gourmand—looked on. His partner, Frosty Hardwick, was nowhere to be seen.

At the back of the garage, a table was laid out with containers of food. Sharee had been right about Chesley having their own caterers. In fact, George Shakes looked like he'd had one for a fair while. I pretended I hadn't noticed the food and approached Shakes.

'Hi. I'm Tara from the food van. Would either of you like to pre-order lunch?'

Shakes scowled at me. 'We do our own.' His red aura was thick and bright like arterial blood but marred by white splotches. That wasn't good.

'Oh,' I said. 'Fair enough.'

He scowled a bit harder. 'Who are you? You look familiar. Have we met?'

Actually, we had. Smitts had forced me along to one of Shakes' jewellery soirées one evening when Henry couldn't make it. The food had been fabulous but the company not so. I'd spent an hour dodging the sticky hands and whiny voice of Phillip Dewar, the drunken idiot my mother had been trying to hook me up with for years. It was all I could do to corral my desire to punch him through one of George Shakes' expensive glass cabinets. Fortunately, Smitty caught my mood and had steered me out of there before mayhem ensued.

'Maybe,' I said in answer to Shakes' question.

He nodded as if to dismiss me, but I wasn't leaving yet.

'Great-looking bike you've got there. Maybe I should put my money on you on Sunday?' I said in the dumbest manner I could manage.

Shakes' aura flared with emotion though his face gave little away.

I continued to prod. 'But I like the black bike too. I can't decide. That Lu Red's such a cute guy. Hey, that's funny, isn't it? Lu Red rides a black bike!'

I got no visible reaction to that, so I tried something else.

'Hey, I do know you—I remember now. Mr Hardwick, isn't it?'

Shakes' red aura turned scarlet and I smelled sulphur rolling off him in waves. Now *there* was something.

'No, it isn't. Now I'm rather busy. Run along.' Outwardly he still seemed calm, but his body energy was giving off lightning flashes. I made a mental note of it and left.

Things seemed to be going smoothly in Team Bennett's garage. Frank Farina gave me a cheerful wave and called out that he'd have the usual and be by to pick it up at about twelve. The general energy inside was all good so I moved on.

The energy in the Riley garage was a stark contrast. Dave, the mechanic, and Old Man Riley were getting into it and didn't even pause when I showed up.

'Who the fuck said you could order these chains from Tex-E?'

'They're better than the crap ones we've been using,' said Dave.

'I don't fucking care what you fucking think. I pay the fucking bills and your fucking wages. I make the fucking decisions about suppliers!'

I cleared my throat and they both turned.

'What are you fucking staring at?' Riley senior barked at me.

A guy who looked identical to Riley senior, only fifteen kilos lighter, emerged from behind several huge cardboard boxes and put a calming hand on the older man's shoulder. 'Dad, get a grip.'

Riley looked like he might turn on his son but he roped in his rage and stalked off past me in the direction of the track.

'Hey, sorry about that,' said Gig Riley, watching his father depart.

'People seem to do a lot of apologising for your dad,' I said tartly.

'He's a passionate man. Afraid it comes with the territory.'

'That's no excuse for being rude.'

Riley junior laughed and his aura stayed mellow. He held out his hand. 'I'm Gig.'

Like Lu Red and Frank Farina, he was a foot shorter than me and a light wiry build.

I shook his hand. 'Hear that you're pretty quick on the tar.'

'Yeah, well, I love what I do, so I try to do it well,' he said with a smile.

His aura had hardly changed in response to my compliment. Even if he couldn't care less what I thought, his ego was well and truly in check. Whoever was threatening Bolo, I doubted it was Gig Riley.

'Good luck on Sunday then,' I said, turning to go.

He nodded. 'Thanks.'

At the Moto-Sane garage, Bolo was deep in conversation with Clem at the back of the bay. I couldn't hear what they were saying but something told me it wasn't about motorbikes. Lu Red was nowhere to be seen. The only other person around was Wal, who was sitting on a drum and leaning against the corner of the rollerdoor, fast asleep. I glanced about. No one seemed to be watching so I gave his leg a swift kick.

He woke with a start and blinked a couple of times. 'Boss?'

'Wal! You're supposed to be watching him!'

'Sorry, boss, damn meds have worn off.'

'Then take some more. He's paying you for this.'

He rubbed his eyes, yawned and began digging around in his pockets for his pills.

'What's going on in there?' I asked, peering in.

'Bin arguin' for a while. Dunno what about, but neither of them's too happy.'

I got out my phone and pretended to be taking Wal's order while I watched them. Their auras were blurry and agitated.

'You have any trouble last night after I left?' I asked.

'Nah. Checked all the windows and doors. Did a few loops of the house, couldn't see nothin'.' His face brightened. 'He's got a cook. Best bacon and hash browns I ever ate this morning.'

I thought of Cass. I'd miss her cooking when she left. I'd miss her.

'Also, boss, I called a local promoter I know from band days. He reckons that Instant Security firm that Lennie Roc works for is full of ex-crims and gym junkies.'

'That's not so surprising, I s'pose.'

'You're gonna love who the silent partner in the business is though.'

'Who?'

'Viaspa.'

I felt sick.

Chapter 19

I walked the length of the straight trying to calm down. Wal's information put a strong probability of a connection between Leonard Roc and Viaspa but not proof. I needed more to be able to be useful to Lena Vine.

I glanced up and down the track. The marshal was out on his safety loop, making sure there was no carrion on the track. On a raceway set in bushland, you never knew what might decide to take its last breath on a hairpin bend. Other than the marshal, there were the usual track officials over near the finish line and a handful of randoms settling in to wait for practice.

As I walked back towards the information booth, I spied Lu Red and his girlfriend, Sally, huddled together by the loudspeaker stand. I got as close as I could without them noticing. They weren't arguing but their body language was charged; a deep and meaningful going on there for sure. Red's hands were outstretched in a pleading gesture but Sally kept shaking her head. Their auras seemed to be keeping their integrity, not merging as they often did with couples. After a while Sally pulled away from their tête-à-tête and walked back towards the pits. Red watched her for a moment or two then slowly followed.

When he'd gone, I veered down to Sharee's booth.

'Morning,' I said brightly.

'Hi, Tara. Gee, you're out early.'

'Didn't get a lot of sleep last night, thought it best to keep going.'

She nodded in sympathy. 'Rough one, eh?'

'Yeah. And I just got a mouthful from Riley senior. The man needs to be locked up.'

Another sympathetic nod. 'Gig is so sweet. Go figure.'

'Met the boss of Chesley too this morning. He was pretty antsy as well. These guys are so uptight.'

'Which one? George? The big guy?' she said, making a pregnant gesture. 'If you think it's bad now, wait 'til Sunday. These guys leave rock stars for dead when it comes to acting out. The owners are worse than the riders. The riders *have* to keep it cool.'

'I guess it's not much fun for Chesley coming second,' I said.

'You mean fourth, really. The other three are on equal points.'

'Hardly worth them going into the last race then.'

She shook her head emphatically. 'Always worth it. Someone could drop out badly on race day or, worse, get a DNR.'

'That sounds bad,' I said. 'What does it mean?'

'Did Not Race,' she explained. 'It happens sometimes. Lu missed round three. Something to do with tyres.'

'But he's still equal first even though he missed a race?'

'Yeah. On points. He blitzed the first two rounds then missed the third. Since then his times have come down towards those of normal human beings.'

I made a mental note to check back over the dates to see if they coincided with something significant.

'You want to put in an order today?' I asked.

She gave me her usual list. 'This your last day?' she asked as I began to move off.

'Yeah. Jim'll be back on Monday.'

'Shame,' she said. 'I'll miss our chats. And your chicken rolls rock!'

I grinned. 'Thanks. I'll tell Cass. Keep fighting the good fight.'

She reached over the counter and hit me with a high five.

Maybe it was lack of sleep but my skin prickled all day. Too many things to worry about. Somehow Viaspa, Lena Vine's security guard and my stalker were all connected but I couldn't work out why. I also felt edgy about Wal, wondering if he was awake and doing his job. And if he did have to defend Bolo, what might it lead to? I didn't have insurance of any kind. Was I likely to be thrown in jail if Wal pulled a gun on someone? Maybe it was time I spoke to Garth, my ex-boyfriend accountant. He was only too happy to tell me when I was out-of-line crazy about stuff. He'd also know about insurance.

'Tara?'

I looked at Cass and then down at where she was staring. I was holding the plastic spatula in the boiling oil.

'Aaagh!' I pulled it out and threw it down on some absorbent paper. It looked like a Dali clock.

'And you put the tray of hot chips into the fridge a few minutes ago.' She pointed to the soggy result.

'Sorry, Cass. Things on my mind,' I mumbled.

'Something to do with you going out in the middle of the night?'

We hadn't spoken much on the way in this morning. I didn't want her involved in my possible Viaspa problem.

'Yeah. I had to drop Wal over to Bolo's. Someone tried to break into his house. He's a bit freaked so Wal's staying with him.'

'Bolo still doesn't want to tell the cops?'

'No.'

'Seems weird.'

'You said that before.'

She shrugged. 'So Wal's your security guy, right?'

'Aaah … yeah.'

'Then I'll be your assistant.'

'Cass—'

'After I've learnt how to read better.'

210

I shook my head at her and began to pack up.

At the gate, I slowed the van to say goodbye to Jase, but there was another security guy there. He said Jase had been called in to work on the weekend so he'd gone home early.

After saying our farewells at Jim's, I drove straight home. I wasn't sad to see the back of the van. A week of serving lunches had confirmed my opinion that I only liked to eat food, not prepare it. Cass, on the other hand, looked a little sad.

'You enjoyed that, didn't you?' I said as we pulled into Lilac Street.

'Yeah. Beats hanging out at Burnside Station. And I got paid.'

'Speaking of which...' I parked near the kerb and handed Cass the rest of her money. 'You did a good job. Maybe you should think about working in the food industry.'

She shook her head firmly. 'Nup. I want to work for you.'

I sighed. 'Look, Cass, it's been cool this week, but I can't afford to keep paying you. Plus you need to get on with your own life.'

Her face took on a stubborn set. 'I'm gonna go to TAFE and get better at reading. Your mum's gonna try and get me a job at the Claremont Growers Market. But when you say I can, I'm coming to work for you.'

She was ready for an argument and I wasn't in the mood, so I let it go. At least she had some short-term direction. She was doing better than me.

When we got home, Cass went off to see Joanna and I called Bok.

'Sweeeeetie,' he said. 'I haven't seen you in over a week.'

'Just checking that you'll be at the photo shoot this afternoon.'

'Course. Can't let you loose around Jenny Munro without supervision.'

I could tell he was smiling, but I wasn't. 'I need to talk to you about Ed.'

'Something wrong?' His tone changed instantly to match mine.

'Yeah … and yeah.'

'Okay. Stay cool and I'll see you at four. We're shooting at Swanbourne, opposite the Vomit House.'

Bok and I had attended a schoolies week party years ago in a house near Swanbourne Beach. Of the sixty teens present, fifty-eight had vomited in the garden, or the toilet, or the sink, from excessive alcohol consumption. We still couldn't drive past the house without groaning.

'Don't be late,' he added. 'The photographer's constipated about the light. We need to be ready to go when he says so—I'm paying him a shitload of money for this.'

'Got it.'

When I hung up, I felt better. Bok would have a plan. He always did.

I collected the address for the Aprilia office in Fremantle, then got changed, planning to go straight on to the beach shoot.

What to wear took some thought. I needed a business suit for Aprilia and then something more casual for the beach shoot. The suit part was easy: a navy blue light jacket and pencil skirt that I hadn't used since my last government job. I got dressed and was relieved it still fit. The beach thing was more difficult. I had a fair bit of hurt ego to dress. That meant my best cut-off shorts with strategic tears, and a sexy singlet top. Eat your heart out, Ed, I thought as I packed them into my beach bag for later.

I walked back up the driveway, pulling faces at the birds as I passed them. Brains steadfastly ignored me, but Hoo flapped his wings and did his Exorcist impersonation.

Out by Mona, the prickling feeling I'd had all day came back with force, as if an acupuncturist had cut loose on my skin. I glanced up and down the street. Was there someone watching me from behind that tree? In that parked car? On that roof? Behind that bush?

I jumped inside Mona and accelerated away from the kerb way fast.

By the time I made it to the highway without incident, I began to settle down again.

By the bridge, I figured I'd been imagining things.

Parking was hard to find in the afternoons in Fremantle and I ended up having a fair walk to Aprilia. Normally I enjoyed the Freo buildingscape but today I was preoccupied.

I stepped up to the counter of the small but attractively appointed office in a businesslike manner. The girl behind it was well groomed and smiling.

'Hello,' I said. 'Beautiful day, isn't it?'

'Too good to be at work,' she agreed and raised an enquiring eyebrow at me.

I flashed my Western Suburbs library card at her so she only glimpsed the large WS letters in the corner. 'Look, I'm from Western State Recruiting over on Fothergill Street behind the prison. I wondered if you could run a reference check on a couple of applicants who said they worked for your company in Europe?' I leaned onto the desk. 'I'd normally ring, but it was such a nice day for a walk.'

She nodded understandingly. 'Sure. Who are they? I'll see if I can help you.'

I read their full names of the two mechanics to her, which I'd gotten from the Motorcycling Western Australia registry, and waited while she searched her database.

She frowned a few times and then held up her finger. 'Please excuse me a minute.'

I was left to enjoy the gallery of motorcycle photos on the walls while she disappeared into another room. When she returned, she was wearing a fixed smile.

'My manager informs me that we can provide reference check for Clem Jonas. With regard to David Bower, however, you'll need to contact his previous employer through the Aprilia main website in Italy.'

Interesting.

'Thank you so much,' I said. 'You've been most helpful.'

'Would you like copies emailed to you? Or I could print them. I'll just need your ID number,' she lowered her voice conspiratorially. 'The boss is here.'

'I'll shoot you an email with my ID number when I get back to the office, and you can reply to that. How does that sound?'

'Perfect,' she said.

'Perfect,' I echoed, and left.

Employers usually only withheld references in that way when they were negative. I wondered what Dave Bower, Riley's wrench, had been up to.

I hurried back to Mona and did a quick clothes change on the front seat. I was late to pick up Ed, so I called Smitty while I was driving and put her on speakerphone.

'I'm on my way to fetch Ed to take him to a photo shoot.'

'Bok told me about it. Swimwear. Lucky you!'

'Smitty, I think he's seeing someone else.'

'Bok?'

'No, silly. Ed.'

'What? How do you know?'

'It's a long story. But can you come down to Swanbourne South for half an hour? I need moral support.'

'Oh, darling … kids,' she said. 'I'll see if I can get away. No promises.'

When I reached Ed's units, he was waiting outside, backpack slung over one shoulder, looking like an advertisement for everything that's hip and gorgeous.

'What happened to your face?' he asked.

'My galah, Brains,' I lied. Explaining my brush with Johnny Viaspa's cactus didn't seem like an option. 'A cat scared her and she scratched me.'

He gave me a quizzical look.

A nervousness of a new kind set in as I drove to the beach. Should I ask him straight out about the girl, or wait and see what he said? If he said anything. After ten minutes, I still hadn't decided what to do. Ed was polite and friendly but I sensed some reserve.

'Did Bok tell you who you're shooting with?' I asked as I pulled into a parking spot opposite the Vomit House.

He shook his head. 'Just that it's a sporting heroes theme.'

'You're paired with Jenny Munro.' I tried not to spit out her name.

He frowned. 'Isn't she the one who you beat in the triathlon?'

Goddamn it! Even his frown was beautiful. It was

216

that mixture of Spanish and whatever else he had in his bloodlines; a divine ethnic interplay.

'Yeah. It goes back further than that, though. She also broke my nose in a basketball grand final in juniors years ago. She's an Ironwoman these days.'

Ed slapped his brow in semi-mock despair. 'Oh, no!'

'It's okay. I'm cool,' I assured him. 'Totally.'

He gave me a more serious look. 'Are you sure? Tara, this shoot is important. Maybe…'

'I'm sure,' I said stiffly. 'I just wanted you to know before we get there.'

His expression relaxed. 'Thanks.'

Bok was already there when we arrived, as were the photographer and Jenny. Jenny's face lit up when she saw Ed then promptly fell into a scowl at the sight of me. I ignored her and gave Bok a wave. Then I sat myself on a towel slightly south of them, close enough to see but not be in the way as they got organised. The swell was moderate and the breeze not too stiff for a spring afternoon. In the distance, a freighter headed off to Sri Lanka or Africa. Right now, though, it looked like a cigar floating out to sea.

The shoot proceeded swimmingly, the photographer oohing and aaahing and Jenny rubbing up against Ed. I managed to contain my jealousy by reminding myself that even though she was all muscle tone, her body was still shaped like a cardboard box.

Not only that, I chided myself, but Ed and I weren't married. We were friends dating, currently without benefits. I wasn't sure how long even that would last now. Part of me was convinced that Ed was just finding his city legs, and that soon he'd spread his wings and fly away. Maybe with a girl named Vonny.

But it still felt bad watching Jenny sliding her hands all over Ed's bum because the truth was I really liked him.

'You doing alright, T?'

Bok squatted by my towel and dropped a kiss on my head. His beautiful face was creased with concern. I wanted to tug his silky dark locks—the envy of every woman who saw them—from their Dior clasp and set them free for the breeze to tangle.

'It's just photos, you know,' he added.

For that I gave him a scowl.

'You'll get wrinkles,' he warned. 'And green is not your colour.'

If we hadn't been at work—Bok's work—I would have wrestled him into the sand. We'd had some epic engagements in our time. He was stronger in theory, but I weighed more and was generally fitter. Bok could eat gargantuan amounts of food but didn't seem to store a single calorie. I, on the other hand, had to run and work out like a demon for every mouthful of vanilla slice.

'The green tinge you see is just handbag envy,' I said.

Bok followed my line of gaze.

Ed and Jenny lay on a large beach towel. He spooned her while she pretended to draw something out of a beautiful patent handbag. The patent seemed incongruent in the beach setting, but I imagined it in a black and white photo, with grains of sand sticking to the leather. It would look sensational.

Bok sighed. 'Gorgeous, isn't it. I picked it up at a garage sale.'

I turned to him? 'Where? Who would sell something like that?'

He grinned at me. 'You have to go to the right garage sales! Her family import accessories from Spain. It's a Balenciaga.'

'Still, why sell it?' I said mystified.

'Oh, some story about moving back east, shedding dead weight and all that. I nearly bought her bedroom suite. It was a Baldacchino copy.'

I had no idea what that was but it sounded expensive. I was about to ask him about it when Jenny's next pose totally distracted me from Bok. She'd laid her body full length along Ed's and was performing a push-up over the top of him that could have doubled as a Kama Sutra position. The photographer sprayed her with oil and murmured encouragement about how sexy she looked. Skin glistening and muscles taut, she tilted her head sideways to give me a wink and a long slow lick of her lips.

Bok saw it and placed a warning hand on my arm.

Before I could react, I caught sight of something monstrous galloping towards me along the beach, dragging a slight figure behind it.

Bok saw it too. 'Jenny,' he shouted. 'Duck!'

But Jenny was so intent on what she was doing that she didn't register. The first thing she knew of impending disaster was when Fridge's giant back paws clipped her body as he jumped over her and sent her spinning like an ice skater in a sideways twirl.

Jenny's flip was worthy of an ovation, but I had other things to contend with, like the approach of a lumbering mammoth.

I dropped to one knee and bellowed, 'Sit, Fridge!'

Fridge dropped onto his haunches and slid to a stop a foot away, leaving a wide furrow behind him.

I stood up, patted his saliva-streaked nose, and saw that Smitty had stopped to help Jenny up out of the sand. Ms Oil-drenched, Ego-maniac Ironwoman had turned into a sandy sea monster dotted with seaweed and bits of broken shells.

'I'm so sorry,' said Smitty. 'Goodness, look at you. I'm SO sorry!'

Ed was on his feet, trying not to laugh, while the photographer made distressed birthing noises.

Jenny shrugged off Smitty and stormed towards me. 'This is your doing. You set this up!' she shouted, her fists balled.

I tensed my muscles. She wasn't above trying to clout

me in public—she'd already broken my nose once.

'Jenny,' said Bok calmly, 'it was an accident. Let's get you washed off. We were pretty much finished anyway.'

She turned her fury on him. 'I should have known better than to work with a friend of HERS. My agent will be speaking to you!'

'Actually, I think you look good like that,' I said innocently.

She ran towards me and thrust her fist up in my face.

Fridge bared his teeth at her and growled.

'Fridge!' cried Smitty.

But Fridge had decided I was in danger and his haunches were set as if ready to spring.

Jenny took a step backwards. And then another. She kept going until she'd grabbed her bag, then sprinted up the beach towards her car.

We watched her drive off.

'I'm sorry, Bok,' I said.

He stared after Jenny without speaking. I felt terrible. Bok's magazine was everything to him.

Finally he looked at me, his face grave. 'There's nothing she can do. The contract is signed. The photos are done. She'll get over it.'

Then, without warning, he smiled and knocked me sideways onto the sand. It was on—a wrestle to the death. In a trice, Fridge joined in, while Ed and Smitty watched, laughing.

Chapter 20

Ed was quiet on the way home and I wasn't sure if he was tired or upset.

'The photos should be great,' I ventured as I parked out the front of his unit.

Unexpectedly, he leaned over and kissed me. It was soft and exploratory, as though he was trying to find out something.

When we broke contact, he sat staring at me. 'I can't work you out, Tara.'

He couldn't work me out?

'Thing is, I'd like to know you better, but you keep brushing me off, like you're not taking me seriously.'

'Do I?'

He took my hand. 'Yes, you do. Can you stop, please?'

I thought about how to reply. Now was the time that I should mention I'd seen him with someone, but the words wouldn't come out. I really didn't want to act like a jealous nutcase. So I opted for a more general approach.

'Ed, you're younger than me and you're … well … you're hot. You're also new to the city and you've got a career about to happen. I'd be stupid not to consider all that.'

'What do you mean?'

'I mean, you're still finding your feet. Things will change for you, and that'll include who you want to spend time with. So I'm just giving you time to work that out before…'

'Before?'

Before I get my feelings trampled all over. Before I get deserted again. Before you run off with someone. 'Before we get into anything.'

He stared out the front window considering what I'd said, and I got a chance to admire his flawless profile.

'Tara?'

'Uh-huh?'

'Why would someone be watching us with binoculars?'

My breath caught. 'Where?'

'Over by the hedge in the next block of apartments. Leaning against the mailbox. You can just see a lens reflection.'

It took me a few seconds to locate the watcher.

I slid the keys out of the ignition and dropped them into Ed's hand. 'Lock the car and go inside. Please.'

'Tara, you can't—'

I didn't hear any more because I was out of Mona and running flat out towards the hedge. It took my stalker a few moments to realise I was onto him. I launched myself and managed to latch onto an arm before he could escape.

I held on doggedly, digging my nails in, but strong fingers ripped my grip away and I fell face-first into the hedge. By the time I'd got to my feet and staggered around the letterbox, my stalker had vanished.

Then a hand gripped my shoulder.

Without thinking, I used Hoshi's *break-hold* to rid myself of the hand and swung around, letting go the same roundhouse punch that I'd taught Smitty's son Joe. The person behind me went down with stunning effect.

Trouble was, it was Ed.

'Oh, fuck!' I fell to my knees alongside him.

He was clutching at his nose while blood streamed out of his left nostril, and coughing horribly.

I held up two fingers. 'How many?'

He pushed me back. 'I'm al-wight.'

'Ed, I'm—'

'Save it. I'm gow-ing.'

'Let me—'

He held out a hand, signalling me to shut up, and tossed me my car keys. Then, fingers pressed to his nose, he got to his feet and headed towards the stairs up to his apartment block. The lobby door banged shut with meaning.

I walked back to Mona. My rear-view mirror told me

that I looked nearly as bad as Ed: fresh bloody scratches from the hedge to add to the cactus scars on my face, and my hair sticking out. Lifting my top, I gently touched the large graze above my belly button. It could have been worse.

I drove home feeling miserable in so many ways. My phone rang as I pulled up outside Lilac Street. It was Wal.

'Yo, boss,' he said.

'Yeah, Wal?' I didn't feel much like talking to anyone.

'Ignatius got another threat.'

'When?' I asked, immediately alert. 'How?'

'Text again. Another picture.'

'Can you send it to me?'

'Hold on.'

I waited for it to come through. It was even more graphic than the last one: a man naked and caught in a vice with a knife resting on his back.

Cass was right. Something about the image seemed like porn. It didn't sit right.

I rang Wal back. 'Does Bolo have a laptop or PC there?'

'In his study.'

'Think you can get a look at it without him knowing?'

'Maybe later tonight. When he's asleep.'

'Good. Check his browser cache for the last few days. I want to know what he's been looking at.'

'Got it.'

I didn't tell Wal about the stalker. He'd be conflicted about who he should protect, and right now I wanted him with Bolo.

After a good look in the rear-vision mirror and several glances up and down the street, I got out of the car. As I walked past the birds, they screeched loudly and jumped around in their cage, trying to attract my attention. I felt guilty that I'd barely given them any time lately.

I offloaded my bag and had a quick shower to clean up my face. I had to go to Hoshi's nightclub job tonight and I didn't want to scare his client.

By the time I got back outside to the birds, I felt a little calmer. I opened the cage door and Hoo jumped straight out onto the ground, as indignant as could be. JoBob mustn't have been around much either. He strutted up the driveway onto the grass and began happily beaking for goodies. Only about a half-hour of light was left, so I changed their water and filled their feed container. That meant scooping into a tub of bird pellets and topping it up with bird mix. They didn't like the pellets (the bit that was good for them) but they'd kill each other for sunflower seeds. Really, they were so human.

Brains tried to bite me as I went to put the filled seed container back in the cage.

'Bad bird!' I said, withdrawing my hand.

We engaged in a strategy-and-dare game where I pretended to take the food to the other end of the cage and she chased me there. I then had to quickly move back to the original position and slot the container in before she—

'Owwww!' I yelled, losing another round.

I left her happily crunching dried corn kernels and went to check on Hoo, who'd found his way along the pool gate to the window ledge above my kitchenette. Cage birds tended to become astoundingly good climbers. My phone rang as I was squeezing along between the pool fence covered in Morning Glory and the side of my flat to retrieve him.

''Lo?'

'It's me. What are you doing?'

'Hey, Bok. Wrestling with a creeper.'

'Say what?'

'Never mind. Are we cool about Jenny?'

He didn't hesitate. 'Yeah, we're cool.'

I believed him. He'd tell me straight out if it was a problem. 'That's good. I don't want to cause you problems.'

'You haven't. But you sound upset,' he said.

I told him about the guy following me and how I'd punched Ed in the nose.

'You have to tell the police this time,' he said in a serious voice.

'Don't be so melodramatic.'

'Don't be such an idiot.'

No one told it to me like Bok. I squeezed along the last bit of the narrow space to the window and reached up to get Hoo. He was chewing on a roughed-up section of the wooden frame.

'Tara? You still there?'

'I'm just getting one of the birds—oh, shit!'

'What? What's wrong?'

'I'll call you back.'

I shoved my phone into my pocket and retrieved Hoo onto my shoulder. He began happily tearing at the vine behind me while I ran my finger along the window ledge. There were gouge marks there, fresh from the look of the wood. Someone had been trying to force entry. I tested the window. It didn't shift, but that didn't stop a cold hand rattling my spine.

I took Hoo back and gave him and Brains an almond each from the treats tin and closed the cage.

Maybe I should ring Fiona Bligh. Maybe Bok was right. This could be getting beyond anything I could manage.

Chapter 21

I went into the flat and locked the door. There was a note from Cass stuck to the kettle, saying she'd gone out with Joanna.

I found the length of dowelling that Dad had wanted me to use as an extra security measure and slotted it into the window tracks. Then I drew the kitchen curtains for the first time since I'd moved in.

Stress made me hungry so I grabbed some slices of bread and turned on my laptop. I had some serious thinking to do and a decision to make before I headed out for Hoshi's nightclub job.

As Google opened on the screen, Bok called back.

'And?' he said.

'And what?'

'Oh, how nice … you're still alive,' he said in an exasperated tone.

I'd clean forgotten that I'd hung up on him. 'Sorry. Look, I've just found that someone's tried to force the window open on my flat. The one with the vines all over it. Hoo was up on the ledge chewing the wood and I saw the marks.'

'Oh.' He dropped the sarcastic tone immediately. 'You want some company?'

'Yes, please. I've got a job to do at the Gallery in Northbridge tonight. Don't fancy going up there by myself right now.'

'What time shall I pick you up?'

'I love you,' I said. 'Ten would be good. I can tell you about it all then. I've got some things to do right now.'

'Promise we'll talk?'

'Promise.'

Ten o'clock left me a good few hours to do some mulling. I opened my Ignatius job file and jotted down some more notes.

To my thinking, Team Riley led the race on suspects. The conflicts between them and Moto-Sane were hard to ignore. Bolo clearly couldn't tolerate Robert Riley and I didn't blame him. But then there was the argument between the mechanics, Clem and Dave, not to mention the problem that Sally, Lu Red's girlfriend, was causing within the Moto-Sane team.

I searched the Motorcycling WA site and went back over the results for the season so far. According to their stats, Lu Red had won the first two races by a large margin. Race three had been a Did Not Race for him, and since then each race had been much closer. The DNR had been in August. That date rang a faint bell for me, so I jotted it down in my file, wondering why his lap time had dropped off so markedly after it.

I moved on to Team Chesley. An hour later, I hadn't come up with anything much about Shakes, Hardwick or Frank Farina, besides an unverified article that Shakes had unsuccessfully tried to buy Hardwick out at one stage.

Frank Farina looked clean of any dirt other than a few groupie messageboards where girls boasted of sleeping with him. Farina was a player, no doubt, but no worse than any other rider from what I could tell. Even if Team Chesley had internal problems, I somehow doubted it would be motivation for them to sabotage Bolo. Shakes' odd reaction about his partner had to be about something else.

I got out of bed and put on my slippers and dressing gown. Time to beard the dragon in her lair.

Dad was washing up with Cass, while Joanna was sitting at the table with a glass of wine, sorting a bag full of buttons into piles.

'Evening all,' I said, staring at her progress.

She saw my expression. 'There's a button expo at the showgrounds on Sunday. I'm donating my collection for fundraising.'

'Oh.' What else was there to say?

'There's some lemon chicken in the refrigerator if you're hungry.'

I licked my lips and helped myself, reheating it with

some leftover rice.

Dad was explaining the intricacies of golf to Cass, so I seated myself next to Joanna.

'Mum, you know George Shakes, don't you?'

She raised her head. 'Georgie Porgie Pudding and Pie. Lord, yes. I went to school with him. He used to eat too much even then.'

I squeezed my eyes shut for a moment. It was such a Joanna comment. 'I believe he went into partnership with his brother-in-law.'

'Frosty, the old sourpuss. Yes, that's right. Why do you ask?'

'It's … err … a job I'm working on looking into some unexplained incidents at Wanneroo Raceway.'

'Wanneroo. That's where all that greenhouse-unfriendly car racing goes on?'

Joanna had recently discovered the conversational value of global warming. 'And motorbike racing,' I said.

'Well, I don't know anything about that, but I do know that Frosty has just left his wife of thirty-five years for a man.'

'The wife being George's sister?'

'Indeed. Poor Sonia. They have five children. It's a scandal of epic proportions.'

I thought about suggesting that it was hardly a scandal, but a little sad that he'd spent all those years denying his true sexuality—and then mentally slapped myself. This was my mother I was talking to. Champion of the

Conservative.

Instead, I thanked her, told her the chicken was delicious and that I had some work to do.

As I walked out the door, I glanced back. Cass looked more at home there than I ever had. And it didn't upset me at all. In fact, in a funny way I was kind of glad for her—and them.

Back in the flat, I added what I'd learnt to my notes. Shakes and Hardwick were definitely having their own problems, which had nothing to do with Bolo Ignatius. I felt happy to demote them to the bottom of the suspect list.

Over the next hour I did more background work on Team Bennett. Bennett's Hardware was struggling to compete against Bunnings, and one motorcycling fan blog claimed the team was up for sale on the quiet. I found a year-old interview with Tony Bennett in which he talked about the family's history in the Western Australian motorcycle racing scene, and how much the team meant to him personally. Securing a berth in the Nationals would no doubt boost sponsorship and publicity but my instinct told me it was already too late. Bennett's Hardware was going down.

I called Garth Wilmot. As an accountant and all-round know-it-all, he liked to keep abreast of who was on the up—and the down.

'Tara? It's Friday night.'

Garth and I had a kind of hate-tolerate relationship.

Even though our romance had failed because we drove each other nuts, I knew he was good at all the things I was bad at, and he knew that I brought some much needed spontaneity into his stuffy life. We stayed in contact because he was my accountant, and occasionally we compensated for each other's shortcomings.

'I need to pick your brains,' I said.

He sighed. 'I was just about to eat dinner.'

'It's nine o'clock.'

'I'm living on the edge,' he retorted.

'What do you know about the state of Bennett's Hardware?'

He took a mouthful of his dinner and chewed in my ear for a bit.

'Well... I've heard the receivers are moving in next month.'

'That far gone?'

'Don't quote me on it. But I don't think you'll find I'm wrong.'

Garth *hated* to be wrong.

'So they'll be selling off their assets?' I asked.

'It's the usual procedure.'

'What about the Bennett racing team?'

'That? Well, I imagine it's been bleeding the company for years. In fact, it's probably the reason things got so bad for them. Always a mistake mixing your passion with your work.'

That was such a Garth comment. Most people aimed

to find a way for their passion to intersect with their work. Garth aimed to keep them separate. Mind you, I wasn't sure that Garth had a passion.

'So even if the racing team had a good result for the season it wouldn't help the company?' I asked.

'Not even a drop in the ocean of their debt. Why? What are you up to?'

Garth always made it sound like I was a criminal.

'Just doing some background work on a client's case.'

'You've got another client? How did that happen?'

Garth thought my whole 'business' was a joke, but he was still happy to charge me for business consultations.

'I need to come and see you soon about insurance and things,' I said.

'I'm an accountant, not a broker.'

'Come on, Garth, you know a bit about everything.'

'That's true,' he said smugly.

'And that's because you have no life.'

I hung up before he could reply. You had to get the last word with Garth or he became insufferable.

I reflected on what Garth had told me before moving on to the Rileys. It seemed my gut instinct was right: Bennett probably had too much going on to be targeting Moto-Sane. I spared a second to mourn the death of another independent business before putting through a call to Crack.

'Sable's Bar, Crack speaking.'

'Crack, it's Tara. I know you're working so I'll be quick. Do you know anything about Frank Farina's reputation with women?'

He hesitated. 'He's a player.'

'He do kinky stuff?'

'Doubt it. Look, I gotta go.'

'You busy?'

'Yeah. Bolo Ignatius just brought in a large group.'

'Bolo? Is there a red-headed guy with him in black jeans and a black t-shirt who looks like an old hard core rocker?'

'Yeah. How'd you know?'

'Is he asleep?'

'Yeah, out cold in a chair near the door. I went by to check he wasn't dead.'

I groaned. 'Do me a favour. Go by again and wake him up. Tell him I sent you.'

'Sure.'

He hung up and I got on with the Riley search, finding only uniformly decent comments about Gig Riley on all the forums and blogs I checked. Seemed as if he was the most loved guy in local bike racing.

And his father the most hated.

I was still leaning towards Riley senior as the architect of Bolo's problems. He seemed to have the strongest motive, and the right disposition to do such a thing. He'd trodden on and likely broken more toes than a medieval torturer. There were plenty of articles about his aggressive business mentality, but it was the business forums that had the more personal comments. One anecdote recounted how he'd sacked an employee for excusing himself to go to the toilet while serving a customer.

A disgruntled customer had posted numerous accounts of Riley refusing to honour warranties, which had resulted in Riley's Tyres being investigated by Consumer Affairs. He'd also gone head to head with the Wanneroo Raceway owners over a number of things including delayed upgrades and permit changes for practice days.

In short, Riley senior was a hostile, argumentative bastard who was in a hurry to get wherever the hell he was going. His one vulnerable spot seemed to be his only child, Gig.

I made a call to a former client Mr Lloyd Honey. Lloyd and I had an arrangement. He had access to a great deal of information. Being a satisfied ex-client, he helped me out, and I tried not to overuse his resources.

'Lloyd?'

'Ms Sharp.'

'Tara,' I said for the umpteenth time. 'How can I ask you for favours if you call me Ms Sharp?'

'Tara then. How can I be of service?'

'I wondered if you could find out the names of all the companies two local businessmen own? Doesn't matter how small. Their names are Robert Riley from Riley's Tyres, and Bolo Ignatius, the sporting goods franchiser.

Also, I need to know who owns a company called Instant Security.'

I could hear him typing the names into his computer. 'As for our arrangement, Tara, I'll do my best. I would ask you, though … how is Lena Vine?'

'You heard … about … Audrey?'

'Yes. Terrible news. Lena and Audrey were very close.'

'I don't suppose you have any ideas who might be behind it?'

'Lena doesn't discuss her business with me. To my knowledge, though, she's an excellent businesswoman with some strong principles.'

'Oh?'

'She's the president of SDIP.'

'SDIP?'

'Stop Drugs in Prostitution.'

I suddenly began to get a tingling feeling. 'Really?'

'Yes. Ninety percent of WA brothels have signed on for it. Lena is very charismatic. Now, let me see what I can find out for you on these gentlemen.'

'Thanks, Lloyd. I'll do my best to help Lena. But I'm not a trained investigator.'

'You have other talents. Goodbye, Ms Sharp. I'll email you through my findings.'

'Tara,' I reminded him, but he'd already gone.

I settled back with Google. Tenuous connections were starting to forge in my brain. Lena was trying to stamp out drugs in her industry. Her security guy was recommended by a company in which Viaspa—Perth's primo drug lord—was a silent partner. And Leonard Roc was conveniently outside checking a faulty security camera leaving Audrey to answer the door and get hit by a drive-by shooter. Unfunny coincidence. If Lloyd confirmed Viaspa's involvement with Instant Security, I'd go back to Lena with what I knew.

But that didn't explain Louise's odd reaction to my questions.

Paralanguage and kinesics could sometimes be misleading. One time I'd confronted my female boss because I thought she was persecuting my co-worker. Turned out his frightened and disturbed body language around her was because, in private, he was happily playing Bottom to her Top. Observing the energies around people was one thing, interpreting them correctly was another. Hoshi Hara had helped me a lot, but I still made mistakes.

Spookily, my mentor rang me right then.

'Missy? Just checking you're still doing the job for me tonight.'

'Yes. I'll be at the club at ten.'

'Good, good. You park behind and use back door. Fat Frog show you around.'

'Cool. I'll be in touch.'

I yawned and stretched. Time to get changed into something club-ready. Bok would be here soon.

As I wriggled into stockings and a tight black dress, a wall of tiredness hit me. I was running on not enough hours' sleep, and Joanna's lemon chicken was sucking all my available blood into my stomach. I went to the fridge and spied a carton of fresh orange juice.

Damn, I was going to miss Cass when she left.

Chapter 22

The Gallery nightclub was just off the main strip of Northbridge in a little side street not far from Ed's modelling agency and an Indian restaurant we both loved. While Bok negotiated the busy streets and found the alley that ran behind the club, I wondered how Ed's nose was and if I'd ever hear from him again. I should check up that nothing was broken.

Maybe in a day or two, when he might consider speaking to me.

'Galah got your tongue?' asked Bok as he pulled into a spot that read Staff Only. We'd changed the old saying about cats a few years ago when JoBob first brought Brains and Hoo home.

'Just thinking about Ed,' I said.

'You really know how to show a fellow a good time, my girl.'

I pulled a sad face. 'Come on—let's go find the Fat Frog.'

Bok trailed me into the club. He liked to hang back and see what was happening from a distance before he got involved. I, on the other hand, hated hanging back and would rather plunge in; which I did as soon as I reached the posse of bouncers and door staff.

'I'm Tara Sharp. I have an appointment with Mr Vatroque.' I waved back at Bok. 'This is my colleague Martin Longbok.'

One of the door staff let out a fan-girl squeal. 'Martin Longbok. Wow! In our club?'

She proceeded to tell the bouncers how famous Bok was, and how having him in the club would be totally rad, especially if he mentioned them in his magazine. Before I knew it, we were sitting in a private lounge above the dance floor, sipping drinks from cocktail glasses while we waited for the Fat Frog. Unfortunately, mine was non-alcoholic. I was working, and Bok and I had already agreed that I would drive us home in his car.

'Why didn't you tell me you were famous?' I said.

Bok gave me a wink. 'Not famous. Just terribly cool. There's a difference.'

'Whatever. Next you'll have groupies.'

'Already do.' He slipped his iPhone out of his pocket, thumbed through some pages, then handed it to me, grinning. His Twitter profile showed fifty-five thousand followers.

'Shut the fuck up!'

He shrugged. 'The magazine's Facebook page is the

same. You should get one going for your business.'

I shook my head. 'It's not the kind of work you want to advertise. Clients don't want anyone to know they're using me. Word of mouth is better.'

'Speaking of clients, how did the brothel visit go?'

I rolled my eyes and handed him back his phone. 'Guess who I saw there?'

'Ummm… I give up.'

'Whitey.'

Bok wrinkled his nose. 'Horny little toad. No wonder June is off her rocker.'

'That's what I thought at first. Turns out he was working undercover.'

Bok's eyebrows shot up. 'What?'

'Creep's been made detective.'

'Kidding? Right?'

I sighed. 'Nope. One of the staff was shot right outside the front door. He's working the job. And so am I.'

'Shot. Like, in cold blood?'

'Uh-huh.'

'I haven't seen anything in the papers.'

'I know. Strange that.'

The door opened and a round ball of a man, whose arms and legs seemed to sprout from his torso, entered. The Fat Frog!

'Mr Longbok. What a pleasure to have you in our club. Can I get you a fresh drink?' His accent was slightly European, though it could have been a complete fake. I wasn't boned up on language intonations.

Bok gave an appreciative nod. 'Thank you ... err...?'

'Vatroque. Claude Vatroque.'

I stood up. 'I'm Tara Sharp, a colleague of Hoshi Hara's. I believe you were expecting me?' I said, seeing that I was in danger of being totally ignored.

The Fat Frog danced on the balls of his feet. 'Oh, of course. Come this way, Ms Sharp. Mr Longbok, I'll send a hostess in to take care of you.'

I raised my eyebrows at Bok. A hostess?

Bok gave a cool nod. 'Thank you.'

Vatroque took me downstairs and showed me the complete layout of the club. The internal fixtures were pretty new, and the DJ was housed in a booth, which, Vatroque explained, moved on a gantry back and forth across the top of the crowd all night. Right now, while the club was still pretty quiet, it was sitting at home base near a set of stairs.

'We believe the same group is causing trouble each week,' Vatroque said, 'but our staff cannot locate them exactly. By midnight, the floor is full.'

'What's up there?' I pointed to the area we'd just come from, but further along.

'We have three private rooms; the one Mr Longbok is using, and two others. They will be of no consequence in your appraisal.'

He was so firm about it that I immediately knew I had to get a look inside them. The fact that Vatroque was one of Lena Vine's—or Kate's—clients was zinging across my radar. 'So the troublemakers are just down here?'

'Yes.'

He led me to the bar and introduced me to the manager. 'The staff will endeavour to help you throughout the night. But feel free to join your friend Mr Longbok at any time should you wish to take a short break.'

His meaning was clear. Keep your behind down here with the ugly masses.

'Would you mind telling Martin that I'll be busy for a while?' I asked.

'Of course. Now, please excuse me. I have things to attend to.'

I spent the next hour wandering around the club and checking the layout: where the toilets were, fire exits, all the various nooks and crannies. The bar ran along one side of the dance floor and underneath the gallery where the private rooms were; a very simple design. Someone had taken a big square warehouse and built in the narrow gallery and some tracks to suspend the DJ's booth.

By the time I'd had a good look around, the place was starting to fill. I hadn't been clubbing in a while and this place was a little younger than my taste. Still, the people-watching was fine indeed. For the next hour or so, I kept myself awake by hanging near the edge of the dance floor and practising reading auras. I hadn't done any cluster readings before; that was Hoshi's specialty. He could walk into any room and pick up the mood and sense the direction proceedings were going to take. Right now I could only see energy and harmony, but it was still early.

By midnight, things were starting to take off and my feet were killing me. I'd worn boots, but the heels were starting to hurt my legs. I could have done with a shot or two of tequila as a pick-me-up. Pity I couldn't drink on the job.

The thought of a drink prompted me upstairs to check on Bok. I hoped he wasn't too bored.

The bouncer at the soundproofed doors leading into the gallery looked like he wanted to frisk me, but I stared him down and dropped Vatroque's name. He let me in and I walked past the other private rooms to where I'd left Bok. I found my BFF in a cosy arrangement with not one but two hostesses, a plate of smelly cheeses and a dozen empty Corona bottles.

'Tara, forgot you were here.' He waved drunkenly at me. 'Thish is…' He slurred two names that sounded like Fish and Chips, then knocked over the table of empties trying to offer me a beer.

I shook my head and eyed the bimbos. 'Can one of you get him a jug of water? I'll be back soon to take him home.'

So much for Bok and me having a strategy session to

manage my problems!

On the way back down to the dance floor, I tried the door to one of the other private rooms. It was open, empty and dark. The next one was open as well, but lit. I peeped in and saw another bunch of elegant couches, low tables and shelves of liquor. There were three people inside, all bent over a glass-topped bar sniffing lines of cocaine. Vatroque was one of them; John Viaspa was another; but the third nearly knocked me flat. Antonia Tozzi … what the hell? I held my breath and waited.

Viaspa was the first to speak. He patted a small knapsack on the bench next to him while Antonia wiped her nose with a handkerchief. 'Tell Dwayne to cut it down before you distribute.'

Vatroque nodded excitedly. 'Yes. This is too good, John. Too good.' I couldn't hear a trace of his accent.

'Not mine,' chimed in Antonia.

Viaspa took her hand and kissed it. 'Of course not. Only the best for you, princess.'

My stomach lurched so hard I wanted to throw up. I pulled myself together and backed quietly away from the door. Nick's wife was supposed to be in rehab in Brisbane, not sniffing blow in the backroom of a teen nightclub with Johnny Evil.

That thought preoccupied me until I reached the dance floor, where a sudden change in the cluster aura claimed my attention. The swirling whirlpool of sexually charged pinks emanating from the crowd had developed a dark brown stain near the centre. I pushed my way through the crowd over to the the DJ's booth and climbed up on it to see better. The stain hovered above two guys who, from this distance, looked no different to anyone else.

I jumped down and threaded my way towards them. But just as I got close, I felt a tap on my shoulder. Swinging around, who should I see but Nice Guy from the gym—Josh.

'Hi. What are you doing here?' I shouted in his ear.

''Bout to ask you the same question,' he bellowed back.

Before I could say anything else, there was a commotion in the crowd nearby—a scream and some scuffling. I grabbed Josh's hand and pulled him closer to the guys I'd targeted.

'Dance with me,' I mouthed.

We did just that and I manoeuvred myself into place next to the guys. It only took a few surreptitious glances to detect that they both had small, concealable electric-shock sticks up their sleeves. When the crowd converged tightly, they stung someone. In the near dark, the other dancers couldn't tell what was happening or who was doing it. But the aura stain I'd seen was emanating from the upset victims.

Before I could go and get a bouncer, one of the guys stung a young girl who collapsed on the floor. Instinctively, I launched at the guy in a below-the-knees tackle. He went down hard and took his mate with him. I grabbed for the hand that held the shock stick, catching a glimpse of Josh doing the same with the other guy. By the time the bouncers reached us, we had them down and out. So much for just observing.

We followed as the bouncers dragged the two guys outside. One of the bouncers spoke into a mobile phone and soon Vatroque came bustling out after us and danced about issuing instructions and making calls.

Josh drew me a short distance away from the pavement circus. He was dressed in jeans and a black shirt that was plain but figure-hugging. His only concession to clubbing was a pair of shiny shoes. 'What was all that about?' he asked.

'The club hired me to see if I could figure out who was causing the trouble they've been having.'

'Hired you?'

'Long story,' I said quickly.

'Well, you take your work seriously.'

I rolled my eyes. 'It wasn't planned.'

'Hey, when you're all finished up here, how about I give you a lift home?'

Just being near his cool green aura was a relief after the turmoil of energies in the club. Maybe I could put Bok in a taxi and…

'Sharpie!'

My BFF was swaying in the doorway, supported by both hostesses.

I gave Josh a rueful smile. 'Can we take a raincheck on

that? I've got to tuck my best friend up in bed.'

Josh's aura thinned a little. He wasn't so happy to be knocked back again.

'You want to hook up at the gym tomorrow?' I suggested, to make up for it.

'Sure.'

'Great. See you around ten.'

'I'll be waiting,' he said.

Vatroque was grateful to me in a jittery, coked-out kind of way. Bok was grateful to me in a drunken, get-me-home-before-I-puke kind of way. So getting out of the club took longer than I'd hoped, especially as I kept looking over my shoulder for Viaspa—but at least I got paid.

As I poured Bok into the passenger side of his car and seatbelted him in, the club's fire door opened and two figures appeared: Toni Tozzi leaving like royalty from the back entrance.

I squatted down behind the open door, so they couldn't see me in the dark.

'Sharpie,' croaked Bok.

'Ssssh,' I said sliding my hand up to his mouth.

His lips moved against my palm and I thought he was going to resist, but after a little surge of being upright, he fell back in the seat, asleep.

Right on cue, a car cruised down the laneway.

I knew Johnny Viaspa's white limo too well from my

recent experience of hanging from his front gate while a dog tried to bite my bum. Johhny V and Toni Tozzi got in together and the car reversed.

Chapter 23

I waited a few minutes until they'd gone, thanking every deity that I could name that I hadn't brought Mona. Then I got into the driver's seat of Bok's car and pulled out onto the street.

I was so tired driving home that the white lines on the road had turned to doubles, so I fished in my bag searching for sugar and found a small packet of red frogs—food-van booty. The frogs gave me a bit of a lift but I was still too exhausted to take Bok to his place, which would mean another hour faffing around getting him up in the lift. Instead, I manhandled him out of the car and into my flat where I dumped him on the couch.

'Don't worry, he's a friend,' I told Cass when she raised her head from under her blanket. 'Go back to sleep.'

We all slept until late.

I woke up less tired but more weighed down by dread.

Toni Tozzi. Johnny Viaspa. Audrey. Bolo. Death threats. The race. It was hard to pick which one to fixate on first, so I crawled out of bed and stumbled to the sink, where I drank a litre of water without stopping to draw breath.

Cass was buried under her blankets still, and Bok's face was buried into the back of the couch. I checked he was still breathing then slapped him across the head.

He surfaced like a drowning man, eyes blinking, mouth open and gasping. 'Whaaa-at—'

'—were you thinking?' I blasted him.

He saw it was me and groggily swung his feet onto the floor. 'Fuck. Who painted the world white?'

I switched on the kettle and started spooning coffee into cups. 'Watch your language. And you owe me a conversation. So get with it.'

'Go easy. I'm delicate,' he moaned sinking his head into his hands.

'Outside,' I ordered without sympathy and led the way carrying cups.

We sat in JoBob's garden chairs, in the sunshine, and he squinted while he sipped coffee. 'Why did you let me do that?' he said.

It was a question we'd often asked each other over the years at various times. Our answer to one another was always the same. 'Suck it up.'

But I let him finish his first cup, and got him a refill and a pair of sunnies, before I started on him.

He didn't speak much as I vented my list of worries,

including seeing Toni Tozzi with Johnny Viaspa last night.

When I'd finished, Bok looked wide awake and a little freaked out. I relied on him to be the calm one; the one with the plan. I didn't like seeing him rattled.

'Right. This is what you're going to do. You ring Ignatius and tell him what you know, then pull Wal off the job and have him watch you,' he said firmly, thrusting his finger at me for emphasis. 'And you ring Fiona Bligh and give her the number plate of the car that's been following you and tell her someone's tried to break into your flat.'

'But that'll bring up all the Tozzi/Viaspa stuff and I don't want to go there.'

'Tara,' he said sternly, 'you have no choice.'

He was right. I couldn't continue pretending I could handle this.

'What about Antonia?' I said.

'None of your business—it'll only make more trouble when you've got more than enough already. Keep out of it. Let Nick Tozzi take care of his own house.'

'But it's Viaspa she's buying her gear from.'

He shrugged. 'Still not your worry. You don't want to give Viaspa another reason for wanting you dead.'

There was nothing sarcastic or melodramatic about his verdict. And he was right.

I stood up. 'Okay. I'm going to the gym, then I'll call Bolo to say I'm done, and Bligh to tell her about the person following me.'

'Why do you need to go to the gym first?'

'I want to have a clear head before I talk to Bligh.' And keep my appointment with Nice Guy.

He narrowed his eyes. 'You promise you'll call them today?'

'By lunchtime. Cross my heart.'

He stood up and gave me a hug. 'Sensible girl. Now find me some Berocca and my car keys.'

Back inside, Cass was wide awake and bubbling over about a job interview at the Claremont Growers Market on Monday.

'It's for the fish department. But I'll be able to move to green groceries as soon as a spot opens.'

'That's great, Cass,' I said, surprised by her excitement.

I settled back to enjoy the ham and cheese croissants she produced from the oven. After eating my fourth one and ascertaining there were no more, I had a shower and unearthed some clean gym gear. Since Wal's departure, the place had fallen back into sad disarray but mess had order, when it was your own.

Bok stayed long enough to polish off a tall glass of soluble vitamin B, before he staggered off.

I was putting on one of my sneakers when my phone rang. It was Lloyd Honey.

'Tara, I have that information for you.'

'Yes?' I said.

'It took a little digging but Instant Security is co-owned

by Jensen Bridges and John Viaspa.'

'Jensen Bridges!' I nearly choked. He was the crooked politician who'd been turning a blind eye to Viaspa's mining lease rort. Crap, this just got worse. I mentally added Lena Vine to my to-call-today list.

'I see you know him.'

'Of him, yes.' Of his dirty exploits.

'I'm also emailing you a list of the companies owned by Riley and Bolo Ignatius. I hope it is of some help.'

'Lloyd, I think I love you,' I said by way of thank you.

'My pleasure, Tara. Be safe. These are not pleasant people you are dealing with.'

'I will, Lloyd.'

I opened my laptop and waited for the list to come through. When it did, the only name that even vaguely rang a bell was Tex-E but I couldn't think why. I sighed, closed the lid and put my beeping phone on charge. Then I told Cass I'd be back in an hour.

Brains squawked at me for a scratch as I walked past, while Hoo hung from one leg and flapped his wings. I opened the door and tickled his belly, which got him screeching in mock protest. Brains didn't like losing the attention and crawled over and bit the foot he was hanging from. Hoo screeched again and fluttered to the floor of the cage.

I laughed, feeling momentarily lighter, and headed out to Mona. She glowed like the rising sun in the morning light. Soon as I could afford it I vowed to get her resprayed.

The orange body and black flames along the bonnet were way too loud for undercover work.

A quick glance up and down the street and back at the house told me that no one was around. I could hear JoBob in the family room with the TV on.

Maybe my stalker had moved on to other tasks.

As soon as I passed the first cross-street on the way to the gym, though, the dark sedan reappeared. My heart started to hammer and I had an overwhelming desire to plant my foot on the accelerator and just flat out race away. Instead, I took the next random corner and ducked and weaved in and out of all the side streets I knew.

I suddenly wished I'd brought my phone with me. If it was Viaspa who'd set this guy on me, it wouldn't be to watch out for my wellbeing. I finally lost the sedan somewhere near View Street and headed back to the gym without being followed.

I parked in the underground car park and grabbed my towel.

'Tara!'

It was Josh, waving me over to the back wall where he was leaning on the boot of a white sedan.

'Are you okay?' he asked as strode over to join him.

'Yeah. Fine. Just some bad drivers on the road.'

'You look like you need a hug.'

He reached out and pulled me into his arms. It wasn't a Nick Tozzi bear hug, but it was comforting and he smelled nice. But as I looked over his shoulder, I realised that the car tucked in behind his was a dark brown sedan. Before I could pull away, my bag was wrenched from my shoulder, and he lifted and dropped me. My head and shoulder collided hard with something. Then a boot lid slammed on me, shutting out the light.

Fuck!

I kicked and shouted and thumped until my voice became hoarse and my hands and feet hurt too much to continue. And even then I kept going. I probably should have kept still and tried to count turns and listen for sounds that gave away my destination, but I was too freaked out. And mad with myself for not realising that Josh had been my stalker.

Eventually, the car slowed and lurched, as if going over speed humps. I felt around for anything that I could use as a weapon. Might only get one chance. But he'd taken out the jack and spare tyre and I found nothing except what felt like a hessian shopping bag.

The car stopped and a few seconds later the boot opened.

'Get out. Quietly,' said Josh, shoving a gun against my ear before I could unstick my tongue from the top of my mouth.

I thought about launching at him, risking being shot and gambling on my size to give me an advantage, but I knew from the gym that he had dense, toned muscle.

So I unfolded my body and climbed out over the lip of the boot. We were in a dark, empty lock-up garage.

He pointed towards an open door that led to a lit stairway. I took a couple of quick steps towards it before he grabbed my elbow and spun me around. The pistol that had been against my ear was now pressed hard against my lips. The sight of his skin-coloured rubber gloves all but closed my throat over. This guy was a professional.

'Try something stupid and no one will even know you're dead until they find you with your guts full of gas, floating in one of those fancy marinas.'

He forced me up the staircase. It finished in the hallway of what looked like a townhouse that was as empty as the garage. There were some Chinese takeaway cartons on the floor, but otherwise he was leaving minimal trace.

'Sit,' he said as he pushed me past the kitchen and laundry and into the smaller of two bedrooms. The only objects in the room were a heavy wood garden chair in the centre of a large plastic tarpaulin.

Josh pushed me over to the chair, then went to the built-in cupboard and opened the door. Inside was a fold-over suitcase. He pulled rope out of one of the zippered compartments and handled it with chilling dexterity.

When he placed the pistol on the floor and began to tie my legs, a window of opportunity flashed before me. A two-feet kick would knock him off balance and then I could dive on the gun.

'Move and I'll break every bone in your body,' he said, reading my thoughts.

His quiet threat paralysed me. I didn't doubt he meant what he said. As he deftly knotted my feet and hands to the chair, I stared at his aura. I hadn't misread his calm—just the reason for it. Unfortunately, auras don't come with 'cold-blooded killer' warnings. A new release of adrenaline vibrated through every part of me.

He felt me tremble. 'Cool it.' He reached into his pocket and brought out a scarf.

'What's this about?' I demanded, the adrenaline finally loosening my throat. 'What kind of a crazy bastard kidnaps someone in a car park?'

He smiled in an empty kind of way. The face that I'd found so pleasant now seemed unfamiliar and cold. I saw a sulphurous yellow snaking through his aura. Not the colour of pus like Johnny Viaspa's aura, but the sickly tinge of jaundice.

'Don't talk, you'll spoil it.' With that, he wound the scarf so tight across my mouth and around the back of my neck that I gagged.

He made another trip to the fold-over case and retrieved a tool wrap, which he laid out carefully on the plastic in front of me. I could see enough of the steel implements sticking out of the pockets to know they weren't made by Meccano. Not unless Meccano had got into scalpels, small hand drills and chisels.

The precision and calm of his movements sent my panic meter spiking off the scale. He was deliberately psyching me out and it was working. Fear made it impossible to think. All I knew was that I wanted to pee. Badly.

A phone started ringing. His. In the fold-over suitcase.

He answered it, listened for a moment, then left the room, shutting the door.

Though I could hear him moving around downstairs, he didn't come back all day. I sat there, slowly getting stiffer, unable to move any part of my body, staring at his bundle of instruments.

Chapter 24

When Josh returned, it was nearly dark. I made a desperate pleading noise and he unwound the scarf.

'Please. I need to … pee,' I gasped.

He shrugged at that idea.

'Let me go to the loo. Please. Otherwise I'll…'

He lifted his shoulders and dropped them again as if vexed then he punched me in the mouth. Pain exploded along my jawline and my head jerked back. He grabbed me by the hair and wrenched my head upright.

'Don't speak to me again,' he said close to my ear, and tied the gag back—tighter.

The smack in the face was a big favour. I no longer needed to pee and somehow it un-stuck my brain freeze. When he left the room this time, I finally began to think.

He'd left the light on, so I could contemplate his choice of torture implements. I needed to get to the scalpel. I started working frantically to get my hands loose from the arms of the chair.

After an hour or more, the rope hadn't slackened at all and my wrists were raw.

I rested for a short spell, wondering how long I had before he came back and used his tools on me. And why he was waiting, anyway? What had that phone call been about? Was he just trying to scare me or did he have another reason for delaying?

I went back to working on the rope, getting nowhere, but refusing to give in.

Some time later, after midnight perhaps, I heard the engine start and the car pull out of the garage below. I counted to fifty and it didn't return. Maybe he'd gone to get food. Or to kill someone else.

I began to work even more frantically, not worried anymore about making noise. My hands remained trapped, but the rope around my ankles had loosened a fraction, just enough that my feet were able to touch the floor.

I began to rock my weight until my momentum toppled me forward. I forced my legs to brace so that I stopped just short of falling on my face, teetering like a hermit crab with the chair on my back. The weight and angle strained my knees to buckling point but I tensed my calves. After a moment of reaching balance, I leaned to one side, attempting to reach the tool wrap. Immediately the chair weight began to tip me over and I had to rock back.

Shit. Move on to plan B.

Plan B involved waddling to the door and positioning myself behind it. When Josh came through it, I'd take him out with the legs of the chair. If I had the strength. If I was quick enough.

With each step towards the wall, my bladder reminded me it was threatening to burst and my back screamed in protest. I gritted my teeth and told myself that peeing my pants was preferable to being sliced up by a psycho.

It took forever to get in the right position but when I did, I was able to lean the back legs of the chair against the wall and take some of the weight off my spine.

Sweat poured off me, even though the air temperature had cooled off. I tried to relax my muscles to give them a chance to recover but a cramp attacked my right foot. I wiggled it around and nearly tipped over again. More sweating and straining to keep balance.

When the next cramp came, I just swore and waited it out, letting the tears flow.

The sound of the car returning brought a welcome surge of adrenaline to my numb legs and crippled back. This was it! He'd come straight up and check on me for sure. I had to get him first swing.

There was a creak on the stairs as he headed up.

I sucked in a quick couple of breaths, bunched my muscles and rose up onto my toes. The door opened quietly and he stood there for a second. Once he realised

I was gone, he stepped into the room and looked behind the door.

With every little bit of force I had in me, I swung the back of the chair around and socked it to him.

One of the higher back legs caught him under the jaw and he fell. I used my momentum to spin right around and dropped the chair down on top of him.

He tried to push me off, but I threw my whole weight backwards and dropped hard again. I was eighty kilos to contend with and this time something cracked—his rib, I hoped, or an arm.

He didn't make a noise, just moved to roll. Fighting to keep balanced, I let his movement push me back to my feet again then repeated my action. This time the crack was louder and, from the groan that escaped, more painful.

Then he stopped moving.

I tried to see underneath the chair. Had I killed him?

From my upside-down view, he looked unconscious but I didn't want to take any chances.

And what the hell did I do now?

It was then that I heard a faint movement on the stairs. Another creak. Quick, quiet footsteps. Shit, there was someone else in the house!

A tight fist squeezed my heart. I had nothing left in the tank for this. I'd beaten Josh but I was still going to die.

When a stocky figure with red hair and too many tattoos commando-rolled through the door, I nearly fainted from relief.

'Arrgh!' I groaned.

'Boss!'

Wal took in the situation at a glance and let out a grunt that sounded like part relief, part satisfaction. A second later he was by my side, cutting the ropes off with a huge knife and removing my gag.

As soon as my hands were free, I leaned down and punched the unconscious Josh in the face, just for good measure. Then I got up from the chair and fell straight over.

While I lay on the floor massaging blood back into my limbs, Wal removed the chair from Josh and tied his feet and hands together. Then he transferred my gag to Josh's mouth. When he was done, Wal surveyed the room and the tool wrap with a low whistle.

'Looks like he wuz plannin' a party. What do you want to do?'

'Toilet,' I croaked.

I struggled up onto my feet and shuffled to the bathroom where I had the best pee of my life.

When I returned to Wal, he was kneeling on the floor delving into his kitbag.

'What's the time?' I said.

'Around 5AM. It'll be light soon.'

'Let's get out of here in case someone else comes. I'll make an anonymous call to the cops.'

'You sure you want to leave him like this? If for some reason the cops don't get him, he'll likely come for you again.'

Wal was right, but I had to get out of here and away from Josh before I started screaming. And I wasn't about to kill him.

'Bligh will get him.'

Wal pulled on a pair of gloves similar to those Josh wore. Then he drew a cloth out of a ziplock bag and began wiping down the chair.

'What else did you touch?'

I thought about it. 'Just the inside of the boot. It's downstairs in the lock-up garage. Nothing else. He had a gun on me the whole time.'

'Go get in the car. It's a white Calais, a block down this street on the right. It's open. I'll go over the boot.'

I nodded. 'In a minute. You got another set of gloves?'

He handed his bag to me. 'Help yourself.'

'I'm going to use his mobile to make the call from here.'

He nodded his approval. 'Smart. Give me time to wipe the boot clean.'

'Where are we?'

'Townhouse estate in Scarborough called Indian Sands. Number thirty-seven.'

I passed his kitbag back and suppressed my urge to follow him downstairs. Even though Josh was hog-tied and still unconscious, I felt sick just being near him.

I pulled on the gloves, and put Josh's tool kit back in the fold-over case in the cupboard, so he couldn't possibly reach it. Then I searched through the case's pockets. The main zippered compartment contained rolled-up t-shirts, underwear, socks and a small wetpack with toothpaste and toothbrush. I guess when you're a paid killer you don't leave stuff lying around in bathrooms.

I moved on to the outer pockets, where I found an airline e-ticket printout for a flight to Sydney under the name Josh Hamilton.

Now for him.

I went back to Josh and, with trembling hands, patted down his body until I located his mobile. He had nothing else in his pockets except for some cash.

I ran quickly through the directory of what looked like a cheap throwaway phone. No contacts listed. His notes section had only a single entry with three names in it:

Sam Barbaro
Lena Vine
Tara Sharp

My shaking got worse as I moved on to calls received. Two numbers only. One unnamed, the other listed under Dwayne. That was the dealer's name Viaspa had mentioned at the club. I rang the first number.

'I told you not to call me.' Johnny Viaspa's voice was as recognisable as his pus-yellow aura.

I hung up and dialled the Dwayne number.

'Roc here.'

Lena Vine's security guard. It hit me then that the name Dwayne was a play on his surname Roc. After the actor

Dwayne Johnson—the Rock. If I'd had anything in my stomach I would have vomited it up.

I rang the Euccy Grove cop shop. Putting on my deepest, most mannish voice, I left an urgent, anonymous message for Constable Bligh, consisting of the address of the townhouse, the sedan's licence plate number and the word 'Hurry'.

Josh began to groan.

I took one last look around to make sure I'd left nothing behind, and placed his phone on the cupboard shelf next to his fold-over bag.

On my way to the door, I stepped close to him and did something any self-respecting, escaping abduction victim would do to her kidnapper. I kicked him as hard as I could where it most hurt.

Then I shut the door on my way out.

Chapter 25

I called out to Wal in the garage as I left through the side door.

'Coming,' he said.

I didn't wait. My nerves were shot to pieces and my legs trembled with fatigue. For the first time since Josh had hit me I registered how sore my jaw was and that my bottom lip had swollen to twice its normal size.

Every bush I passed seemed to hide another madman; every shadow made me fear that he had an accomplice.

I was in tears by the time I found the Calais and fell into the passenger seat. When Wal popped up at my window shortly after, my heart stopped altogether.

I couldn't speak as he got in.

He squeezed my shoulder. 'Done.'

And we were out of there at last.

Wal made two calls on the way home. The first was

brief, and consisted of him mainly listening. The second was to Bok, whose panicked voice I could hear from the passenger seat.

'I've got her,' Wal said, cutting him off. 'Be home soon.'

I wet my lips and forced sound from my dry throat. 'How did you find me? Whose car is this?'

'Like to say that findin' you was off me own bat, boss. But if it had just been down to me, you'd still be sittin' in that chair wonderin' what to do when The Finisher woke up.'

'The Finisher?'

'That's what they call him.'

'T-tell m-me e-everything,' I stuttered.

He sucked in a long noisy breath and slowed down to under the speed limit. 'Well... Cass got worried when you didn't come back after the gym. She called your mate Martin from your phone.'

'Smart kid.'

'Martin rang me and we met at your place. Then your rich guy turns up.'

I had to think for a minute. 'You mean Nick Tozzi?'

'Yeah. Turns out he's had someone watchin' you for a few days. Some ex-Forces guy. The Forces guy saw you go into the car park at the gym. When you didn't come out he went to have a look, caught sight of The Finisher leavin'. Apparently he recognised him. Knows him from ... you know ... around.'

'He called Nick?'

Wal nodded. 'Forces guy tailed you to the townhouse. Rich guy and me jumped in his car and caught up with the Forces guy outside the townhouse.'

'There was someone else with you?'

'Forces guy took downstairs; I went up.'

'I didn't see him.'

'Yeah. He prefers it that way. When I told him you were okay, he vamoosed.'

'Wh-where was Nick?'

'Outside. We told him to watch the back in case someone came out that way.'

No wonder I hadn't seen him. 'So where is he now?'

'Right behind us. He picked up his guy and they're following us.'

I twisted in my seat but could only see headlights. 'Can you pull over? I want to talk to him.' I suddenly wanted to cry again.

Wal shook his head firmly. 'He told me to take you straight home and that's what I'm doing.'

I sank back into the seat, really beginning to shake now. I was safe but I didn't feel it.

'Wal, Leonard Roc's number was in Josh's phone.'

'Shit.'

'Yeah.'

'The only other number was Viaspa's.'

'Shit. So what's that mean?'

The pieces began to fit together. 'I think that Viaspa hired Josh to get rid of Barbaro and me and Lena Vine.

Our names were on a list in his phone notes.'

'Lena? Why her?'

I thought about it. 'She's active in a lobby group called Stop Drugs in Prostitution. Maybe it's affecting his trade. What if The Finisher hit Audrey by mistake.'

'Pretty dumb mistake for a pro.'

'At night, in the dark, they could be mistaken for each other. They are the same age.'

He shrugged. 'Maybe.'

'And I bet Leonard Roc's one of Viaspa's dealers. He could have lied about the camera malfunction so he was out the back when Josh did his drive-by. Why else would his number be in Josh's phone.'

'He's in on it somehow,' said Wal grimly.

'I think that Kate rang the doorbell, thinking Lena would answer, then went back into the lounge.'

'Why would she do that?'

'When I interviewed her, I could tell she was a user. Leonard's probably supplying her. He's getting his stuff from a nightclub owner in Northbridge.'

'Shit,' said Wal for a third time. 'Murderin' bastard.'

I wanted to agree but my teeth began to chatter.

They didn't stop until I'd got home, had a shower and let Cass force-feed me a litre of water, a sweet Milo and a bacon sandwich.

She was pale and quiet and didn't ask any questions.

When I'd finished eating, I let her give me some ice for my lip. After that, she stopped hovering over me and cooked breakfast for the others.

Bok and Wal ate together on the couch as I filled them all in on what had happened from the moment I was pushed into the boot of the car. I didn't leave out anything.

Bok looked a bit sick, and Cass was whiter than my bed sheets.

'You've got nine lives, Sharpie,' said Bok, kissing me on the head. I think we should all get some sleep. I'll come back this afternoon and we'll talk more.'

Wal lay down on the couch once he'd locked the sliding door, and Cass got up to wash the plates.

I climbed into my own bed, hugged my pillow, and rolled to face the wall so neither of them could see my tears. I stayed like that until they subsided, then I carefully patted my eyes dry with my fingers. I hadn't dared look in the mirror when I'd got home. My face was still grazed from the brush with the cactus garden and the hedge, and now my lip was fat and my chin bruised.

I wanted to cry again at the thought. More than that, I wanted to see Nick.

But Tozzi hadn't stopped as Wal and I pulled up outside Lilac Street; he just gave me a wave and kept on going. I wanted to thank him but it would have to wait. There was something I had to do that was much more urgent.

I rolled up and out of bed and grabbed my phone, dialling Madame Vine's number.

'Lena?'

'Yes, Tara.' She sounded remarkably awake for 6AM. 'Have you made some progress?'

'Yes, progress has been … made.' I told her my theory about Leonard Roc's connection with Kate and Viaspa. 'I think you shoud call the police. Get Roc out of your place. He's dangerous.'

'What about Louise?' asked Lena.

'I'm guessing that she knew about Kate ringing the doorbell and didn't want to say anything. What I sensed in her was … guilt.'

Lena was quiet for a moment. 'And you think they meant to kill me, not Audrey?'

'Yes. Your lobbying against drugs in prostitution is a threat to Viaspa.'

'I knew I would tread on toes but this is extreme… Oh, Audy,' her voice trembled. 'I owe you a great deal, Tara. I'll call Detective Whitehead immediately about Leonard.'

'Don't be surprised if they can't make anything stick to Viaspa. He's slippery. I know from experience.'

'The worst ones always are.'

'Watch your back, Lena. He'll lay low for a while, but not forever.' It felt like advice I should be giving myself.

'You too, Tara.'

I hung up and shivered into a kind of sleep.

A few hours later I woke up gasping for breath as someone

tried to choke me in my dreams. I sat upright and blinked away the nightmare, waiting for my brain to orient itself.

Home. In my bed. Safe. Daytime.

Cass was asleep on her fold-out bed and Wal was out cold on the couch.

I massaged blood into my facial muscles and blinked a few times. Then I grabbed my phone. Maybe a bit of Facebooking might help cure my fear hangover.

Instead I found myself looking over the list of companies again. Tex-E. I remembered Riley had mentioned them as one of his suppliers.

I quickly Googled it and found out it was a small company that sold motorbike chains and electrical parts such as speedometers, switches and headlights. What I hadn't expected to find out was that Bolo was a part owner.

A lightning bolt of suspicion struck me. I got up and shook Cass awake.

'What?' She sprang up out of bed and almost knocked me over.

'Cass, it's me. Shhh. Listen. What time does the race start today?'

She crinkled her forehead. 'Umm … 10AM, I think. Why? You're not—'

'What about the superbikes?'

'Around 1pm. That's what T-Dog said.'

I checked the clock on my computer. It was 11.15am. An hour's drive should get me there before the main race.

I raised my voice. 'Wal, wake up! Wal!'

He opened his eyes without moving a muscle. 'What?'

'I know why Bolo wouldn't go to the police about his death threats. We've got to get out to Wanneroo. Now!'

He zipped up his jeans, ran his tongue over his lips, and cracked his knuckles. 'Let's go.'

I was beginning to think maybe I'd actually struck gold when I met Wal.

He never quibbled over important things.

Chapter 26

Wal drove me down to Fresh Flesh in the Calais, where I picked up Mona. Those few moments spent back in the shadowy gym car park got me shivering all over again. How close I'd come to disaster.

I managed to get control of my reaction by the time I arrived back to Lilac Street.

Cass and Wal joined me.

'How did Bolo act when you were watching him?' I asked Wal as we hit the highway north.

He shrugged. 'Jumpy. But I put that down to the death threats. Why? What are you thinking?'

'Did you check his browser history and his files?'

'Yeah. A lot of porn. Some of it pretty hardcore, though.'

I nodded. I wasn't prepared to share my hunch yet. There was still a missing piece of the jigsaw to put in place. Something that Smitty had said kept coming back to me. When a guy falls hard … he'll do just about anything to please her... except I wasn't thinking of Sable and Crack this time.

As we passed through the main gates at Wanneroo I knew I had to pay Sharee a visit. I pulled into the visitors parking area.

'Cass, can you go find Jase and take him to Riley's bay. Make him wait until I get there.'

'What should I say?'

'Anything, just get him there. Wal, I want you to hang around outside Riley's too. Don't let Gig Riley leave until I get there. Do whatever you have to.'

I checked the time on my phone: twelve forty-five. Fifteen minutes til race time. The bikes would start rolling down to the start line in five minutes.

I sprinted past the pits down to Sharee's booth.

'Tara! Hi!' Sharee hung out over her counter and waved at me as I approached. 'Wow, you look terrible.'

'My cat scratched me,' I said. 'Sharee, this is really important. What's Lu Red's girlfriend's name?'

'Sally,' she said.

'I mean her surname.'

'Ummm. Lemme think ... Rowan, no ... Rowe. Yeah. That's it. Red and Rowe. Always thought it'd make a funny surname if they put them together.'

'Thanks.'

'Why?'

'Can't explain but I owe you,' I said. I walked away from her and rang Bok.

He answered sleepily. 'T?'

'The place where you bought the beautiful handbag … was the woman who owned it named Sally Rowe?'

'Yes. Rowes are a name in the industry. That's why I went to it. I knew I'd find gold in her cast offs.'

'How long ago was that?'

He paused for a moment. 'About a month, I guess.'

My heart skipped a beat. 'I love you!' I said.

'Oh,' replied Bok suspiciously. 'What have I done now?'

'Gotta go,' I said, and hung up.

I bolted back towards the pits entrance and flashed my pit pass at the gate guy.

In the Moto-Sane pen, Clem was wiping the Honda's faring while Bolo hovered near the tyre rack watching Lu Red zip up his suit in preparation for the race. Red's aura was how I expected to find it: dark brown with fear.

Bolo swivelled when he saw me. 'Tara? Is something—'

'I know who's been sabotaging your team, Bolo,' I blurted, conscious that I was out of time.

He took a step towards me, frowning. 'Who? Are we safe to race today?'

I turned on Lu Red. 'I guess it depends on what Lu's planned. Might be he's dirtied the fuel again.'

Bolo stared at his rider then back at me. 'What do you mean?'

'Lu wants to go back east with his girlfriend when she leaves.'

Red blinked, taking in my accusation. His aura began

to pucker unhappily.

'But that's ridiculous,' said Bolo. 'Lu's not leaving. And even if he wanted to, why wouldn't he just tell me he wanted to leave?'

'I assume you have a contract. Wouldn't he have to pay it out if he wanted to break it?'

Red crossed his arms. 'This is crazy, Bolo. You need to get her out of here. I can't have this kind of nonsense right now.'

'Think about it,' I said, refusing to back down. 'If you lost your sponsors because the team was doing badly, you'd be forced to let him go. Then you'd be the one breaking the contract.'

'What proof do you have?' demanded Bolo, colour rising in his face.

'Timing, mainly. Everything was going well until Sally decided to sell up and go back home to Victoria. Ever since then you've been having problems.'

Clem straightened up and stared at Lu Red. Understanding dawned on his face, like he was seeing the possibility that I was right. Bolo's eyes continued to dart between me and Red while he put things together.

'That proves nothing,' said Lu Red. 'The woman is mad. Get her out of here.'

Bolo wavered. I could see him thinking it through. 'Are you the one who's been sending me death threats?' he said to Lu.

But I wasn't going to let Bolo get away with that.

'You made those threats up, Bolo,' I said. 'You wanted it to look like you were a victim in case you're investigated.'

All eyes settled on the team's owner.

'What are you talking about now?' Bolo blustered.

'You thought it was Robert Riley who was sabotaging you, so you're planning to get him back today. You covered yourself by bringing me in, and agreeing to Wal acting as a bodyguard. Who'd ever suspect you'd do something to Team Riley in an effort to win? Not when you were the poor guy getting the death threats and having the mechanical problems.'

'Ridiculous,' he said, shaking his head.

I ignored him and directed a question to Clem. 'You worked with Riley's mechanic, Dave, in Europe. Why did he leave?'

Clem stared at the ground, clearly not wanting to answer.

'Was he sacked for taking bribes?' I asked.

He glanced up, shocked. 'How did you know?'

'I heard you'd had a fight with him, so I asked around. He came back to Australia and tried to badmouth your reputation, didn't he?'

He nodded mutely.

'See I checked with your previous employer. They said you were the best mechanic they'd ever had from down here. When they wouldn't discuss Dave, though, I figured he was the one who'd been sacked. That right?'

Clem shrugged then nodded again.

'Then I wondered if he'd been spreading rumours about you to hide the truth. Bolo knew the truth—that's why he hired you, because you're good. It's also how he knew he could bribe Dave,' I added.

Bolo's aura had turned the colour of grey smoke. But I didn't wait to press home my accusations.

'Clem, quick,' I said. 'I need you to come with me. We have to stop Gig Riley from racing.'

We sprinted the short distance to the Riley pen. Wal was loitering nearby, and Jase and Cass were standing right outside. Jase looked annoyed and a bit stressed.

'What's going on, Tara?' he said. 'I'm real busy.'

'I want you to be a witness to a conversation I'm about to have. Are you prepared to do that?'

'What about?'

'You should know that I'm actually an investigator.'

'A private investigator?'

'Yes.' Kind of.

His eyes lit up and the annoyance vanished from his face. 'Okay. I'm in.'

'Follow me,' I said.

Wal drifted closer as I strode into the pen.

Riley senior was having a last-minute word with Gig, who was sitting on his bike preparing to put his helmet on.

'Stop!' I shouted.

Riley opened his mouth to give me a blistering serve but I lunged at Gig and latched onto his arm. 'There's something wrong with your chain. You can't race—it'll break.'

'Get this crazy bitch out of here,' Riley senior bellowed at Jase, who'd appeared behind me with Clem.

'Tara? What the—' Jase began.

'There's a faulty chain on the bike. Gig,' I pleaded, 'just take a look at it. I'm a private investigator.'

Gig looked around for Dave, but the wrench had disappeared.

'Please. Just let Clem double check it,' I said. 'No harm in that.'

'That bent bastard isn't coming anywhere near my bike,' spat Riley senior. 'Now clear out, all of you.'

'Clem isn't the one who's bent,' I said. 'It's your guy, Dave.'

Gig stared at me, and I could see him deciding whether to trust me or not. His aura reached out to mine. 'Dad, just let him check. It's my arse out there.'

Riley gave me a disgusted look but nodded. He loved his kid more than he loved winning. I'd banked on that.

Clem grabbed a spanner from the workbench and squatted down to test the Z-rings. On the fourth light tap the chain broke.

'Jees-us,' Clem said. 'That could have been nasty.'

Riley trembled with barely restrained fury. 'Where's Dave? I'll…'

'I can change it,' said Clem quickly. 'If you want. Only take few minutes.'

Gig looked at his dad and gave a quick nod.

Riley let out a breath. 'Do it.'

While Clem and Gig searched the cartons for a new chain, Riley turned back to me. 'After this race, you and I had better have a long talk.'

Chapter 27

Gig Riley won and broke the race record. Lu Red was recorded as a DNR.

After it was over, I explained to Riley senior that I'd been working on a case that led me to suspect his mechanic was taking bribes. I refused to go into any more detail, other than to say that he shouldn't let Dave near one of his bikes again. He gave up questioning me eventually, but I knew he hadn't let it go. Dave would need to put some serious distance between himself and old man Riley.

I hadn't given up Bolo because he was my client, however bent. It'd be up to Riley to dig around and find out the truth for himself.

One thing I knew for sure: I was going to have a hell of a time getting my expenses paid in full on this job.

I did slip Crack's card to Riley senior as I left though. 'You'll be needing a new wrench. This guy's good. Been around bikes all his life. Used to sleep with his Ducati.'

Wal and I caught up with Bolo in the car park, door of the Beamer open, engine running. He looked angry and a little scared.

'I don't like being lied to by my own clients, Bolo,' I said calmly. 'But if you pay me the rest of my money, I'll let it slide this time.'

'Why you piece of—'

Wal wagged a warning finger. His eyes gleamed at the possibility of violence. 'Don't you get nasty with my boss, now, mate.'

'You've got nothing on me,' he said.

'I know you're a part owner in Tex-E and that you arranged to have a faulty chain delivered to Riley's. Then you bribed Dave to fit it. I haven't told Riley or the police, but I could do both. They'll find the proof.'

Bolo took an unsteady breath then he reached into his pocket. Pulling out his wallet, he pulled out some notes. 'No paper trail. No more talk about it. Right?'

I took the money. 'I won't say another word. Whether Riley looks into it further though is out of my control.'

He gave me a look that told me he knew what he'd do to take care of that. I pitied Dave. Well, actually I didn't. Gig Riley could have been killed.

Wal stepped reluctantly away from the car, and Bolo was gone before I could stuff the cash in my pocket.

Cass, Wal and I left the track soon after. On our way

home, I drove through McDonald's for soft-serve, much to Cass's delight.

When we got back to the flat, I went to bed after telling Cass to lock the doors and draw the curtains. She did as I asked, taking the key with her to another 'appointment' with Joanna.

Persistent knocking woke me up five hours later.

I forced myself vertical and staggered over to the sliding door.

'Sharp?' It was Fiona Bligh.

I unlocked the door and stepped out. She was alone.

'What in hell's name happened to your face?' she asked.

'One of the birds scratched me. Then I fell over and hit my chin. What's up? Where's Bill?'

'In the car,' she explained. 'And I hope you're telling me the truth. About your face.'

'This a social visit?' I asked.

'You don't happen to know anything about a tip-off to the station telling them to go to a townhouse in Scarborough?'

I did my best attempt at listen, stretch, yawn and react with mild interest. 'No. But it sounds interesting. Do tell.'

She gave me a sceptical stare. 'Well, whoever it was did us a good turn. The guy we caught is wanted for aggravated robbery and rape. And without wanting to pre-empt anything, I think he may be able to help us in one or two murder investigations. Either way, he'll be put away for a while.'

Jeez! 'Glad to hear you've had a win,' I said. 'Anything else I can do for you, Fiona?'

She gave me another raking appraisal but didn't pursue it. She'd delivered her message to me. They had Josh, and he was going down.

When she left, I had to sit for a bit. It was just as well I did, because my phone rang and it was Nick Tozzi.

'Can I come and see you?' he asked.

'Now?'

'Are you alone?'

'Yes.'

'I'm outside. There's a police car in your driveway.'

I sighed. 'They're just leaving. Wait a minute and then come in.'

I didn't know that I was ready to talk to him, but putting it off wouldn't make it any better.

When I opened the door, he looked so worn out that I slipped my hands around his waist and hugged him for a long time. He hugged me back just as hard.

When I was able to let go, I asked him if he wanted tea.

He shook his head. 'No. I just needed to check that you're alright. Do you want to talk about what happened?'

We sat on the couch and I recounted the kidnap details, and how I'd knocked Josh out with the chair. 'The police have him now,' I said. 'He's wanted for robbery and rape as well. Plus they're going to try and get him for some murders.'

'Are you sure you don't want to tell the police the whole story?'

'I don't trust the cops to be able to prove Viaspa's connection to him. If I go to the cops and tell them everything and Visapa goes free, he'll never let it go. This way, I've still got some leverage at least. It gives me a chance.'

'That's a dangerous game, Tara.'

I shrugged and we sat in silence for a bit.

'Thank you for having my back. You saved my life,' I said eventually.

'I was worried. You've taken some serious risks in the past to help me, Tara. I won't ever forget that.'

'To help both of us,' I corrected.

'When my investigator called and said you'd been taken, I…'

I waited. Would he be able to say it? Would I be able to hear it? Neither of us was very good with our deeper emotions.

Turned out he couldn't. But he pulled me back into his arms and stroked my hair. 'You're giving me grey hairs, you know.'

'Me too,' I said in muffled tones.

I felt his chest move as he took a deep breath, then he kissed the top of my head.

'I have to go and pick Antonia up from the airport,' he said.

I froze. 'Oh? Is she back from Brisbane?'

'Yeah. She sounds great. Maybe this will be it. Lord knows, I could do with some good news.'

Couldn't we all.

I sat on the couch for a very long while after he left, wondering why I hadn't been able to tell him that I'd seen Antonia at The Gallery with Viaspa. Maybe for the same reason he hadn't been able to tell me how much he cared what happened to me.

Neither of us wanted to take a risk on what would come next.

My phone beeped a message and I flicked it open. It was from Lena Vine, telling me that the police had taken Kate and Leonard Roc away for questioning. I hoped that meant Johnny Viaspa would be on the police's radar as well. But knowing my luck, he'd used an untraceable phone.

Another beep. This one was from Ed: Let's get together soon and talk.

My spirits lifted. I took that as a good sign. Now I just had to work out what I wanted from him. Before I could get any further on that thought, Wal and Cass clattered in the door together.

'Martin's coming too,' said Cass, smiling.

'Wonderful!' I said, my eyes moistening.

Bok walked in a second later carrying an esky from which he produced two bottles of Roederer champagne, an ice cream cake and beautiful black Miu Miu handbag.

I cried a little bit and hugged him too.

'I just saw your mum in the driveway. She said you missed a dinner engagement.'

'Crap.' I would pay for that in untold ways.

Bok gave me a sympathetic back slap. 'Cass, we need glasses and spoons.'

We sat on the floor around the coffee table, eating the cake and sipping our way through the first bottle of champers. Cass begged off the champagne saying it tasted like petrol, which relieved me. She went to the fridge and got a Coke.

'I just heard the news on the car radio,' said Bok as he poured another round. 'The police arrested a guy called Finn Fiegal who goes under the name of Josh Hamilton for the suspected murders of Sam Barbaro and Audrey Ponting. They found him tied up in a townhouse in Scarborough. Apparently he's wanted for all kinds of other things too.'

'I heard. The cops have just been here,' I said.

Bok raised an eyebrow. 'Problem?'

I shook my head. 'No. Everything's shiny.'

And it was, really.

For the moment.

Acknowledgements

Many thanks to Alisa Krasnostein and Tehani Wessely for breathing life and pizazz into this reissue. Also to Prof. Michael V. Henderson for specialist answers and the memories of Wanneroo back in the day.

Australia's Marianne Delacourt delivers the laughs and action with her sassy, unorthodox PI Tara Sharp in her novel Sharp Turn.
– The Herald Sun

Sharp Turn is suspenseful, hilarious and absolutely impossible to put down! This book left me desperate to know what happens next. A must-read!
– Author, Nansi Kunze

Delacourt has invented a Stephanie Plum character who is just as ballsy and loveable but this one lives in Perth and has 2 pet Galahs instead of a hamster. An easy read with multiple story layers, Sharp Turn will keep you guessing till the end, pick it up this summer if you like Janet Evanovich and Val McDermid's, Blue Genes.
– She Said magazine

Too Sharp

Also by Marianne Delacourt
Book 3 in the Tara Sharp series
Coming 2017!

It's too hot for Tara Sharp in Perth; the local crime boss is out for her blood. So when a friend offers her a gig 'minding' an international rap star on the come-back trail, she jumps on a plane for Brisbane. It's not Tara's usual line of work but the money is good and she's a sucker for a backstage pass. She's soon caught up dealing with the bizarre habits of the 'artist', not to mention his crazy fans.

She's in too deep, and one of the men in her life is about to drop a bombshell...

Chapter 1

Wal let me into his flat above the empty antique shop. He cast a furtive look into the night then quickly closed the door and locked it.

A little shiver tap-danced along my spine. My security chief was confident he could handle himself in any situation. It came from having been a roadie for some hardcore bands and a misspent youth developing an unhealthy obsession with weapons. Wal didn't lock doors quickly unless something bad was going on.

Had I been followed? I wondered. Was there a sniper on the roof across the road? Someone hiding in the rosebushes along the fence? A stream of scenarios flashed through my mind, none of them good.

'Got your text. 'S'up?' I hissed, glancing at the window as if someone might suddenly rappel through it.

My paranoia was accentuated by a bunch of different things. For a start there was the crime lord, Johnny Viaspa, who wanted the worst for me. And the wealthy businessman, Bolo Ignatius, who would happily see me locked up. And the hit man who was locked up—because of me.

On top of that stuff was my psychic ability, which let me read auras and body language. That kind of affliction ... er, gift ... left a girl a little sensitive to all the nasty things in life. For example, on my way to Wal's, I'd stopped at the petrol station to fill up my beloved 1970s Monaro, Mona. The guy behind the mound of lollies and lottery tickets on the counter had a stark white aura that glowed like a halo. In my experience, white auras meant health problems. I tried to ignore it, but then I spotted a black mole on the back of his hand as he gave me my receipt.

'You should get that checked,' I said before I could stop myself.

'You should mind your own business,' he said, scowling at me.

I left. That kind of thing happened all the time. People thought I was either nosy or kooky, neither of which made for good first impressions.

'Don't open the window,' said Wal now as I walked across the room and peered behind the blind.

'Sniper?' I asked.

He gave me a funny look. 'Nope. Glass is cracked. You touch it, it'll shatter.'

I sighed and reined in my imagination, feeling foolish. 'How did that happen?'

'Someone tried to break in last night.'

Aha! My imagination was vindicated. I gave Wal a hard stare. His aura was busy; sparking and sputtering around him like he was about to short circuit. Normally he favoured the bogan Russian mafioso look—tight black jeans, black shirt, black cigarettes with gold filters—but today he was all Australian in faded, baggy denims and a singlet. I didn't know how old he was but the skin on his arms and shoulders was scarred and spotted. He had a naturally brawny physique and long red hair that came from his Irish ancestors. The snarl, though, was all his.

'Problem?'

'Nothing I can't handle.'

'Then why am I here?' I usually called Wal to help me, not the other way around. He'd started as my part-time security chief a few months back when narcolepsy had forced him to quit the band life. These days he was living on the pension, a bit of cash I was able to send his way, and my rich Aunt Liv. It seemed to be enough to keep him in cigarettes and ammunition. I sure as hell never asked about the latter.

'Got this mate who's in a spot,' he said.

'And?'

He slunk across to his tiny kitchenette and put a pan of water on to boil. Looked like I was getting a cuppa whether I wanted it or not.

'Sugar?' he asked as he took a chipped mug from the

cupboard. 'Milk?'

This had me even more worried. Wal didn't do tea parties.

'Raincheck on the milk,' I said as he sniffed at the carton he'd pulled from his tiny bar fridge. 'Tell me what you want.'

He didn't answer, but carried on going through the tea ritual. In fact, not until I was sitting on his Liv-donated overstuffed armchair with a scalding cup of black tea in my hand did he even look at me.

'Stuart—my mate—he's a music promoter in Brisbane,' he said finally.

'And?'

'We go back. He was a roadie with me, though he was younger; started managing a garage band a few years ago. One thing led to the next and he turned to promoting a year back. We keep in touch.'

I didn't ask what that meant. With Wal it's always better to know less.

He took a sip from his cup. His was rum, though, not tea.

Something about this Stuart guy was really bothering him and I waited for him to get it off his chest—not that he seemed to be in any great hurry to do so. I watched him for telltale signs of dozing off, but his narcolepsy had been better since Liv had made him promise to take his meds (and promised to pay for them). Not sure that the rum was a good idea but that wasn't really my business—at least, when he was off duty it wasn't.

'He's a bulldog once he gets his teeth into something,' Wal went on. 'Never known a bloke to be so dogged. Stuck at the business for a year with nothing much happening and now he's finally landed a big act.'

'Great!'

'Would be,' said Wal, glowering. 'But some prick's trying to squeeze him out.'

'How so?'

'Venues aren't returning his calls, equipment places won't hire to him.'

I didn't say anything. No point in asking what he wanted me to do. He'd get to it.

'Thing is, there's a few big guys on the block and he can't pick where it's coming from. If he could, maybe he could deal with it.'

'Uh-huh.'

'So I said I was working for someone who'd be able to help him. Said you was good.'

'Wal, you're killing me with compliments.'

He shot me a narrow-eyed look. 'Can't talk like a woman to him, boss. Blokes don't get that. I said you was good, he knows what that means.'

I pulled a face. 'Joking. You want me to chat to him?'

His frown lifted. 'Would ya, boss? It'd mean a lot.'

'Don't know if I'll be able to help.' I took a sip of the tea. 'Not to be rude, Wal, but can he pay?'

'Mates rates.' Wal framed it as a given.

I sighed. I couldn't really afford mates rates right now, but how could I refuse Wal a favour when he'd worked for me for nothing on some jobs? Besides, he could torture me in a million different ways.

'Okay. But that means your cut will be less.'

That was my little joke. He didn't get paid unless I did, and that wasn't often enough for either of us. That's why I was still living in my parents' garage putting up with my mother trying to matchmake me with wealthy losers.

Mother dear; Joanna Sharp, heiress of highbrow and Super-Snoot. I did love her. I did! But we were different animals. In fact, she confided in me once that she thought they'd mixed up babies at the hospital when I was born. Her little joke. She laughed in her twinkly, silvery, refined way when she said it. But I never found it all that funny. I also figured that dark thoughts would get me nowhere fast, and life was full of enough landmines without stepping on one deliberately. So I let it go. She still drove me insane though!

'I'll get him to call you, then,' said Wal, knocking back the remainder of his rum.

'Fine,' I said. 'Tomorrow. I've got a date tonight.'

'Huh?' His eyebrows rose. 'Which bloke?'

I gave him my most quelling look. Which bloke indeed! 'Ed.'

'Poor sod.'

'What do you mean?' I asked, and immediately

wished I hadn't. Wal told it like he saw it, with no real consideration for feelings.

'Doesn't know if he's coming or going with you.'

'Ed and I are in the early stages of a friendship,' I said primly.

He shrugged. 'Well, don't string him on too long on account of that rich fella.'

'I have to get going,' I said huffily, putting my tea down on the table.

He saw me out, unperturbed by my stiff manner. 'See ya later, boss. Thanks.'

The door locked behind me.

Once I was back in my car and on the road, I calmed down a little. Wal didn't often comment on my personal life—never, actually. Maybe I should take his comments under advisement.

Thing was, I had a Clayton's love life: the kind you have when you don't have one. First there was Eduardo (my date), a sweet, gorgeous model and former country boy whom I'd rescued from a bunch of marauding gym ladies. Since then we'd been dating on and off. He found my work hard to stomach and I found his stomach … hard!

I chuckled at my own witticism and turned off Stirling Highway at the Jarrad Street traffic lights.

The Ed thing should have been perfect for a girl whose life was in a state of flux, but there was this other guy I couldn't get out of my head. It wasn't because, as

Wal said, he was rich. In fact, I found the whole rich thing a tad tiresome because it brought with it a coke-addicted wife and way too much baggage. Thing was, there was this kind of electricity between Nick Tozzi and me. Truly! Not the kind of electricity you read about in romance books but the real kind. When we touched, my aura gave me a hundred-volt shock. I got all tongue-tied and quivery and ... well ... messy. It was embarrassing. I tried to stay away from him but we had history. I saved him from losing his business and he ... well ... saved my life.

Now it'd got complicated. We'd talked about it a little; agreed that we were attracted to each other but that it didn't have to mean anything in the grand scheme. He'd gone away happy and was trying to sort out his marriage. I went away more confused than ever. I mean, I liked Eduardo a lot. Really a lot! And found him smoking hot. But this 'thing' with Nick Tozzi kept stopping me from committing.

So right now, before my date with Ed, I was on my way to a Smitty and Bok therapy session. My two best friends weren't ones to hold back on the subject of my love life, and even I knew it had reached the point where I needed intervention.

I pulled up outside Bok's apartment block and sat for a moment to summon my courage. This is necessary, I told myself. I need help.

My last relationship had ended worse than badly, on

account of The Bastard running off with our housemate and my furniture. That, combined with the whole I-can-read-auras thing, left me pretty wary of starting over. It was hard to feel good about someone when their aura was telling you they were hot for the girl next to you.

I did a quick check in the rear-view mirror. Make-up still intact (Bok hated it when I didn't wear lippy). Hair scraped back in a ponytail—must remember to brush it out before I met up with Ed later.

Okay. Let's do this.

I key-locked Mona—no central locking on a 1980s Monaro—and caught the lift to Bok's apartment.

Smitty opened the door with a glass of champagne in hand. 'Darling, hurry in and start drinking before I drain the well dry.'

'Smitts?' Her normally flawless complexion was blotchy and her cute nose red and runny. My frightfully decent and usually immaculate bestie was looking a mess.

She hiccoughed, sniffed and then screwed up her face. 'Henny and I had an awful fight.'

I put my arms around her and she fell against me, her head in line with my armpit. I steered her backwards inside and let the door close behind me.

Bok came out of his bedroom with his phone to his ear. He took one look at us and the champagne bottle upside down in the ice bucket and told whoever he was talking to that he'd call them back.

'Smitts,' he said. 'You murdered a whole bottle of Bolly while I was on the phone.'

The only reply he got was a heartfelt sob.

Bok and I exchanged looks as I gently lowered Smitty onto the couch. My t-shirt was getting snotty and tear-wet so I tried to ease her away, but she clung to me like a limpet with separation issues.

'Come on, Smitts. How long have you two been together?' I asked, knowing the answer full well. Smitty, Henry and I had been through school and uni together. They'd been a couple forever. And a great couple at that. Three gorgeous kids, no mortgage (on account of him being a well-heeled doctor) and an out-of-control dog named Fridge. They had everything I thought I wanted ... except moments like these.

'Jane Smith, stop being a drama queen. What's a little disagreement between the perfect couple?' Bok's lame attempt at stern just caused further sobs.

In the twenty-plus years I'd known Smitty she'd only cried like this once before, and that was when her mum passed away.

'Hey there, Smitts. No one's died.' Then a terrible thought assailed me. 'Is Claire alright?' Hen and Smitts' eldest suffered from Crohn's disease, and had been in hospital on and off all her life.

Smitts actually stopped crying for a moment and raised her head. I took the opportunity to extract myself from her embrace.

'No, Claire's fine,' she said. 'As fine as a nearly sixteen-year-old can be.' Sniff.

'Then what's wrong with you and Hen?'

'I think...' She paused as if having trouble getting her tongue to pronounce the words. 'I think Henny is having an affair.'

Bok and I were silent for a full minute before Bok disappeared into the kitchen and returned with another bottle of champagne. A cheaper bottle. I'd planned to drive to my date with Ed, but something told me tonight wasn't going to go according to plan.

'He can't be,' I said after a large swig of sparkly goodness.

'He thinks you're a goddess, darling,' added Bok.

Smitty looked unconvinced.

I finished my glass and poured another, ignoring Bok's withering frown. 'Okay, let's examine the evidence. Lay it on us.'

Smitty reached into her purse and withdrew a dainty handkerchief. After a less than delicate blow of her nose, she took a breath.

'I took his suit jacket to the dry cleaners. They found something in the pocket, so they pinned it to the front in an envelope. I don't read his mail, you know that,' she said. 'But...'

'But?'

'I didn't know what it was, so I opened it.'

'Smitts, you're killing me,' I said. 'Get to it.'

'It had Belle Bussey's name and phone number on it.' She curled up into a ball, hugging one of Bok's silk-covered pillows.

'Is that it?' asked Bok. 'You're having a crack-up about that?' He stared at the crumpled pillow like he wanted to wrest it from her grasp and possibly hit her on the head with it. Bok was not the patient type.

Nor was I, actually. In fact, we weren't the greatest pair to help with heartbreak, but I knew Belle Bussey and Bok didn't. I understood why Smitty was in the foetal position on the couch.

'Honey, I'm going to make you something stronger. I'll be back in a jiff.' I turned to Bok. 'Unlock the booze cupboard,' I ordered.

He preceded me into the kitchen and planted his back to the pantry, arms crossed.

Bok was gorgeous. Long, silky black hair and a beautiful face gifted from his mixed Asian-Latino heritage. Girls went mad for him. So did guys. I knew that stubborn, impatient look.

'You do not get near any more of my booze unless you tell me what's going on,' he said.

Being a magazine editor who entertained visiting models, clients and industry people, Bok always kept the booze cupboard well stocked. He also shifted the hiding spot for the key on a regular basis, in case I found it. Not that I was a big drinker or anything but there are … occasions that require certain measures—of the spirit kind. Now was one.

'Belle Bussey caught the same bus as us but she was a year older and went to another school. The father owned a bank. According to JoBob, the mother was connected to the Swedish royals, though I doubt it. Nothing naturally blonde about her.'

Bok looked thoughtful. 'You mean Spanders Bank?'

'Yeah. Wouldn't touch them with a barge pole. Anyway, Belle had it bad for Henny. When we left school she offered to take him to Europe for summer hols.'

'And he didn't go?'

'What? And leave Smitts here alone? Our girl was something else when we were teens. I mean ... she still is.'

'Yes, she's always had the Grace Kelly look going on,' he agreed. 'So this Bussey bitch is a would-be ex-flame. If he didn't go for it back then, why would he go for it now?'

'Well, the summer we finished high school, Henny and Smitts had a huge fight. Can't remember what about but it was epic. They didn't speak for nearly two months.'

'Don't tell me. He slept with Belle.'

I rolled my eyes. 'You got it. But it gets worse. Belle proposed to him.'

'Sweet,' said Bok, narrowing his eyes.

'Smitts is sweet. Belle is a Venus flytrap.'

'So what did our bachelor boy do after she got down on bended knee?'

'What any average young bloke would do—he ran a mile. All the way back to Smitts.'

'Did she welcome him with open arms?'

I remembered Smitty's agonising. 'Not one bit. She made him work for it, but the deal-breaker was Belle. He had to promise never to make contact with her again. Ever!'

'Oh.' Bok produced the key from his jeans pocket. 'In that case there're some decent reds on the bottom rack. Or we could crack a bottle of bourbon.'

I gave the pantry a quick squiz. Above the shelves of booze was a single shelf with two different breakfast cereals, six tins of salmon, a box of ginseng tea bags, an open packet of water crackers and some Tim Tams.

'Remind me not to come here for dinner,' I said, grabbing the bourbon. 'Got any Coke?'

'Dry ginger ale?'

'Sounds good. I'll get the glasses.'

I returned to our foetal friend and plonked the grog and glasses down. 'Okay,' I said. 'He's up to speed.'

She uncurled, took a glass and held it out. As I poured, Bok appeared with the mixer and a plate of brie and stale crackers. We huddled in and got to it.

'Could be a bunch of explanations, Smitty,' I said. 'Give him the benefit.'

She shook her head. 'We had a deal. Never her. Never again. I can't believe it.'

'Tara is right, Smitts. There could be a good reason.

Henny isn't stupid. He knows what would happen.'

'Maybe he's sabotaging our marriage. Maybe he wanted me to find out. Have I got too fat? Am I terribly boring?' Her lips quivered and she took a gulp of bourbon. 'It's the pearls, isn't it? He always said he hated women in pearls because they reminded him of his mother. I wore pearls to the Maynards' wedding.'

'No, Smitty, it's not the pearls.' I sighed and topped up her glass, and my own. It was going to be a long night.

We talked back and forth for an hour or so, Bok and me defending Henny while Smitty vacillated between blaming herself and him.

When Bok's art deco clock chimed 8PM, I got out my phone to send Ed a text. crisis talks. cn u pick me up @ boks. drunk t

Smitty bumped my elbow and I pressed send.

'Whatcha doing?' she asked, squinting at the screen.

'S'posed to be meeting Ed.'

'Oh my god!' Her shriek had me plugging my fingers in my ears. 'How selfish of me!'

'Calm down,' I said, unplugging. 'He'll come and get—'

My phone beeped a reply. My car is in garage. Another time.

'Ooooorrr NOT,' I finished lamely.

'Nooo,' moaned Smitts, rocking from side to side in the grip of alcoholic dramatis. 'I've ruined your date.'

She'd never been able to hold her liquor as well as Bok and me.

'Shall I slap her sober?' whispered Bok from behind his hand.

I sighed and shook my head. 'Put the kettle on.'

Bok nodded and weaved a slightly erratic path to the kitchen. As he disappeared Smitts grabbed my hand and hauled me close. Suddenly she appeared sober.

'T, you have to do something for me.'

'What?' I asked, feeling slightly muzzy and annoyed by Ed blowing me off.

'I want you to spy on Hen.'

Also from *deadlines*

Deadlines is the crime imprint of the award-winning Twelfth Planet Press specialty small press. We aim to promote quality, fun writing in fresh, exciting projects that seeks to raise the awareness of women's voices, and demonstrate the depth and breadth of Australian fiction to a broader audience.

Tara Sharp 2016

Sharp Shooter

Sharp Turn

Coming in 2017

Too Sharp

Sharp Edge

Café La Femme
by Livia Day

A Trifle Dead

The Blackmail Blend

Drowned Vanilla

Keep Calm & Kill the Chef (coming soon!)

www.ingramcontent.com/pod-product-compliance
Lightning Source LLC
Chambersburg PA
CBHW020536020726
47494CB00006B/1788